CW00969762

# RECOVERY

# STANLEY
# MIDDLETON
## RECOVERY

HUTCHINSON
LONDON    MELBOURNE    AUCKLAND    JOHANNESBURG

First published in 1988 by Hutchinson & Co. (Publishers) Ltd
an imprint of Century Hutchinson Ltd, Brookmount House,
62–65 Chandos Place, London WC2N 4NW

Century Hutchinson Publishing Group (Australia) Pty Ltd,
PO Box 496, 16–22 Church Street, Hawthorn,
Melbourne, Victoria 3122

Century Hutchinson Group (NZ) Ltd,
PO Box 40–086, 32–34 View Road, Glenfield, Auckland 10

Century Hutchinson Group (SA) Pty Ltd,
PO Box 337, Bergvlei 2012, South Africa

Set in Linotron Plantin by Input Typesetting Ltd,
London SW19 8DR

Printed and bound in Great Britain by
Anchor Brendon Ltd, Tiptree, Essex

ISBN 0 09 173528 9

Who would have thought my shrivel'd heart
Could have recover'd greennesse? It was gone
   Quite under ground; as flowers depart
To see their mother-root, when they have blown,
     Where they together
     All the hard weather,
Dead to the world, keep house unknown.


*The Flower*
George Herbert

# 1

Job Turner, a widower, closed the front door behind his daughter and then, wrestling with the catch, immediately jerked it open again.

Alison had traversed the few yards to the garden gate, where she now turned, a look of handsome enquiry on her face. The two stared at each other.

'Yes?' she called, as from a great distance.

'Oh, nothing.'

'You opened the door again.'

'I know.' He grinned, foolishly, not pleasantly, drew in a lungful of air. 'Just checking that you made it off the premises.'

The trees in the avenue to his right rose black, wintry still; thorn hedges showed no touches of green. Job trotted out, patted the stone sill of a leaded window and examined the small, greyish patch of grass between the house and the front palings.

'You'll need to paint this fence again,' Alison said, now in the lane outside.

'Don't remind me.'

A tall girl, she touched her upswept hair and made round the far side of her car.

'It's March,' she spoke loudly. 'Spring's here.'

'You wouldn't think so.'

He wished she'd get into her vehicle, not prolong the conversation, or the topic which they had already exhausted twice. There were people about, striding it, loitering, making the most of the dry Sunday afternoon, visiting the country park to stare at the Hall, at the ploughed hillock, the high trees which marked the beginning of rusticity, the verge of the town.

''Bye, then,' Alison shouted. 'Let me have the tin back.'

'You can have it now.'

'Inside the next week or two.'

She darted down into the driving seat, and instantly drove off. That was typical, he thought; she knew what she was about, had a large Volvo which demonstrated her status. The tin she had mentioned contained buns she had baked for him. They would be excellent, crisp on the outside, deliciously softer in the middle, currants unburnt. Grudgingly he cleared away the teacups, emptying the pot, stowing the milk-jug in the refrigerator. He decided against washing the dishes until after his next meal.

His living room was small, dark, uncomfortably crowded with furniture. Job poked at his coke fire, felt the burst of heat, fixed his gaze on the dead, grey eye of his television and considered Alison, his eldest daughter.

He approved of her in that she was successful, bossed her husband, the family, the au pair, the nanny, the dog and called in two or three times a month to lay down the law to him. She had done well at the university, then trained as a solicitor, and now worked for the firm in which Geoffrey Greene, her husband, held the senior partnership. Alison had known all along what she wanted.

Job Turner looked round his possessions as he did every Saturday and Sunday. He lived in this, the East Lodge of Bentwood Hall; his house was a cramped, damp, Victorian place that had been left to him, out of the blue, by the will of a not very well-regarded schoolfellow.

At the time, two years ago, Job, recently widowed, grieving, maddened by his loneliness and the efforts of his friends to keep him company, had relinquished his house in the town, letting it furnished, and had moved into this, Alison's words, 'poky hole'. He did not know yet whether he had done well. When she had scrutinized it earlier this afternoon, he had felt both put in his place and yet congratulated on his individualism.

He had been surprised to learn from the evening newspaper that his friend and namesake, Ian Turner, had died from a heart attack. They had started in the same class at the grammar school forty-six years ago, two smart boys in their

8

uniforms, Turner I. and Turner J. T., had been evacuated together for a few months during the war, taken School Certificate in the same summer, had both been rejected at eighteen by the forces. Ian had never married, had looked after himself, worked hard in a bank, had been promoted and was within an ace of achieving what his last Christmas card described as the life-long 'ambition to be a retired manager', when he had been killed by heart failure while driving from work. It appeared that he had invested wisely, and had bought property here and there, almost randomly. When Job's wife died, Ian had apparently altered his will to bequeath the lodge to his friend together with a sum of money to be spent on its repair and repainting 'and on nothing else'. Flitting had been a difficult decision, and Job, lacerated still by his wife's death, had let the huge Victorian semi-detached where he had brought up his family, and moved into the cramped rooms without knowing exactly what he was about.

Alison, who had wanted him to move from Oak Villa, had asked him at the time if he were wise, and he had answered, out of character, that Ian had set him a test from the grave. The conditions of the will bound him to live in the house before he sold it off and to spend the whole of the quite considerable sum for repair and improvement within that period of residence.

'Test of what?' Alison demanded, humorously grim.

'Living out of the way. Something I'd always said I'd wanted.'

'Not a good choice on his part then.'

She spoke the truth there; she usually did. A housing estate, partly private, partly council, had been built during the last ten years within a few hundred yards of the lodge. If Job Turner stood at his front gate and looked right the impressive line of trees in the squire's avenue came almost within touching distance; in front was an irregular, hedged field, where three horses grazed. To his left, if he kept his eyes low, were the blank, blackish walls of farm outbuildings, flanking one side of the lane, which quickly widened into a kerbed road serving lines of red-brick boxes sprawled across the hillocks.

Ian Turner had bought the lodge ten years before, at a knock-down price, just when the building of the estate had begun. He'd rented it out, kept it in goodish order, though it had stood empty when he died. Job wondered whether his school-friend had feared he'd not long to live.

That was ridiculous.

They had hardly kept in touch, enclosing a note each year inside a Christmas card, Ian's invariably the longer. On Gillian's death, Ian had written a sensible letter of sympathy, had attended the funeral service but had not attempted more than a few words to Job, but had gone home, forty miles away, and had added the codicil about the lodge. Odd, odd.

Once he had made up his mind to move, Job allowed Alison to take over. She decided what small amount of furniture was to go, what pictures; she chose the new carpets; she instructed the central-heating, the double-glazing, the damp-course experts; she decided on colour schemes, picked the decorous garden fence. Within two months Job had found himself installed, warmly comfortable, intrigued by his daughter's ingenuity, his nostrils tickled with the smell of new paint. His old house, which he had mulishly refused to sell, had been let for a year to a visiting American professor with a family. It had all been efficient and painless inside the grief which clawed him still.

The house was minute, well built, modernized now, convenient in every way, but he would have done better to have settled for a flat in the town. The size of the garden worried him, and he had begun to plant trees and shrubs to lessen his weekend labour. Here again he had been advised by the indefatigable Alison who, as usual, demonstrated her omniscience. He'd never done much in the garden at home, had left it to Gillian; the children had shown no interest at all. And yet here was his eldest, larger than life, producing catalogues, reeling off lists of botanical names, dragging him round to nurserymen whom she impressed without difficulty. Job kissed the rod, was gratified, even comforted.

A trace of his daughter's perfume hung sedately about the room still. A brief flash of sunshine brightened the furniture, the chimney breast, the ornate gold frame of the landscape above the fire. Job saw to it his hearth was safe, placing the guard, tapped the table-top and quoted out loud from a School Certificate poem:

> 'O for a lodge in some vast wilderness,
> Some boundless contiguity of shade'

and, laughing at himself, made for the small square of hall by the front door where he kept his top coat. He was adjusting his scarf when the bell pealed with a deafening intensity in that confined space. Job swore, dug a little finger into his right ear and opened up. His son-in-law, Alison's husband Geoffrey Greene, faced him.

'Have you got my wife here?'

'No. She left five minutes back.'

'Hell's bells.' He exaggerated the liquid sounds, cheerfully.

'Come in, then.'

The two of them crowded the hallway between them, for Greene was a large man, six foot two or three and broad-shouldered with it. His wavy hair was grey, thick, and held in place by a modicum of cream or oil. Nearly fifty years of age, he had the appearance of a former rowing blue, or rugger forward, though he had never shown any interest in sport. As he stood in highly polished brogues, cavalry-twill trousers, excellent tweed overcoat with white silk neckerchief, towering over his father-in-law he exemplified robust health.

'Have you lost her?' Job asked.

'No. I knew she was coming here.'

'Where are the children?'

'Dawn, the nanny, is walking them round. I see you're just going out.'

Job Turner completed the buttoning of his coat.

'Ten minutes up the road and back.'

'I'll join you if I may.'

'I thought you were searching for Alison.'

'I knew she was here. I thought it gave me the opportunity of looking you over. It's some time since I saw you. How are you keeping?'

'Well. Very well.' Turner spoke gravely. He was no more

11

than nine years older than his son-in-law. 'And not grumbling.'

'Good.'

Greene opened the front door, stepped back and blocked the path outside. As Turner occupied himself with two keys, the other man watched but made no comment.

'Off we go then.'

Greene's Audi occupied less of the lane than his wife's Volvo but, like his shoes, the car shone, burnished daily. The two men pushed past it on the minuscule pavement that extended the length of the Lodge and set off towards the avenue.

'It's not warm yet,' Greene said.

In spite of the sun's aura of chill gold, a gelid stillness nibbled face and finger-ends.

'Is all well with you?' Greene's rubicund features, redder neck, twisted at his father-in-law's question. 'I mean it's not often I see you.'

'That's why I'm here. When I inquire from Alison she invariably says you're fine. But you know what women are like. I wanted to see for myself.'

'What's likely to be wrong with me?'

'Nothing. Nothing.' Greene punched one fisted kid-glove into the open palm of the other. 'But I like to make sure for myself.'

Job Turner did not answer. A young couple with a push-chair rattled past them; further up the lane a boy shouted to an unseen companion, a warning or call of delight. People appeared suddenly, muffled, the ends of their noses pink with chill.

'Handkerchief weather.' Greene, using his. 'I often wonder how you like this place.' His soft, confident solicitor's voice. 'You seemed to be shunted into it.'

'It would have been silly to stay in that barrack.'

'Oh, yes. I often meant to ask you this: that friend who left you the place, was he given to eccentricities?'

'No. Utterly conventional. And complacent.'

'Then why did he . . . ?'

'Who's to say? It came as a surprise. I didn't expect him

12

to die. In my book he was a survivor. No. Right out of character.'

'That's what Alison implied.'

'And you didn't believe her?' Job placed his question mischievously.

'Alison doesn't like mysteries.'

'Only muddles. You lawyers thrive on them.' Coughing, laughter stopped him. He'd heard some lecture about this, and the two words had stuck.

'No.'

Turner did not explain for he was moderately certain that his son-in-law had picked up his reference, and that his denial merely signalled a hope that Job would go on to say something interesting. The beefy exterior disguised a cultured mind.

They had emerged from the avenue, passed the well-spread stables, and come within two hundred yards of the back of Bentwood Hall. Notices on raw, planed boards warned them to go no further. The two men stood and stared at the randomly placed windows, the oblique patterns of water pipe, the patches of white on the red brickwork.

'I wouldn't like to foot the bill for the upkeep of that.' Turner.

'The other ratepayers will help out.' Greene laughed, throatily. 'Have you ever been inside?'

'No. Have you?'

Greene shook his head.

'A caretaker and his family live in,' Job continued. 'Until such time as alteration begins. I pass the time of day with him when I'm out walking.'

'Ugly.' Greene was scratching his face. 'And I can't understand why this road approaches from the back. Presumably there'd be others. Unless they were demonstrating their bluntness to visitors. All superior houses have posteriors.' He laughed again. 'As with superior persons.'

'Keep it clean.'

Job Turner enjoyed this man's company, little as he saw of him.

'Been to church today?'

'No, thank you.' Greene spoke with moderation. 'My

13

religious observances will begin and end with a social midnight service at Christmas and the *Saint Matthew Passion*.'

'You surprise me.' This was a lie; Turner knew that his companion saw no sense in the doctrine of the atonement. A God who sacrificed his son offered him no hope, indeed little sense. He did not exactly lose his temper when arguing these matters, but had been known to bite his lips or point a stiff finger at his opponent. His wife found some mild amusement in this, blamed it on his father who had the reputation of a tyrant. Geoffrey did not deny this, either, but would go on to examine, in the quiet tone he used in his office, the oddity and diversity of the ways people acquired their most cherished beliefs. Alison, like her own father, a token believer, attended church at Christmas and Easter. 'It's the music, is it?'

'I go to worship Bach, yes.'

'Who was mistaken in his religious credos.'

'In my view. But he was a product of his age.'

'As you are.'

'Exactly, exactly.' Greene laughed at himself. 'I am utterly influenced by a science about which I know nothing.'

'Let's turn back,' Turner said.

'Literally, I hope.'

They had reached a small parking space with room for eight cars. A dog barked, wildly, scampering as its master let it out of his back seat. Its tail wagged with violence as its owner clipped on a lead.

'Do you ever think of a pet?' Greene.

'Too much trouble. I'm out all day. Wouldn't be fair. The house is very small.'

'A cat wouldn't mind.'

'I'm too much of an old woman these days. Don't like dirt.'

'Did you never have an animal as a child?'

'No. My parents weren't keen. But my mother did have a dog after I left home.'

'Draw what conclusion you will.'

They were swinging along now, both men puffing slightly, pleased with each other. Greene talked about his children, Sarah and James, and the difficulties and advantages of

14

becoming a father for the first time at the age of forty-five. Turner listened; they had flitted over this several times without Greene giving an inkling of why he had remained a bachelor so long. If Geoffrey had not met Alison he would have been celibate to this day, cheerful with it, everybody's favourite uncle. She had no truck with that nonsense; the principal of the firm she had joined was a good man, who deserved more from life than he derived at present, and she saw that he received it. This big, intelligent, cultured man invested his faith in her, and was rewarded.

'I expect you spoil them.' The father-in-law.

'You should come up more often to inspect the damage.'

'I leave that to a more competent authority.'

'Your daughter?' Yes, I approve the terms.'

'My daughter.'

Even more pleased with themselves, their feet cracking twigs on the lane, they reached the Hall once more.

'I can't understand anyone wanting a place that size,' Turner said.

'It's not large as country houses go. Three of my clients have bigger, even in these rough days.'

'What do they do?'

'A furniture manufacturer, a stockbroker, and two "landed gentry".' He mocked the term with his tone. 'That's four. I just remembered. No, five now. I forgot Lord Averham. No, six. Goodness. I'll stop before it sounds like boasting.'

'There must be some money somewhere.' Job, as one willing to be instructed.

'Make no mistake about that.'

They kept up their spanking pace, too breathless to talk easily. When they arrived back at the Lodge, Greene refused to come in, but stood shaking his keys by the car in the late afternoon sunlight.

'My father was asking about you,' Greene advanced the sentence offhandedly.

'How is he, then?'

'Not too well, really. He's eighty next year. But he said he'd like to see you again.'

'Did he mean it?'

'Oh, I should think so. Would you go up with me?'
'I'd be glad to.'
'I'll phone you.'

# 2

Job Turner, back from his work on Monday evening, had hurriedly prepared his high tea so that his table could be cleared, dishes washed, floor swept clear of crumbs in time for the BBC 1 News at six o'clock.

At ten to the hour his son-in-law rang. Job was not pleased, but Greene did not delay him long.

'Are you free Wednesday or Thursday night to go up to see my father?'

'Yes.'

'Choose your day.' Turner did so, Wednesday. 'He doesn't want me there, he says. Will seven-thirty do? He'll kick you out at ten, because that's when God has ordained his bedtime.'

'Are you ringing from home?'

'No, the office. Some of us have to earn our living.'

Greene, sounding less than cheerful, immediately rang off. Job fetched out his street map to be consulted once he'd heard the news bulletin. Perhaps the Almighty had also ordained that.

At twenty-seven minutes past seven on Wednesday evening Turner stood, in a grey suit and raincoat, at the door of Frederick Greene's large bungalow. It was too dark to determine the state of the spacious, surrounding grounds, but they would be neat, beds already hoed, lawns treated with spring fertilizer, trees and shrubs symmetrical with winter pruning. Old Greene employed a firm of jobbing gardeners and kept them up to the mark.

He appeared now at the door, lifting spectacles and dropping them back on to the bridge of his prominent nose. He wore excellent green tweed trousers, but a baggy, unmatching cardigan with sagging pockets. Like his son he was large, but the balding head and the scraggy neck now perched uncouthly small above the breadth of shoulder, the barrel of chest.

'Ah, Turner, Turner. Glad to see you.'

'You were expecting me.'

'I'm not senile yet. And Geoffrey's capable of delivering a message. Hang your coat up, if you can find a peg.'

He led the way into the living room.

'I'm glad to see you, Turner,' he announced again. 'I don't have many visitors. And most of them I could do without.'

'Doesn't Alison bring the children up?'

'Occasionally. But she doesn't stop long. There's nothing much to occupy small children here.'

'Sarah will look at pictures in books with you now.' Critical.

'Nothing suitable,' Greene snapped, glaring at his book-cases, slapping his chair arm, establishing that his ways were not to be changed for grandchildren, however favoured.

'And doesn't Alison bring something?'

'Apparently not. She doesn't want to waste time here. She makes what might be called a "duty visit". What can I get for you to drink?'

Greene had struggled up again from his chair.

'Nothing, thanks.'

'Gin, whisky, sherry?'

'No, thanks.'

'Your good example's wasted on me.'

The old man splashed about with gin and tonic water.

'How's the work?' he asked, still on his feet.

'I'm busy, but it's dull. I look forward to retiring.'

'When's that, then?'

'In three years' time when I'm sixty.'

Job Turner was headmaster of a junior school, a thriving, well-regarded place in a good catchment area. More than twenty years ago, when he had been the music specialist at a secondary comprehensive school, the area education officer and the music adviser, impressed by his achievements, and guided by a current educational whim about the value of musical training in the early years of a child's career, had pressed him to apply for the headship of this new, purpose-built primary school and had seen to it that he was appointed.

At the time he had been uncertain of the move. A transitory difference with his new headmaster over the allocation of

18

practice times rather than ambition or educational idealism had finally prompted his application. Now, looking back he had done all that was expected of him, and more; his choirs had shone in festivals; his open days were exemplars to the world. His pupils sang in solo and in concert, played instruments, danced to loud parental applause and did so to this day. They also efficiently practised the three Rs. Turner, the expert, directed with *élan*, but had sidled into boredom. He knew this clearly, hid his disappointment, kept his charges, subordinates and pupils hard at work and the classrooms shipshape in spite of strikes and low morale. If anyone had put the question to him he could not have said whether or not his staff liked him. 'I try to be fair,' he'd answer. 'I suggest schemes that are possible and can be seen to be so. I do a bit of teaching myself. Like or dislike don't come very forcibly into the argument.' They had, however, gone out of their way to show sympathy when his wife died, a little to his surprise.

'I didn't retire until I was seventy,' Greene continued.

'Why so late?'

'I was as capable of a good day's work then as I was at fifty. My father never did retire. He was down at his printing works on the day of his death. Seventy-eight.'

'You never thought of joining the family firm?'

'He never thought of it. I was sent to the grammar school and then into a solicitor's office. He was clever, and he liked the idea of formal education. Latin and Greek. And then the law. And I suspect he didn't want me down at Bluebell Hill, poking my nose in where I didn't understand.'

'You didn't feel the same about Geoffrey, I take it?'

Mr Greene held his glass of gin and tonic high, squinting.

'No. I sent him to the university. "MA (Cantab)" looks well on our letterheads. Or did at one time. He's conscientious. He's a good lawyer. But he's no innovator. He wouldn't want to change things unless there was some overpowering reason for it. It's your Alison who sees to it that the firm is up to date these days.'

'Do you approve?'

'You mean because she's a woman? She's the one who'll

19

keep them up to scratch. And run her home and family. Was she always like that?'

'She was never openly bossy,' Turner answered, 'that I noticed. She knew her mind, was very quick and never relished wasting her time. Exactly like her mother.'

'She didn't set you right?' Greene guffawed, but dry as dust.

'Oh, she would often suggest alterations to schemes I put to her: about my school, or the house or the next holiday. She'd think for a minute or two and then, "Why don't you do it this way? Or that?" Almost invariably her suggestions were worth listening to. Even as quite a small child she'd see ways of improvement. She has a tidy, or a mathematical mind.'

'Yes, yes. Yes.' Greene had stretched his legs out straight in front of him, and directed the affirmatives at his slippered feet. 'Geoffrey's a good man. In every sense. I don't want to put the idea into your head that he's a fool. He isn't. He would always have made a living because he works hard. He's a conservative. We've always done it like this. What the old hymn says: "Experience will decide." '

Job Turner pulled a face, surprised at the mention of hymnology.

'You always got on well?' he asked.

'No.' Greene's voice acquired sudden strength. 'We didn't.' He sniffed. 'I bullied the boy. He wouldn't stand up to me, even as a man. It encourages tyranny, you know.' Again he laughed, like the rustling of paper. 'My temper was short. I admit that.'

'And do you regret it?'

'Regret it? No, I don't think so. Why should I?'

'Geoffrey doesn't hold it against you?'

'I expect so. I would, if I were in his place. But once you get old you're a confounded nuisance, in any case, saint or sinner. So it doesn't make much difference. I still keep a financial finger in Boyce, Greene and Hardy. That doesn't please. Old age is a bloody blight. As you'll soon learn. Does Alison visit you?'

20

'Yes, when she can. She came last Sunday and brought me some buns.'

'Lucky you.'

Greene screwed his face into a mask of distaste, while Job Turner remembered that this old man, according to Geoffrey, used to beat his wife. The son had made the confession a few months ago when Turner had visited Alison in hospital, after the birth of her son. Geoffrey had seemed both elated and yet vulnerable too, a victim of his own glad feelings.

'Has your father been up to see them?' Turner had asked, a question more out of sociability than as a requirement for information. They were walking together to the car park.

'No.' Greene seemed enormous. 'I don't suppose he's interested.'

He continued in this grumbling vein until they reached his Audi.

'One thing I shall never forgive him.' He slapped the roof of his car, then leaned on it, as if to be searched. 'He used to beat my mother. Ritually.'

Turner murmured disapprobation, looking in embarrassment at the dust on the ground.

'If she displeased him in some way, cooked him a meal that wasn't to his liking, or spent money, in his view wastefully, or even just answered him back, he'd get her on her own, roll up his newspaper, the *Daily Telegraph*, and beat her about the head.'

'Hard?'

'Quite violently. I don't know how much it hurt, physically, but it was utterly humiliating.'

'And she put up with it?'

'For years. Apparently.' Geoffrey blushed, stabbed with his toe at the asphalt of the car-park floor. 'I caught him at it not long after I'd qualified and joined the firm. I was living with them, but they thought I wasn't at home that evening. I walked in on it. It seemed, at first . . . I thought it was a kind of daft game they were playing. Once I found it was serious . . . well.'

'Did you do anything about it?'

'I threatened him with the police. Then he went berserk.

21

Shouted, raved. I thought he'd assault me, but perhaps I was too big, I don't know. My mother ran from the room. Under his bluster, there was an element of sense. If I went to the police what would be the effect on our good name, and that of the firm? If I'd any nous I'd keep my bloody silly mouth shut and mind my own bloody business. I didn't answer and that made him worse. Even more odd was that after he'd stormed off my mother came back in and begged me not to take any steps against him.'

'Had he sent her?'

'Very likely. She said, and I don't forget this, in a trembling sort of way, "It doesn't hurt, Geoffrey. Really it doesn't." It had been going on for years.'

'And?'

'We, that's the three of us, have not mentioned it from that day to this.' Geoffrey had pushed himself away from the car. 'This is confidential, of course. I hope you won't say anything to anybody, not even Alison. I don't come out of it well. I ought to have been more positive.'

'I don't know; it's difficult. One's own parents.'

'If I'd really stood up to him, it might have made him more unreasonable.'

'Did he continue?'

'Not in my presence. No. But I could never look on him in the same way again. Not that I think about it much. I don't dwell on my failures. . . .'

'It's nothing of the kind. You probably did the right thing.'

'I don't know. I don't know. But please treat all this as confidential.'

The big man had lowered himself into his car, blushing again as he slammed the door.

Frederick Greene had replaced his gin on the table. He drank it with his eyes as if the almost full glass held significance for him.

'How's the music?' he grated.

'I still play a bit to amuse myself.'

'Have you got a piano in your present place?'

'A small one. An upright.'

In the past ten years since the death of his wife, Father

Greene had taken up concert-going, record-buying and was experimenting now with compact discs. He'd played the piano as a child, had always been capable of rattling off a few Beethoven sonatas, but had rarely patronized choirs or orchestras, local or national, in his prime, never belonged to the Music Club, the Operatic Society or the Philharmonic Circle. His wife, oddly Cecilia by name, claimed to be tone-deaf. On the rare occasions Greene met Turner he'd ask for some information, randomly, once about Beethoven's 'Pastoral' Symphony, once *The Ring*, then about Webern.

'Do you play it much?'

'I try to do twenty minutes or half an hour every day. I don't always succeed.'

'Is Alison interested?'

'Well, yes.'

'She and Geoffrey don't often go to concerts.'

'Don't they?' Turner fought down a gust of ill-temper. 'I thought they did.'

Greene bared his yellow teeth, and ran a left-hand arpeggio round the arm of his chair. 'What do you know about Elgar's Cello Concerto?' he asked next.

Turner told him in a few succinct sentences.

'How does it begin?' He nodded towards his piano; Turner rose, lifted the lid of the old Steinway grand and played the first solo chords. Greene nodded, eyes bright, nostrils flaring.

'That's it,' he said. 'That's the chap.' He had heard a performance, he said, on the television that had been impressive. Elgar was a great man. 'Think,' his voice uncalm. 'I can remember quite clearly times when that work did not exist.'

Turner mentioned Elgar's scribble in the nursing home.

'What was he there for?'

'Throat, I think. It's all in Kennedy.'

'Elgar's a great composer.' Greene spoke to the air, not to his companion. 'That's what I wanted to know. I couldn't be sure. I needed your opinion. I'd always thought of him as an empire-builder. Or a purveyor of oratorios. It's not so, is it?'

The old man allowed his tongue to run away with him. It was odd that he had made so wide a misjudgement, that it had taken all these years to disabuse himself of these wrong ideas. He had heard the Introduction and Allegro, and had been affected without his knowing.

'Play that opening again,' he asked.

Turner did so.

'Great, great.' The old man jigged on his feet. 'We'll have a cup of coffee.'

'You haven't finished your gin,' Turner objected.

'What difference does that make?'

Greene slugged towards the kitchen as Turner resumed his seat in the half-lighted room. Pictures on the walls were no more than rectangles of gloom; the furniture loomed dark, the carpet subfusc, books navy blue or blue-black. The old man's enthusiasm touched Turner unexpectedly. When Geoffrey telephoned, he'd thought that he'd been asked to witness some document. Quite wrong, he was cheered, stretched his legs out, enjoying the warmth, the closed-in smell.

Now Greene shuffled back with the coffee.

'Instant,' he grumbled. 'Can't be bothered with the other stuff. Get to like the taste of this.'

'Like Elgar.' Turner took his cup from the dark oak tray, transferring it to a carved Muslim, Arab or Indian, stool. 'Didn't you know the "Enigma Variations"?'

Frederick Greene shook a finger twisted with arthritis at him.

'I knew it. But I had never opened my mind to it. That means I never heard it, I suppose, doesn't it? Water off a duck's back?'

'This surprises you, does it?'

'It shouldn't. Human beings are extremely rum. I learnt that every day of my life down in that office of mine. I'm not so near normality myself if it comes to that. But I ought to have been more receptive to Elgar.'

'Has this conversion altered your view of the "Pomp and Circumstance" marches?'

'No. Not really. They're good of their kind. Well, they are, aren't they?'

'Oh, yes. I wondered if you approved of their kind, that's all.'

24

'You can be sarcastic, Turner.'

'I'm sorry.' Job wondered at the flash of temper, at the squinting eyes with lids wrinkled by anger. He had followed an interesting line of inquiry without thought of hurt. 'Elgar is a genuine popular composer, with "Salut d'Amour" or "Chanson de Matin", and something of this immediate melodic gift is marvellously carried over into the complexity of the variations, the concerti, the symphonies.'

Again Greene questioned his visitor about the genesis of the Cello Concerto, pursuing detail, excited as an adolescent.

'You say Elgar used the decline of his powers to advantage.'

'That's what the critics claim, and probably rightly. He felt with deep poignancy that his artistic life was as good as over, done for by age, illness, his wife's infirmities, her imminent death, the war, and this with craftsmanship which he never lost, produced an eloquence of despair in him. There's no fluency, no high spirits, though he tried, he'd been a joker, and the result of these broken snatches is a masterpiece.'

Greene picked up his cup, put it down unlipped.

'I understand,' he said. 'Or I think I do. Drink your coffee, Turner, or it'll be cold. That's right. I'm sure it is. Thank you. Thank you.'

Job drank, had his cup whipped away and refilled by his still-muttering host. That the old solicitor had grown so excited gave pleasure; here stood a man who had maltreated his wife, but who could enthuse over a composer he had formerly despised. His thoughts lacked logic, or steadiness, balance.

Greene returned with his guest's coffee, a fair spillage in the saucer.

'Are you comfortable here?' Job Turner asked, waving arms at the walls.

The old man had been in his bungalow a bare three months, having sold his last, three times the size, to advantage.

'Yes. How do you like your place?'

'It's small and dark, but warm in the winter.'

'So you're not sorry you moved. Neither am I. You cook your own meals?'

'In the holidays, and at weekends.'

'I have a woman in every morning except Sunday, and she cleans and cooks lunch for me.'

'Well?'

'I beg your pardon?'

'Does she do it properly?'

'She passes muster. Now and again she stays to a meal herself. We get on without too much trouble. I put my arm round her waist, or stroke her backside.'

'She doesn't object?'

'No. Why should she? I rather imagine she's anticipating a little something in my will. She might even enjoy my advances. I'm not dead yet, you know.'

'How old is she?'

'Forties. She's always telling me how badly she gets on with her husband.'

Frederick Greene had spoken without boasting or emphasis, without facetiousness or prurience. His coffee and gin rested on the table before him untasted. The brightness that possessed him about Elgar had disappeared.

'I'm getting old,' Greene said. 'Bible-backed.' He held out his fingers. 'Look at these. Can barely play the piano now. Takes me all my time to put a record on.'

Now he began to boast, though vaguely, about his former strength, his success at money-making, his love of women. His head wobbled, his crooked hands moved unsteadily as he picked up and put down undrunk both his coffee and his gin. He talked quickly and breathily, darting glances at Turner, opening his nostrils to breathe deeply. The performance, though theatrical, was amateurish, with overdone arm-movement.

Turner emptied his cup, looking for an excuse to leave, but even as he stood, Greene opened a new line of conversation, which recording of the Elgar to buy, to delay him.

Turner answered brusquely, thanked his host for the coffee, went out. He put on his coat and scarf in the hall, without hurry, but still Greene did not appear. Job fiddled impatiently with gloves, decided to call his goodbyes through the door he had left open, but as he bent forward the old man made an appearance.

26

'I don't move quickly these days.'

Certainly Greene's spine looked much more curved than an hour or so ago. Once again Turner ran through his sentences of thanks, inviting Greene to visit him.

'Geoffrey would sooner visit you than me,' Greene whined.

'He doesn't come very often. Not even with Alison and the children.'

'But you like him?'

'Oh, yes. No doubt about it.'

Turner moved to the front door, called out again, opened up.

'Do you ever think about dying?' Greene spoke throatily, in his last attempt to delay.

'When Gillian . . . I . . . No, not often. No . . . but. There.'

Callously Job stepped outside, pulling the door shut behind him. The night froze round small stars, and he heard no sound, no fastening of bolt or catch, indoors.

# 3

Job Turner had given his daughter Alison an account of the visit to her father-in-law's. He had kept it, he thought, lightly amusing.

'Geoff's worried about him,' she said.

'Are you?'

'I can't be other. He's at an age now where he could do something silly. This Elgar business, for example, it's not stable, is it? Over-exaggeration, at the least. Nobody's better pleased than I am that he's taken up an interest in music, but. . .' She fixed him with her pretty scowl. 'I know he's got little else to occupy himself with.'

'Was he a good lawyer?' Job asked, hoping to learn.

'Yes, in his limited way, I suppose he was. Hopelessly provincial and without much interest in pure law, but he'd an eye to his main chance. Good at investment.'

'And you think he's lost his touch there?'

'I can't say. In any case it's his own money. No, we're a bit afraid that he might set the house on fire, or on the other hand he might entangle himself with a woman. He's always been something of a rip, though he was very careful, I admit, to cover his extramarital jaunts.'

'He'd be attractive as a young man.'

'For all I know,' Alison said, unimpressed. 'He led Geoffrey's mother a dog's life, poor woman. She left all her money to Geoff, nothing to him. Drew up the will once while she was away on holiday, not saying a word.'

'Was the old man annoyed when he found out?'

'Possible. She left a good deal of property that really takes a bit of looking after these days. I guess he'd be hurt or angry at the time, or she'd hope he would, but the inheritance would not have changed his life style. He was very rude to Geoffrey about it, or so Geoff says.'

'Did he hold it against his son?'

'We don't know, if you're talking about wills. He could leave his money to Battersea Dogs Home or some Charismatic chapel, but it doesn't seem altogether like him. He has a distant relative or two who might profit.'

'So, if he married some unsuitable woman and left her his money, it wouldn't matter much to you?'

'I think it would to Geoffrey. He would not want to see the old man make a fool of himself. He doesn't altogether like his father or approve of him, but he doesn't want him a target for scandal or scorn, or even to be cheated.'

'It would upset him?'

'Sometimes, Daddy, you do talk foolishly.'

'And that upsets you?'

They laughed together, but guardedly.

'Do you get along with him?' Job Turner asked. 'Is he likely to ask your advice?'

'Yes and no to your questions. He once paid me what I took to be a compliment when he said, "I should have married someone like you." I don't know exactly what he meant by that. In his view I'm still a woman. A poor, weak vessel.' She smiled with vinegary, thin lips.

'He told me you had much more initiative than Geoffrey.'

'Yes.' Her mouth grew grim. 'He'll take any opportunity to run Geoffrey down. Did he act eccentrically? Apart from this enthusiasm for Elgar?'

'He poured himself gin and coffee, and drank neither.'

'Could be worse. Keep your eye on him.'

'If past form's anything to go by, I shan't see him for the next three years.'

'Did he make a favourable impression on you?'

'Not really.'

Alison wished him goodbye; he was unsure about her motives for the inquisition, certain she had left something unsaid. At the door he promised to call round to see the children.

When his daughter had gone, Job Turner sat by his fire, a solitary, bemused. Alison had filled the small room, with her quick movement, resonant voice, her expensive perfume. She

29

represented another world, richer, more diversified than his. Since his wife's death he had realized how much of his own energy and success had been in his partner's gift. Gillian had been quick, knowing her own mind; she had made the family decisions for them and he suspected had regarded his career in schools as an easy option. Beautiful, tall and almost unageing, she had enhanced the quality of his life, had made an interesting man of the dull schoolmaster, an artist of the musician, a Prospero of the father. When she had died, in hospital after a road accident, he was left to wander in a landscape of broken projects. She had kept him full-tilt at his work, because he needed to prove to her that his schemes and events had worth; a word of praise from Gill outranked all official congratulation. Now she was taken away from him, and his lonely life was lived by habit.

He snatched at his weekday anorak and marched out towards the Hall, along the avenue. A few children dawdled in groups in this their Easter holidays. The wind had shifted from the east, but blew cold now out of the northwest, massing black shower-clouds. Job Turner walked hard until his incipient depression began to fade in the intensity of action; his cheeks glowed; his breath came short.

'Hey, there. Hey-up.'

Job slowed down, but did not look round. Headmasters are unused to bawled greetings or warnings.

'Can you give us a minute?'

Now he turned. The caretaker from the Hall was advancing, crisscrossing his arms about his head. Turner watched the progress, the breathless arrival. For a short time the man stood in front of him, incapable of speech but indicating by jabs with his hands that he would soon remedy the defect.

'I just wanted a word with you,' the man said finally. Short, overweight, he was rather younger of face than Job had expected from his casual observations at a distance as they had exchanged greetings. 'Mr Turner, in't it? They tell me you're something of a musician. Is that right?'

Job modestly made noises of acquiescence.

'Do you know anything about pianos?'

'I've played a good number.'

'I wondered if you could come in some time and look at the one in the Hall.'

'When?'

'Any time you're free.'

'Now, for instance?'

'Yes. If you please.'

They set off across a grassy hillock, on to an asphalted drive which led through a brick archway into a wide yard, quite bare, and overlooked on three sides by blind, dusty windows. The caretaker led up four worn steps, through a heavy door and into the main building.

'Tradesmen's entrance,' he said.

'Why these steps?' Job asked.

'They didn't think o' servants' legs in them days.'

The room they had entered was large, utterly empty, the shelves naked, the walls a yellowish brown rather than the county cream of the original paint. Footsteps echoed under the high ceiling, but the man did not pause for explanation, pushed out into a dark corridor.

'The kitchens was through there.'

They walked, a dark length, then up again by uncarpeted wooden stairs.

'They had to carry the food all this way. Ridiculous, in't it? Even from the point of view of keeping it warm.'

Now they were in a spacious foyer, half-lit by distant, stained-glass gothic windows. The main door stood opposite; a double, curved flight of stone-balustraded stairs led regally upwards.

'That was the dining room.' A black thumb pointed briefly right. 'We go this way.' The caretaker led to doors under the staircase which were broad enough to drive a lorry through and still, in spite of damp, dust, darkness and neglect, highly polished as glass, beautifully grained.

'The large drawing room,' he said, hand on an ornate, immense brass knob.

They entered, quietly, cowed by the size of the room. Five large windows on the south side cast a faint light through the drawn, heavy, faded-red velvet curtains. One of the four

31

windows on the north wall, uncurtained, lit the room. All the furniture was hidden under dust-sheets.

The caretaker led towards a grand piano, whisking away its cover, dropping it to the floor with a flourish.

'It's this I want you to look at,' he said and dragged out the stool. 'It's not locked.'

Job Turner lifted the lid of the Bechstein. The keys were yellowish; when he struck a chord he found it badly out of tune. He jangled into a Bach minuet, without pleasure. The caretaker stood at his shoulder.

'Who's that by then?' he asked.

'Bach.'

'My favourite's Chopin. Ballades, impromptus, nocturnes.'

Turner struck the opening chords of the Polonaise in A flat, but gave up at the tuneless racket he created.

'It's badly in need of tuning.'

'How much would that cost?'

'Twelve, fifteen pounds. But one tuning might not bring it up to concert pitch.'

'Does it need repairs?'

Between them they lifted the lid and peered inside. It was dusty and there were indications of rust. Back at the keyboard Job Turner rattled through a chromatic scale from top to bottom, then down again. He struck another chord.

'These instruments are beautifully made,' he answered. 'And though this one has been neglected, it doesn't look too bad.'

'So fifteen pounds would make it playable?'

'With luck.'

The caretaker, in a solemn flurry of thanks, closed the lid and replaced the cover before asking the name of Turner's own tuner. Turner drew out his pocket-diary and gave the information, telephone number, a reference to efficiency.

'It's like this, Mr Turner,' the man answered, smoothing with rapid hand movements the top of the piano. 'My name's Smith, by the way. I've a daughter who's done very well on the piano, passed Grade 7 with distinction, wants to do eight and then her diploma. Now our piano's all right, y'know, for an upright but it isn't a Bechstein. This one's standing here

32

useless, and likely to do so for some time. If I could set it right at the expense of a few pounds then she could come in here every day and practise on it.'

Smith's voice had acquired a gentility, as if once again he served the squirearchy.

'I see.'

'Is it wise?'

'Aren't they selling the Hall and contents off?'

'In time. It'll take a year or two. You know what corporations are like. They're dealing with the grounds after a fashion. So they'll probably hang on to this. As a show-place. I'm only guessing. But I like to back my hunches.'

Smith explained that his daughter's teacher, Noelle Waters, now thought she should retire, that Susan needed someone younger, more energetic to put the girl through her diploma. 'She mentioned your name.' Turner felt surprise; he had met Mrs Waters occasionally, at musical festivals, at the county music school, knew her reputation as an outstanding teacher, but had no idea she rated him so highly. 'She said we needed an all-round musician, not just a pianist for these final exams.'

'My experience is exactly the opposite.'

'That's what she said.'

Without hesitation Smith continued with his argument, pressing Turner to phone Noelle Waters and to grant Susan an audition. He led back through the foyer, down the stairs and into the servants' domain, then the yard. Job realized that he had been put through some sort of test.

'I'll take you round one of these days,' Smith promised, once they were in the open air. 'It's worth a glance. That I can tell you.'

'Does it take much looking-after?'

'I'll say. The wife and I are supposed to keep the dust down. And in the winter it's my job to put the central heating on. But that's as old as the hills. Must cost a fortune.'

In the end he held out a plump hand, taking it for granted that Job Turner had fallen in with his wishes.

'You'll ring Noelle Waters, won't you, and let me know?'

Out here, in daylight, he looked younger, fatter, more formidable, aggressive.

Job Turner gave his word.

Since his wife's death, he had done some piano teaching at the Saturday morning music school. Already he had two pupils, younger than this Susan Smith, one thirteen, one fourteen, both gifted, and he enjoyed the effort he spent on them. Preparing another talented musician for examinations would occupy his time, but he felt the need for caution. Smith's last words rang in his head.

'It seemed like an act of Providence when I found out you lived just on our doorstep.'

The pair shook hands again; Turner returned straight home.

Later in the day he telephoned Noelle Waters, received a favourable report and therefore wrote to Smith asking Susan to present herself.

# 4

The Saturday Susan Smith came to the Lodge had been bright, warm with sunshine, brilliant with daffodils, windless, charming. Job Turner had walked out both morning and afternoon and had returned sweating, pleased even with the knots of people who were making their first venture into the country park. He sang out loud, touched his hat to the one or two pedestrians he met whom he recognized. Dogs scooted about; the riding school dispatched its young people, black-hatted, into the sharp light and shadows.

By seven-thirty, the appointed time, Turner lounged, almost tired out by the excitement of the day.

At seven-thirty-six Susan rang his door bell.

She smiled, apologized for her lateness, saying she had miscalculated the time it had taken her from Hall to Lodge. She removed her coat, and sat straight, primly, on the edge of a chair. She answered questions about her education, present work, ambitions with a clear voice, grammatically but with a local accent. She had good teeth.

Susan was not sure that she wished to make a career in music, but thought she would like to be good enough to teach the piano, at least locally. She didn't collect classical records, no, and she was interested in some pop. Mrs Waters had spoken very highly of him.

'She spoke highly of you,' Job answered. 'And she said she would continue to give you consultation-lessons, if I agreed. But whether or not you stick by me depends on how well we get on with each other.'

'I shall work hard.' Susan spoke sharply, as in rebuke.

'I'm sure. But one never knows. We may not see eye to eye.'

'I shall do my best.'

The girl leant forward, her blouse open one button too low, revealing a black brassière.

'Would you like to play for me?' he asked. 'This piano's rather small in tone, but I had to fit it to the size of this place.'

'I've never been in this lodge before.'

'Did you bring some music?'

She pointed to the case she had propped against the chair. He pulled out the piano stool. She edged in to the keyboard, music on her knee.

'Have you any preferences?' she asked.

'I leave it to you.'

She did not take long, but pulled out a book, opened it on the stand, and began. A Chopin waltz. She played it through rapidly, accurately, with signs of musicality.

'Good,' he said, when she'd finished.

'I'm not quite used to your piano.'

'We'll take that into account. I liked that. Let's hear something else.'

Now she chose the Brahms Rhapsody in G minor, and performed it, face set, elbows determinedly in, with some power.

'We could do with a bigger piano for that,' he told her.

'I'm beginning to like this.'

'Do you enjoy Brahms? Have you done very much?'

'No, I haven't. But this is good. It's strong music.'

'You're right there. Play something else, please.'

She fiddled inside her case, extracted Debussy's 'Golliwog's Cake-Walk', did it well, but solemn-faced. He praised her, laughing. She did not join in.

'Can you memorize music easily?'

'I think so.'

'Would you show me?'

Susan sat for a moment, rubbing her lip with the index-finger of her right hand, making the choice. The stillness, the indecision made her look younger, an eight-year-old hesitating between cream cakes. Quite suddenly she began without fuss on the Schubert B flat Impromptu.

The girl played easily, almost as if she herself improvised

36

Schubert's inspired simplicities, the only sign of strain an occasional snort of breath.

'Shall I go on?' she asked, after the third variation.

'Can you?'

She smiled at that, picked hands from lap and continued.

'I'm impressed,' he said, stopping her. She nodded, but returned immediately to her playing.

'I like that last variation,' she answered, when she had completed the coda. 'It suits my fingers.'

Again he praised her, and asked her to stand with her back to him while he gave her ear-tests, of Grade 8 and Diploma standard. She was in no trouble there, her only two errors he put down to his own inaccuracy with rhythm.

'Have you got perfect pitch?' he asked.

'No. I don't think so.'

He played a note, asked her to name it. She did so immediately. They giggled together. Once more he sat her at the piano while he searched in the cupboard for the Forty-Eight.

'Have you done any Bach?'

'A bit. For exams.'

Turner opened the book at the E major, No. IX of Book Two, setting it on the stand in front of her. She studied it, eyes half closed, and bowed her head towards him before she started. Again she played well, muttering at and correcting her occasional mistakes. She commented on the unusual typography of the mordent on the last chord of the prelude. When the fugue was done he asked her what she thought of the music.

'It's not very difficult, technically. But I don't know how to play it. Except to make each part clear.'

'That's not a bad start.' He asked if she knew the term 'suspension' and they discussed the best way to deal with Bach's on a modern piano. He was surprised, a little later, that she did not seem conversant with 'stretto'. She listened, hands in lap, as he explained something of the principles of fugal writing.

'Now,' he said, 'just play us the major scale of E as for your last exam.'

She rattled up the keyboard with one slight slip.

'Again, please,' he ordered.

This time the flow was flawless.

'Would you like a cup of coffee?' he asked her. She stared, strangely, as if he had asked the question in a foreign language one had once studied.

'Yes, please.' The voice was thin, almost nonexistent.

'Play, if you wish, while I make it. Or have a rest, That's better. I've worked you hard.'

When he returned she was sitting on the piano stool, staring at one of the Forty-Eight. He signalled her to another chair, telling her to make herself comfortable. She looked into the proffered tin and chose a chocolate biscuit.

Without delay he made it clear that he would accept her as a pupil, half at the piano, half on theory at the same rate she had paid Noelle Waters.

After a quarter of an hour Susan began to talk freely. She had done well at 'O' levels, but had not considered staying on in the sixth form. 'I want to concentrate,' she said. 'Other subjects like history or English Literature seem a waste of time. You don't agree with that, do you?' She laughed, as if she'd already heard and dismissed from her own school-masters his expected answers.

'Perhaps you'll change your mind. Later on.'

Susan said how satisfying it was to be financially independent. Both her mother and father had jobs, and had paid for her lessons while she was at school, but now she could do as she liked. She worked in a solicitor's office, where she was in charge, for the old dear who had slaved there for 'donkey's years' had died suddenly and had not been replaced. Yes, she could manage. There was responsibility certainly, but she'd been shown the ropes and now appeared sure that she gave her employers what they wanted. The principal partners, a husband and wife, were a pair of oddities, but absolutely fair, and knew what they were about. 'Dry as dust, they are, both of them.'

'Have they no children?'

'Yes. Two. Both grown up, and living away.'

She supposed her employers were in their fifties.

'Do they look older than I am?'

She screwed up her eyes, but answered that she did not know. Susan's demeanour suggested to Turner that he had no business putting such questions. When she had finished her coffee, she said she must leave.

Hurriedly he fixed her next lesson for the following Tuesday. He said he would consult Miss Waters about the timing of examinations and choice of pieces. He asked the girl to prepare a Beethoven sonata, or part of it. She chose the 'Pathétique'. 'I've heard it, but I've never studied it.' Yes, she had a copy. At home they had a complete Beethoven piano sonatas which she would use.

'Is it a good edition?' he asked. She did not know.

'But there's nothing wrong with my eyesight.'

Now Susan looked young as she went out into the darkness. He thought he ought to accompany her, but made no offer.

# 5

Frederick Greene telephoned asking Turner to come up to his home.

'What is it this time?' Job demanded. 'More Elgar?'

'No. Though I've started on the Violin Concerto as well as the Cello.' He sounded satisfied. 'No. I'm in a bit of trouble, one way or the other. Can't talk about it over the phone. But I'd be obliged if you'd pay me a call.' The voice was cheerful enough.

'You come to see me.'

Greene's voice whined now. He was old; he did not go out much; the weather was cold.

'Get a taxi. Door to door. You'll enjoy the outing and it'll do you good.'

'I'm quite capable of driving my own car.'

'I'm sure. But use a cab. Easier all round. Make the effort.'

They fixed the day and time of the appointment.

Job watched Frederick Greene's arrival from the front window. The old man was helped from the cab, staggered the two steps to the gate, but looked the white house over carefully. Illuminated by the two outside lights, the visitor swayed on the path, his long topcoat half-buttoned, his scarf loosely tied. Turner opened the door before the bell rang.

'You've made it. I told you so.'

Greene flung his arms about in imperfect circles, but said nothing. Turner helped him out of his coat and through the door into an easy chair where the man sat without speech, breathing heavily, dead to the world.

'Can I get you a drink?'

The visitor opened his eyes, pushed at the air with his right hand.

'Coffee please. Black. With a spoonful of whisky or brandy in it, if you have such a thing.' The voice sounded normally strong. When Turner reappeared with the drinks, Greene was hitching his trouser-legs and staring at his glossy shoes, light as dancing-pumps. The two men, settled opposite each other, exchanged sentences about health, the late spring, heating-bills. Greene looked at his coffee cup, but made no attempt to drink.

'This is a cramped place,' he said, rudely.

Good-humouredly Job gave some account of its provenance. The old man, pulling at his wrinkled jowls, bottom lip wet, lisped questions about the other Turner and why he had lumbered his namesake with this out-of-the-way place.

'I've never been left property before,' Job said. 'I can't sell this until I've lived in it. That's the wording. No specific period.'

'But does it suit you?'

'Yes. It does. Why not?'

Greene nodded his head at the foolishness of mankind.

'The making of wills is the cause of eccentricity in some people,' he pronounced. 'The power to surprise or harm appeals, perhaps. Not that they'll see the result of their machi-nations.' For some ten minutes the old solicitor talked from his experience, interestingly, with a clarity of mind and strength of voice. He sat upright; he might have been at the desk in his office advising some favoured client. Then his voice faded, his hand sawed, the straight back bent.

'There you are, then.' His voice whined.

'Don't forget your coffee.'

'No. It'll be too hot, still.'

'You wanted to ask me about something, you said.' Job Turner set it plainly out.

'I did?'

'Yes. On the phone. That's the reason for your visit.'

The old man scratched his face, gathering his scattered wits.

'I don't know now,' he replied, at length, 'whether I want to talk about it, whether it would be wise.'

'You'll have to decide that for yourself.'

'Oh, I shall, I shall. Make no mistake.' He paused, rolling in his chair, groaning. 'I'm in my eightieth year, and old for my age. Physically, I mean: I'm terrified now if I have to cross the road. Fearful. I'm so slow.' He looked across to see the effect of these confidences. Turner picked up his cup, drank socially. The other stared out into the far top corner of the room as if something hovered there which he had not quite latched on to. 'Because I'm so uncertain I thought it would be sensible to talk to someone, and so I rang you on the spur of the moment.'

'I see.'

'You'd be surprised how many people get relief by coming out with their secrets. They would sit in my office all day and let their tongues wag. It cost them money, but I suppose we don't consult the doctor or the parson these days.'

'In America or Switzerland you find a great many psycho-therapists who are never short of clients.'

'I'm not surprised.' Greene's eyes shone dully, with moisture. 'But it's indiscreet sometimes. To confess. To put yourself into someone else's power. I'm feeble now, tottering. I thought of you.'

'Yes,' Turner answered, hardly following.

'Not that you could do anything to help me out. You could give me your advice, and though I'm sure it would be sound, I don't think I'd of necessity follow it. It's just I'd like some-body standing by me when I cross a road to make certain I won't fail to spot a road-hog, and get bowled over. It's dangerous and frightening is old age. But what do you think?'

Job Turner, impressed by the old man's cunning, took out his reading-glasses and perched them on his nose. His staff, his pupils, his parents often sought advice from him, some-times on topics about which he felt ignorant, but he knew the importance of giving the appearance of close attention, of concern.

'I don't . . . I can't answer you until you've told me more.'

'On the general principle?'

'I wouldn't confess an indiscretion on my part,' Turner said, slowly, 'to somebody else without very good reason.'

'Because their confidentiality is not to be trusted.'

'That comes into it. But mainly because I should find neither relief nor satisfaction in making the confession. I'm secretive. If I'm ill, I'm like a cat. I creep off to my own corner.'

'Are you to be trusted?' Greene demanded, straight up, but holding broken-scarecrow fashion to the arms of his chair.

'I make no great claims.' Job picked up his cup. 'Drink your coffee. It'll be cold.'

'You're an old woman. What my father used to call "an old hen clucking for daylight".'

'Oh, thank you.'

Greene picked up his coffee and sipped it as if it were poisonous. He returned it to its table.

'We're no further forward, then, are we?' he asked, slyly smiling.

'No.'

'Aren't you curious to find out what I've been up to?'

'Of course.'

'But you still think I shouldn't tell you.'

'You've decided on that yourself. And, if I may say so, you don't seem to need me.'

'At this moment, no.' Greene, fingers perched on thumb, wagged a whole hand. 'But I'm pleased with myself. I've made the effort and emerged from my prison without breaking any bones. I'm in congenial company. But that's a different kettle of fish from the small hours or when I'm a bit off, when I can't cope, when I've no energy to raise a finger to fend for myself.'

'I see that. But if I were in your shoes I'd postpone the decision and find out if you can manage. If you can't, you can always come back.'

'And waste another cab-fare.' Greene wheezed, grinning. He might have been an actor hamming up old age.

'If it's not worth that, it can't be very serious.'

'I didn't say it was.' Greene studied his coffee over the top of a pair of glasses he had now farcically donned to match Turner's. He pinched in his lips. 'I think I can tell you.' Turner removed his spectacles, tucked them into the case and waited. Greene smacked his lips, drew in a lungful of air, sat straighter.

43

'It's that woman,' he began. 'The cleaning woman.' He squinted slyly over the glasses.

'Does she have a name?'

'Harper. Mrs Harper.' He gave the information grudgingly, glancing about him. 'We had sex.' Job Turner, not knowing whether to laugh or cry, sat silent. 'I felt like it one morning. She was free and easy. She stayed to lunch and, well, it happened.'

'Just the once?'

'Yes. I've kept out of her way these last few times. I think I may have acted unwisely.'

'What leads you to suppose that?'

'Sexual intercourse is a dangerous social proceeding. At least with mature adults. It involves emotional charge. It did not, as it happens, in my case. I enjoyed it, mere hedonism. I might even say I was proud of myself. I mean I'm nearly eighty. But what about her? Money changed hands. I added something to her weekly account.'

'She didn't take offence?'

'No, not that I noticed. She mentioned the increase, and smiled. Conspiratorially. Thanked me.'

'Did she . . . show pleasure during the . . . ?'

'Look here, Turner, I'm not going to give you a blow-by-blow account just to satisfy your lubricious imagination. She was willing enough. You can always tell when a woman's ready. And, yes, she enjoyed it.'

'What's the problem, then?'

'You can see bloody well what it is. Here I've got a cleaning woman who's regular, does her work adequately, cooks lunch and now look where we are. It won't be long before she starts to make demands, and I'm in no sort of state to resist them. All because I dropped into old habits or had to prove something to myself. I've done that all right. I've shown myself what a bloody fool I am.' He spoke without heat, reasonably.

'Don't forget your coffee,' Turner warned.

'Bugger you and your coffee. I don't want it.' Now Greene flapped his hands in a tantrum. 'I've something more to think about.'

'Is that so?'

Greene trembled with anger, but his rage quickly subsided and he was left muttering, a low, fierce, incoherent chatter, more frightening to the onlooker than the overt manifestation of his irascibility. Job Turner sat staring at the other man's shoes which in this small room were only eighteen inches from his own.

'I've always been what they call a ladies' man.' The sentence, unexpectedly delivered, caught Turner's attention. He nodded. 'It's nothing to boast about insofar as it troubled my wife. Elgar lusted after other women, but. . .' Greene seemed to fall asleep. 'I don't think he committed adultery. Did he? And he fancied women of rank. Gentlewomen. He was a mixed-up creature. Had the worst of all worlds.'

'Except that he composed.'

'He lost faith in that. Why he. . .' Greene sighed, made a clucking noise with his mouth, and moved his head, deliberately it appeared, in a sharp zigzag, before shaking it mournfully from side to side. 'Still, Elgar's troubles won't sort mine out. Worse luck.'

'What are you going to do?'

'First, if not foremost, I'm going to set your mind at rest by drinking your excellent coffee.'

'It must be stone-cold.'

Grinning, as if he'd scored a point, Greene drained his cup, replaced it, wiped his mouth with the back of his hand, and composed himself. 'Secondly, I shall try to act as if nothing has happened. Thirdly, I'll listen to what you have to say.'

'Go on.'

'Two and three are, I admit, difficult. Two, especially. I'll paddle along for a week or two, and then get a rush of blood to my head, or some other part of my anatomy, and away we go again.'

'How do you know that these casual encounters don't suit your Mrs Harper?'

'I don't. My experience is that women will make trouble or gain advantage if they can.'

'More so than men?' Turner pressed.

'Yes. No doubt about it. Isn't that your view?'

'No.'

Greene hummed and nodded, as if he expected as much, but still asked how he was to proceed. Turner, intrigued and vaguely annoyed, praised the old man's clarity, said he'd do well to keep out of Mrs Harper's way, and hope.

'I tend to be a pessimist,' Greene said, almost complacently. 'But we'll drop the subject.' He inquired about Turner's school. Job told him about his new commitment to teach Susan Smith to diploma standard. Immediately Greene subjected him to a long series of technical questions, as if testing Turner's qualifications for the task. Both men were thoroughly enjoying themselves, cut and thrust, when the doorbell interrupted them.

'My taxi-driver,' Greene said, looking at the clock. 'I wish I'd left it rather later, but I'm slow. I need to be in bed on time. Nor did I think it would be as interesting as this. Go and answer the door, man. I can get up on my own. And don't mention the other business to Alison.'

'Is it likely?'

'You're used to too much power and too little responsibility.'

'Many thanks.'

By this time the cab-man was hammering on the door.

'Sorry,' he apologized to Turner, 'but the old gent's a bit deaf.' He nodded inwards where Greene, struggling into his overcoat, took in every word.

'I'll let you know,' the visitor sighed, did not shake hands, made steadily for the taxi, 'any developments.'

# 6

Job Turner's lessons to Susan Smith brought him pleasure. The girl showed not only talent and assiduity, but an immense willingness to learn. He lent her books which she read, rather slowly in her limited time, but very thoroughly. She was competitive, hated her mistakes, fought to set them right, was determined to please him. He consulted Noelle Waters and between them they decided on Susan's examination pieces and plan of campaign. Moreover the weather brightened; occasional days were warm at last.

Susan now practised on the piano at the Hall which had been tuned.

'I'm not thumping away in their ears every spare minute of the day, now.'

'Didn't they like it?'

'Well, you know. My Dad does. He creeps in to listen. He doesn't say anthing, but I leave the doors open so he can sit in the foyer and hear it all.' When she spoke like this she seemed younger than her years, a tricky schoolgirl.

'Does he ever discuss it with you?'

'No. Not really. He's a very good brass player. You knew that.' Turner did not. 'But if I ask him about something to do with the piece I'm playing he'll just say, "You'd better ask Mrs Waters or Mr Turner." But he loves music. Has Radio 3 on all day.'

'And your mother?'

'She used to sing in a choir and play the piano. But not now. "My teachers were no good," she says. "They'd no idea." '

When he found out that Susan had never been to a concert, he repaired the damage at once. He chose the next popular programme: overture to the *Thievish Magpie*, Schumann's Piano Concerto and Beethoven's Fifth.

47

Susan turned up at his house in her rather old-fashioned Sunday-best; obviously her mother had had some say in the choice. She looked young and pretty, with a copper light in her hair.

'They were always going to take us to a concert from school,' she said, seated in the car, 'but our class missed it. Always somebody else.'

After her last harmony lesson, he'd played the Beethoven on his stereo-set and they had followed, side by side at the table, the score. She was quick, convinced and delighted by his explanation of sonata-form, to make suggestions or query his conclusions. Much of what he taught her, elementary to him, seemed new to her; she had been well instructed but only within the strict limits dictated by the examination syllabuses. The Smiths had no record-player at home, for her father had said there was enough good music on the radio and that he knew what would happen if he bought a stereo, his daughter would waste her money on, and blast his ears in, with 'pop'.

'Is that the truth?' Job asked her.

'I expect so.'

This evening they occupied good seats, in the middle of the upper circle, and arrived early so that he could park his car and she enjoy the preliminaries. She sat rather straight, and nervously, unsmiling, unwilling to miss a striking dress, a handsome man, the polish on the double-basses already lying on the platform, the casual arrival and chat of the players as they turned and sorted their music. She clapped, making no noise, for the advent of the leader, and again on the appearance of the conductor, checking with her programme.

She did not move during the Rossini, her eyes glistening. The cliché 'riveted' exactly described her pinned-back immobility.

'What do you think of that, then?'

Her excitement barely allowed her to talk.

'Marvellous,' she got out. 'The sound. The sound of it.'

She did not look at him in her exhilaration but kept her eyes on the platform where the piano was being wheeled centre-stage. Turner noticed three rows in front of him his daughter

Alison and her husband. Susan's knees were neatly together; she held on to her programme as if it might drift away. Rossini's crescendi had conquered her.

'Do you know the Schumann?' he asked.

He needed to put the question twice; she broke from her rigidity to say, programme to mouth, 'We studied it for 'O' level.'

Why had she not told him this before? Why had he not inquired? He said nothing about his daughter's presence; Susan fixed her eyes on the reassembling orchestra. A violinist on the first desk tapped A on the piano.

'Is it in tune?' Job whispering, jovial.

She opened her eyes wide as she turned her head towards him. He might have been speaking Greek. The soloist and conductor bustled forward; both seemed big young men, brawny, ready with their white bows and tail coats to wrestle with the music. The pianist adjusted his seat, wiped his hands on a folded handkerchief. The raised baton descended; Schumann's fantasy zigzagged down across the hall. Susan did not move. Her lips were slightly parted. She caught him looking at her, smiled, and immediately set her face into solemnity. Time and eternity coalesced.

At the end of the concerto she applauded with vigour, impetuously slapping her hands. He thought she might shout out. The pianist's formal bow, his dignified reappearance, the puppetry of his acknowledgement had nothing to do with the music or Susan's rapturous violence. She was the last to cease clapping, and when he touched her arm, motioning her to accompany him outside, she barely seemed able to draw her breath.

'Good?' he asked in the foyer.

'Perfect.'

'You didn't hear any wrong notes?'

She shook her head at the blasphemy.

Alison made for them, beautiful in black, fair hair upthrust. She touched her father on the arm.

'My word. Lill can certainly play.'

Turner saw Geoffrey Greene leading his father towards them. He introduced his daughter to Susan who now looked dressed for the kitchen compared with Alison's elegant simplicities. The older woman spoke warmly, moved by the music, as she shook hands.

'That was very good, wasn't it?'

'Susan said it was perfect.'

Alison's surprise was interrupted by the arrival of husband and father-in-law, two more big men. She made the introductions.

'Wasn't that superb?' Geoffrey.

'I've heard of you,' the old man wheezed. 'From Job here.'

Susan shook hands shyly. Geoffrey began to talk immediately, setting the girl at ease. His father joined him, voice strong, recalling a performance in the 1930s by Gieseking.

'Was it better than this evening's?' Turner.

'How can I tell?' The old man laughed. 'I was fifty years younger, and that was an advantage.'

'To hear this made me feel young again.' Geoffrey spoke warmly as he and his father continued reminiscence or banter, all directed towards Susan. The two were out to impress, inform, make the girl feel important, and they succeeded. Alison encouraged them like a manager. Their laughter turned heads towards them. Susan looked from one to the other, entranced, but prim with it. Job Turner had not realized how attractive Frederick Greene could appear. He was quite unlike the figure who had tottered in on his son's arm.

Turner felt quite annoyed when a bell signalled the end of the interval. The Greenes, one either side, both talking volubly, led the silent, delighted Susan back into the auditorium. Alison touched Job's arm, holding her father back.

'Look at them,' she said. 'The ladies' men. They're really enjoying themselves with that young woman of yours.'

'It's good for her.'

'I'm sure. And for Fred. Just look at him. Straight and spry as you like. Whereas when we came in he could barely breathe, had to be helped up a stair at a time.'

'Whose idea was it? For you to bring him?'

'Geoffrey's. His conscience troubles him now and again. Besides, he didn't think the old man would take him up on it. He'd be too exhausted or Beethoven's Fifth wasn't worth crossing the street to listen to.'

'But he surprised you?'

'Yes. Just as you do, bringing pretty young ladies out to concerts.' She smiled, impishly, so that he remembered how the clever Alison and her mother would at one time dissolve into fits of giggling.

'One only. A pupil.'

'Don't excuse yourself. Fred wouldn't.'

She gave him a little push towards the door, and held his elbow, pleased with herself. The Greenes, expansive and in everybody's way, still talked in the aisle; by the time Job had prised Susan away from them, the leader of the orchestra had made his appearance. Job had just time to wonder whether the soloist would stay to hear the performance, or was already on his way to London down the M1.

Bows bit strings; clarinets supported; heads were flung back. Beethoven spoke his iron law. Susan, engrossed, sat still as a stone. At the end of the slow movement while the players returned she looked at him for the first time, full face. She wished to say something, but could not.

'Now we'll hear some real Beethoven,' he said, helping her out. Tears glistened. He nodded, patting her arm, delighted that he could observe the effect of Beethoven's andante con moto on this gifted girl. He thought of Schubert going to see the great master's corpse and begging for a hair from a body already turning blue with corruption. But now the composer lived again, scherzando and then magnificent with trombones. Turner wished that he had listened, as his pupil had, to the symphony for the first time in his life in a concert hall. As a schoolboy he had studied the Beethoven Fifth and the César Franck in class; they were now fixed as the music of his spring, of love, blossom, cotton-wool clouds.

They exchanged a few words with the Greenes; Susan walked down the stairs with Geoffrey while Alison and Job piloted the old man, who puffed and blew for their sympathy. On the way home the girl three or four times expressed her thanks, trying to phrase the ineffable and choking in shyness. Turner watched her walk under the brick arch into the lighted court-yard of the Hall, where she turned and waved. The sight of the dark silhouette with hand raised pleased him beyond all bounds.

Job Turner spent the Thursday, Friday and Saturday of the next week in London attending a committee on the teaching of music in schools. He found the meetings dull, but the talk between and in the evenings made the jaunt valuable. A professor of piano at the Royal Academy and a lugubrious, witty Glaswegian, lecturer in music at Liverpool University made contact with him over lunch and he revelled in their company. The pianist, a large, red-faced extrovert, told Turner that the schools, public or private, did their best to kill music, and argued for 'centres of excellence'. The Scotsman, who looked no more than thirty, and who had been pushed on to the committee because his head of department did not want to attend, said drily that the trouble with teachers of all sorts was that they had inordinate difficulty in recognizing outstanding talent. 'Look at Britten,' he warned them, his voice lilting, 'and what they told him at the Royal College. That his work was too continental, too European. It makes me despair.' Job described his dealings with Susan Smith; the other two listened carefully, even courteously, to what he had to say, but as if they did not understand his problems. The pianist made practical suggestions about requirements for the licentiateship, and the changes of fashion amongst examiners, 'I know. I'm one of 'em.' and told Turner that if the girl was as good as he thought, she should be entered for a scholarship at one of the colleges. 'Not that there's much of a living to be made with the piano these days.'

'Is the standard as high as ever?' Dr Mackenzie asked.

'Remarkably so. And that means that other factors besides technical skill or even musicianship are those which bring success. Resilience, character, dedicated assiduity, luck; paranoia sometimes.' Walter Wrangel laughed, 'Believe you me.'

That evening, Wrangel had retired to his home in Kentish Town, Mackenzie walked the lighted streets about the Euston Road with Turner after dinner. The young man was writing a symphony, but did not know what chances of performance it had.

'I'm not in touch with enough influential people,' he whispered. 'A friend of mine on Scottish Radio managed to organize a passable broadcast of my Rhapsody for Cello and Orchestra, but a longish symphony is another matter altogether.'

Mackenzie grumbled gloomily from a dour face, but Turner guessed he was an optimistic character. He'd reach forty this year, Mozart and Purcell were long dead by that age, and nothing would stop him.

'You'd like to become famous?' Turner mocked.

'Who wouldn't?' He dropped his head. 'I think I have some ideas worth hearing. I'm not always sure, but. . .' He slapped his mac. 'If I'm not, who else will be?'

Job Turner glanced time and again at Mackenzie's face, at meals or in meetings. One would not guess that he was a musician, a composer – the pallor of the skin, the lank cheeks, the slightly balding head gave him the appearance of a costing clerk, a woodwork-teacher or a backstreet grocer. From time to time in the course of a speech or argument he'd pull out a small manuscript book from his inside pocket and jot down notes, ignoring the curiosity of his neighbours. He never hurried his hand, wrote his fill, sometimes a mere half-dozen crochets, once two and a half lines, reread it and now and then made an additional bar available to himself for future use. It seemed important, this bit of private enterprise, compared with the continuing strong speeches. As the two assembled their bags in the foyer of the hotel before leaving for home, Turner asked Mackenzie if he would describe these fragments as inspirations.

'No.' The voice was tuneful, quiet, friendly. 'More like pointers. If there is inspiration it will come in the long periods of writing. Or waiting. These are suggestions I might use, and which I can't afford to neglect.'

The composer shook his head, as if somebody hadn't got it right.

On his return, Susan said that she had received two extra lessons, in lieu of his, from Noelle Waters, who was now concentrating on her scales. 'She's a fanatic,' the girl complained, half humorously, 'and says scale-technique, rhythm and speed, is one of the real essentials, that musicianship is useless without this and other basics.'

'What do you think?'

'It seems obvious. But Noelle had been somewhere, I've forgotten exactly, and had been talking to Fanny Waterman, she's been a friend for long enough, and she said that it was lack of technique that made English pianists do so badly in international competitions.'

'She should know.'

'I sometimes get bored with scales.'

'I'm not surprised. I'll think about it.'

The following week she excitedly showed him a book on Beethoven by Romain Rolland, which Frederick Greene had sent her.

'Have you read it?' he asked.

'I've started. He, Mr Greene that is, asked me to go round to his house to play duets with him. Is he any good? As a player?'

'I believe he wasn't bad, but he's old now, nearly eighty. One's not quite so energetic, but he's an interesting man, in his eccentric way.'

'His son, your daughter's husband, is very handsome, isn't he?'

Job Turner had never thought of Geoffrey in that way.

'That's the sort of man you'd like to marry?'

'He's too old.' She blushed deeply. 'My dad wondered if you'd like to hear the Hall piano now it's been tuned.'

He promised to give her a lesson there some time, instructing her with a chuckle that he'd pay attention to her scales.

# 7

Job Turner lunched with Alison and her family on Sunday.
He enjoyed reading to Sarah, who sat on his knee with all the
straight-backed attention of her mother while he dealt with
trains, zoos, new babies and Rapunzel. After the meal the
whole family took a stroll in the nearby park; Turner was
allowed to push the baby in the pram. Geoffrey and Alison
swung Sarah along between them, walked her on the top of
flat walls, hid from her behind trees and whirled her high on
the swings until she shrieked with delight. In bright sunlight
Geoffrey's brogues glistened, and in spite of his size he moved
with the speed of a man twenty years his junior. He laughed
and jumped with the child, while Alison watched him
indulgently.

'Do you always come out together on Sunday?' Job asked
Alison.

'If it's possible. It depends on the weather.'

'Did your father take you out for walks?' he inquired of
Geoffrey.

'Not that I remember.'

'Oh, Daddy did.' Alison spoke as if he weren't there. 'In
fact I can remember coming several times to this park.'

'All three of you clamoured for the swings and slides.'

'Poor you.'

He told them of Frederick Greene's present of Romain
Rolland to Susan Smith. Alison and her husband acted out a
comical pantomime of eyebrow raising.

'Is it a suitable book on Beethoven?' Alison wanted to
know.

'Yes. It's old-fashioned, but it's short. And it has letters
and quotations. And *The Heiligenstadt Testament*. She's not
preparing for an examination on Beethoven, otherwise she
might need more up-to-date books. No, it's right for her.'

'When was it written?'

'Early 1900s. And Rolland's a real writer. This led to the Jean-Christophe books.'

Alison questioned him about Rolland's work. She seemed capable of amusing Sarah, tending her husband and probing her father, learning quickly, exposing the gaps in his knowledge. He could not help admiring both her energy and her intelligence.

'You should ask Fred about it,' Job advised.

'I wouldn't be so foolish.'

'Why's that, darling?' Geoffrey, rueful.

'He'd take umbrage and accuse me of poking my nose into what wasn't my business.'

'You could handle that.'

'I'm not looking for trouble.' And Alison chased off to catch Sarah, whom she swung into a thrilling circle.

'Is your father keeping fit?' Job asked Geoffrey.

'He's better than he's been for months. He's not well in winter. I know he puts it on a bit, suits his health to the mood of the moment, but his heart's not good and he suffers from bronchitis. He smoked a great deal. He's done well to live as long as he has.'

'A strong constitution.'

Alison and Sarah trotted back, winded, wreathed in smiles, mildly noisy. Geoffrey's offer of a piggy-back ride to his daughter was accepted.

'We called it a donkey-ride when I was a boy,' Turner told Alison.

'Children are more polite.'

'Or diplomatic.' Geoffrey, bouncing his daughter. The baby, James, struggling upwards in the pram, smiled suddenly.

Job Turner found his own house quiet after a spell with grandchildren, and was grateful. He wondered how Geoffrey, who was almost his generation, managed to drum up the necessary energy for parenthood. The children, there was no doubt, were fond of their father, even if it were true, as Alison half-jokingly claimed, that it was because she had to reprimand and punish.

'Slide the responsibility on to the nanny. That's what you pay her for.'

Alison looked pityingly at her father.

'We're none of us as simple as that.'

Now sitting over a solitary tea, Job Turner wrestled with the Sunday newspapers, glancing out to his neat back lawn, the blossom-laden apple trees, the still high brightness of the sun. The Lodge seemed dark with its small leaded windows, cool without fires; he wondered what the Greene family were doing at this hour in their spacious house. They made Sunday a great day, and when the children were in bed and read to on this evening by father, husband and wife would sit and open their Sunday papers, and read out pieces each to the other, and taste glasses of wine in civilized ease.

He settled to the piano for his daily practice, now religiously observed since he'd begun to teach Susan. Bach, first from the Forty-eight, then the Beethoven sonata she had begun for her examination, then Liszt 'La Campanella' which he was determined to master. He worked hard, repeating insecure passages, trying all the time to make his fingers think for him. At the end of an hour, he felt exhausted and wondered how much Father Greene could manage at a time. He'd ring and find out. He decided against it, though he had nothing better to do.

About nine o'clock, when it was still light outside, he heard a knock on the door. Susan's father stood there dressed for the pub.

'I just wanted a word with you,' he began. 'About Susan.'

Job Turner ushered him into the living-room.

'I'll be quick,' Smith said. 'I know you're busy. But I thought I'd like to ask something. It's about this Mr Greene.'

'What about him?'

'He's sent Susan a book, and he's invited her up there to play duets with him. Now we wasn't sure. Her mother got on to me. What do we know about him? I mean you hear such things these days. Is he a man of good character? The wife was quite worked up. She said, "Go and ask Mr Turner." Isn't he a relative of yours, I mean?'

'He's a retired solicitor almost eighty years old. His son, also a solicitor, married my daughter.'

'You think it will be all right, then?'

'As far as I know.'

'Is that exactly a straight answer, Mr Turner?' Smith's face reddened, aggressively.

'As far as I can give you. I take it that you and your wife were thinking of some kind of sexual assault. I've no reason to suspect anything like that. After all, he's eighty and she's not eighteen yet. No, I think it unlikely. But I don't know for certain.'

'Is there anything that makes you say that?'

'No. Native caution.' Job covered the lie with a guffaw. 'After all, you could have suspected me of something similar.'

'You're quite well known. In school circles. You're a man of good character. You wouldn't hold your job if it wasn't so.'

'And yet you can read in the papers of respectable head-masters who . . .'

'I know, I know, Mr Turner. But it was worth the asking. Thank you very much. We're very grateful for all you're doing for our Susan. She's a different girl altogether after this month or two she's had with you.'

'In what way?'

'She's more grown up. More serious. She even speaks better. Not that we've much to write home about when it comes to that.'

'Perhaps that's her job. Her employers might know Mr Greene. She might ask them. It was I introduced them; you know that. At a concert. He's quite well-to-do. It might be to Susan's advantage if he took an interest in her.' *Multum in parvo.* 'Are her employers interested in music?'

'You don't mind my inquiring, do you?'

'Not at all. It's very sensible. I'm sorry I can't be more helpful.'

Smith, now on his feet, made for the door. He walked strongly, like a rugby forward, as if expecting opposition.

'I s'll have to go, Mr Turner. The wife's outside in the car. We're on our way down to the Deerstalker.'

'Why didn't you bring her in?'

'She sent me on my own. "You'll talk easier and franker without me," is what she said.' They stood outside now. 'You wouldn't like to come down to the pub with us for a quick 'alf. We shan't stay long.'

Turner refused, but walked out to the car where he waved reassuringly to Mrs Smith who acknowledged his greeting but did not wind down the window.

A few days later, unexpectedly meeting Geoffrey in the street, Job Turner mentioned the conversation. Geoffrey licked his lips, fingered the knot of his tie.

'I should think it's in order to give him a clean bill nowadays.' He did not look at his interlocutor. 'He's nearly eighty. Still, one never can be sure. And as you know you won't find much admiration for the old rogue in me.'

They walked along together, Geoffrey slapping kid gloves on his driving coat. The weather had struck chilly again.

'He was always what's known as a bit of a lad.' Geoffrey spoke with embarrassment, reflected in the colloquialism. 'You knew that?' He waited until Turner had acknowledged that he did. 'He was pretty discreet on the whole, but people knew, or suspected. Or tattled.' Turner admired the quest for accuracy. 'Only once did it approach anything like a scandal. It's thirty-odd years ago, nearly forty. I knew nothing at the time, of course.'

'How did you find out? From your mother?'

'No. She would never say a word against him.' Geoffrey seemed enormous, in height, across the shoulders. 'Listening in. At first. It's amazing what you can pick up if that's what you want. And then I faced an old colleague with it when he'd had one or two more than usual, and he came out with the story. Willingly enough, I may say.'

Job Turner waited for the climax, but Geoffrey strode forward, donning his gloves.

'He put a girl in the family way. Then she was married off to someone else. He saw to it that they were financially, er, sound. Bought a little house. The child survived. He owns or manages a petrol station. I see him sometimes.'

'Does he know anything about it all?'

'Shouldn't think so. I don't think the husband had any idea either. He's dead.'

'Is the girl about?'

'I believe so. She'll be getting on for sixty. Still lives in the same house.'

'With the son?'

'No. He's married.'

'I see. Does your father still contribute to her upkeep?'

'I can't honestly say. I doubt it, but. . .'

'Does your father realize that you know the story?'

Geoffrey smiled, to himself, as if some favourite tune played inside his head.

'Of course. From whom do you think I have the detail? He broached the matter some years ago, asked me if I'd heard anything of it and to say exactly what it was I knew. Then he gave me his account and allowed me to question him, at least briefly.'

'Why, do you suppose?'

'He was not boasting, if that's what's crossed your mind. He spoke dispassionately, almost as if we were discussing a client. I wondered at the time if some question of blackmail had arisen.'

'From the woman?'

'Yes.'

'But didn't you ask him?' Job Turner, with an earnest, enthusiastic, naïve curiosity.

'I did.' Geoffrey put him in his place. This big man in his smart clothes was nobody's fool. 'He denied it.'

'And you believed him?'

'No. I didn't press him because I am as I am, and because I was sure he was capable of looking after himself. She wouldn't have got far with threats. He'd have had the police in in no time. He could be quite terrifying, if he so chose. And blunt. She'd be in no doubt. If he paid her some mainten-ance still, and here I'm guessing, he would have had no compunction about stopping it, or threatening to do so. He'd blast her off the earth. As I heard no more of the business, I took it that it had settled itself.'

'Why did he tell you? Is it like him?'

'In case it came into court. He wouldn't want me in the dark.'

'I see. Interesting.'

'That's not the word I'd choose.' Geoffrey answered magisterially.

'If you don't mind my asking, does Alison know anything of this?'

'Yes. I told her a year or two back when we were discussing my father.'

'What did she think?'

'Apart from legal points? She showed no surprise. As I expected. This is my destination.' Geoffrey pulled off a glove to shake hands with his father-in-law, wheeled into a large printing-works. 'Mustn't be late for a valued client.' He beamed ironically at his little maxim.

Job wandered down the street, discarded, as puzzled why Geoffrey went to visit a client as why he had made the revelation about his father. In spite of his polish, Geoffrey was as careful as Frederick with his time and money. Perhaps he was going as far as his code of behaviour allowed in issuing a warning. Turner walked uncomfortably, not pleased with himself, incapably morose.

He forgot his suspicions in the turmoil of school. In this term he would discharge his senior pupils to the secondary school, and he therefore wanted to make sure that every one of them was well drilled in reading and writing. He had instituted a series of summer term tests, in arithmetic, composition, reading aloud, against the wishes of his staff who had argued that delight in learning, pleasure in art, in free expression of thought or emotion were best at this stage, and that examinations with marks and positions and competition suited the academically-gifted only, but put off the majority. He rode roughshod over his teachers. 'I'm not against art and music and games and emotional development. We'll have them by all means. But the greatest pleasure in literature is gained by those who have a sound basic knowledge of grammar, who can read and write correctly as well as fluently. In the same way, the musicians who profit are those who practise and are encouraged into good habits by their instruc-

61

tors. I'm not telling you that strictness, rigour is all, but we'll have more of it.'

His staff had done as they were told; parents, mostly middle class and wanting value for money, approved so that he now had more applications for places in his school than he could satisfy. The adviser, unenthusiastic if not hostile at first, had fallen in with his ways, and now, it was said, preached the Turner doctrine in other places. Job Turner produced the tests, different each year, and marked or moderated a large number of the scripts; he was not idle and saw to it that his teachers were not. Once the system was established it became popular with the staff, and once the headmaster's choirs began to win trophies at the musical festivals doubts about the diminishing part aesthetics played had disappeared. Art exhibitions were mounted; dancing displays given; drama throve. Other schools showed jealousy when they failed to reach the standard. 'Turner's sweatshop,' defeated rivals mocked. 'The Oxbridge of the junior schools.'

This kept the headmaster occupied, and he was grateful, but now he had trained his assistants, so that the work was less demanding and, since his wife's death, he had continued by habit rather than from conviction.

When his wife, Gillian, had died after a car accident something over two years ago, people had remarked how little difference it made to the public figure. Job Turner was as efficient, or ruthless; if he was asked to carry out a task, it was done as swiftly as before. He forgot nothing; he helped and encouraged with the same strength; he'd rebuke as powerfully. When friends or colleagues offered sympathy, he received it seriously with a firm handshake and a warmly-voiced sentence of thanks. It seemed to observers almost natural that this strongly integrated character should be capable of bearing his tragedy with fortitude. Even his huge house was kept as polished and dust-free as in his wife's time. Neighbours marvelled, as they had during the three weeks Gillian had lain in hospital before her death, at his normality, his social cheerfulness, his appearance of ordinariness.

His daughters, all away from home, had discussed their father's calm which they had not expected. They knew that he both depended on and admired Gillian, always consulted her though he knew that her advice might well contradict his own practice. Sharp, still pretty in her early fifties, she had ruled the house which she had chosen, arranged her children's careers, made supportive appearances at the functions at her husband's school, taught biology as head of department in the private school her daughters attended. For the last ten years of her life she had worked as a lecturer in the university department of education. She had a first class honours degree in science, a doctorate, and had filled in the corners of her life with charitable concerns, so that her house clattered with committee meetings. Sometimes Job Turner wondered, even asked her, if she regretted not following an academic career.

'Of course. But if I were a professor, with a whole shelf-ful of highly regarded scientific papers I'd regret not being a mother.'

'You might have managed both. Some women do.'

'I'd have had to have married a different husband from you.'

That was typical of her; she spoke the truth even when it wounded, though her warmth could as easily heal. He comforted himself with the thought that if she had really wanted a career in academe she would have chosen it, and not him, even at the age of twenty-five when she accepted his proposal of marriage. Moreover, this paragon had inherited money so that the family never went short; two cars, foreign holidays, visits to London were the order of the day. The children prospered in their studies. Alison at law, Phyllis in medicine at a London hospital, and Hilary as a biochemist at Imperial College, where she now taught. The two eldest were married, and had children. It seemed as if Gillian arranged condign success for her nearest and dearest, without in any way surrendering her own ideals or schemes.

And yet, as his daughters, highly intelligent women, warily noticed, Job Turner took Gillian's death without reeling, picked up his pieces, and continued in his own small circle of success. They did not believe it possible; they were glad for their own sakes for they had expected trouble and interruption of their own careers, but it had seemed utterly unlikely that their father could make his way without guidance from that gifted, lively partner.

# 8

On Gillian's death Job Turner had felt himself ruined.

During her lifetime friends mocked him behind his back, saying that though he might rule the roost at work, he took a low second place at home, and he admitted there was an element of truth in the gibe. But it cut nowhere deeply enough. Gillian saw to the meals, the garden, the children's lives, the holidays; she ordered in workmen for repairs and alterations. She paid the bills, took the decisions about furniture or the choice of pictures, invited friends, refused or accepted invitations and all this together with her own work at the university, her charitable committees, her visits to some elderly pensioners and her support of his concerts and festivals. Yet she never seemed in any hurry; she understood perfectly when she could spend five minutes listening and her attention was so keen, so cheerful that the five minutes appeared to the recipient as twice, three times its real length. Her head was packed with lists, kept separate but exactly correlated. He guessed that the twenty minutes' drive to the university in the rush hour sorted out the day's dilemmas. Such balance and grasp baffled him.

And yet in Gillian's presence he never felt himself inferior. She genuinely admired his musical ability, occasionally asked him to play the piano for her, and encouraged her daughters to sit in with her to listen. She carefully attended to anecdotes about his school, and was not afraid to be seen there supervising her practising teachers or adding lustre to the nativity play, the summer festival, the spring concert. People took to her at once; her memory, unlike her husband's, was a perfect instrument, so that she made no mistakes about the names or illnesses of his teachers' offspring. If his staff wanted her advice, she gave it modestly, sensibly, willingly, not concealing her cleverness but never flaunting it. 'Have you talked to Job yet?' she'd ask, blue eyes wide. That became an ironic shibboleth amongst the clever young people attracted to his school; if one consulted Gillian, there was no need for a second shot with Job. There was nothing expansive about her, no rhetoric, no gush or rodomontade; she meant what she said and without exaggeration.

Of course she attracted envy. It took the form of criticism of her clothes, 'a headmaster's wife has no business wearing a suit or slacks on this sort of occasion' from those less gifted, and from the clever-clever the sneer, suitably disguised in a caricature of her own demure phraseology, 'If only the world were as simple as Gillian Turner thinks it is'. She ignored such enmity, noticing it, but unmarked by it was able to dismiss it, without even a sarcasm at the expense of its probable motivation. She could speak with emotion, but the emphasis was never self-regarding. If she lost her temper, which happened rarely, she'd say afterwards that she hoped it had been in a good cause. The head of her department, the vanity-riddled Professor Emsworth, had pronounced after her funeral that he now found it infinitely sad that while he was engaged everlastingly and inanely administering trivia he could no longer count on Gill Turner at work tirelessly doing real good to somebody somewhere.

This life had ended one foggy evening on the motorway.

Gillian had been to a lecture and exhibition of paintings in Yorkshire. Job Turner had considered accompanying her, but she had said that her friend, Joan Phillips, wanted to drive her there and talk about some problems. Mrs Phillips, a widow, a magistrate, a retired headmistress, liked to run some of Gillian's philanthropic errands for her to prove that she was not altogether past hope. She insisted on driving, too carefully for Job, and endlessly asking for advice without listening for answers. When Job Turner groused, not for the first time about this, his wife checked him.

'There aren't any answers I can give. She finds her solutions by setting her problems out.'

'At boring length. She should buy a tape recorder.'

'Job Turner, you can see why that's not true.'

Gillian's smile had flashed, winning him over.

An accident had taken place in the fog just ahead of Mrs Phillips's Metro, and she had edged behind a lorry on the hard shoulder. Before Joan had applied the handbrake, a huge tanker had hit them from the back smashing them into the vehicle in front. Mrs Phillips had been killed outright; Gillian had lingered for three weeks.

Job had expected her to survive. Spirits such as hers were not quenched by skidding tons of wood and metal. He had visited the unconscious figure day by day, had come only gradually to accept that she would not live, but had continued to hope against all sense. Her death had been tranquil enough, as still as those last three weeks of life, and the hospital staff had shown kindness, consideration beyond duty. He felt, with a tremor of nervous excitement, that he had made a dozen and a half new friends amongst those dedicated people, and he half-regretted, with such sensibility as he had preserved, that they would continue their work with equal zeal amongst people unknown to him.

At the funeral he learnt for himself the strength of the truism he'd heard on other such occasions: 'How Gillian would have enjoyed having us all here'. His daughter, Alison, properly subdued, had tried in the week following the burial to question him about his views of an afterlife. She had called in first, having phoned every evening. He could not answer her question. That a life as scintillating, as modestly powerful, as good as his wife's, could be put out by a momentary lapse of care on the part of a decent man – he had heard the driver's evidence, had spoken to him – seemed to suggest that God, if he existed, amused himself with malicious pranks, while at the same time Job could hear the gentle expostulation Gill, an atheist, would have put forward: 'But perhaps I'd done my time here exactly. It might have been downhill all the way from here on. Aren't you blaming God out of ignorance? You don't know the whole of the circumstances, the universe full?' And he knew that he would not have been able to answer her in life, as he could in death, 'I'm blaming God out of love'.

He wondered why Alison seemed so insistent. He wished he could reassure her, if that's what she needed. Perhaps Geoffrey, usually the soul of tact, had come out with some sentence from his agnosticism that the believing Alison had been unable to bear in the first agony of grief. Job dared not question her. She could, he believed, have shredded Geoffrey's arguments into ruin had she so wished, but her sense of overwhelming loss proscribed intellectual games. Job felt pity for his daughter while lacking the ability to soothe her. Gillian would have known what to say, had he died. But he suspected that neither would have been so radically crippled by his death. His mind sparked uncomfortably like a distant thunderstorm over a solid, unalterable world of grief.

After the first few days, when he was petrified with shock, he was able to continue his work. Good habits had re-established themselves; he could conduct a morning assembly, take a choir practice, hold a staff meeting, attend a parents' evening or governors' committee in full control of himself. But this sense of icy loss afflicted him for hours on end; he had no one to work for, nobody on whom to make an impression. Adjudicators, advisers, colleagues, the director, friends or rivals did not matter as Gillian had; they could offer their approbation, but the final arbiter was missing. As far as he could tell, Turner did not work less hard or satisfy himself with lower standards; from now on, it seemed, he must be judge and jury of his own achievements, and he did not like it.

Alison had pressed him to leave his house.

'It's a barn, Daddy, and it needs all that cleaning and maintenance and heating.'

He had agreed, but did not want to move. The huge, semi-detached Victorian villa, in a tree-lined avenue, had been Gillian's choice; she had put down the deposit, had directed its redecoration, organized the repairs, replanned the garden.

'It's so inconvenient. And for one.' Alison.

'It's where the family were brought up.'

'Yes, I know exactly how you feel.' Alison smiled, teeth as large and hygienic as in a dentifrice advertisement. 'But we must be sensible, really.'

He hung on at first in the place even as she persisted. When Ian Turner left him the East Lodge, Job compromised, deciding to let not sell.

'I don't know if you're wise. With a house of that size, it means children, for certain. And with children, damage.'

'Put the price up then, so we can recover.'

In the end she had entrusted the letting to a house-agent, who, she said, was trustworthy, efficient and a friend. An American academic and his family rented Oak Villa, and now a television administrator had taken it. Alison arranged for her gardener to attend regularly for weeding and trimming the lawns.

Job Turner had decided he would pass the old home often, to look it over, but in fact tended to avoid the district. His three favourite photographs of Gillian, one suitably enlarged, stood in steel frames on his mantelpiece, but he needed no reminders. Now, nearly three years after his wife's death, he would look up, in this new cramped house, from his book or his piano to wait for the rattle of her keys in the front door. It seemed barely possible, but it happened. Regularly, two years and nine months after the event, and in a strange place she had never, to his knowledge, even glanced at in her life. He amazed, frightened, mystified himself.

Recently he had observed in himself a failure to respond satisfyingly to success. After a choir practice, both in his own school or the local authority's music college, he realized that, though he had achieved all he had set out to do, and often more than that, with his gifted pupils, he lacked something, vaguely felt that life was amiss, askew. He could not report, however modestly, his accomplishment to Gillian. While she was alive he had taken it for granted that he would give his wife some account of his attainments and would listen to her comment, her praise. Not until she had been dead for eighteen months did he realize how important to him this had been. Had he died first, he never would have known. Amongst his other discomforts this discovery surprised him.

In a small way, he admitted it only grudgingly, Susan Smith replaced his wife. He filled in his time in new fields, preparing to instruct her, pursuing enquiries about examinations, making sure that his lessons wasted nothing. This seemed now different from his work at school, more testing, more tiring and yet satisfying. He dressed formally to teach the

69

girl, and though he joked about it to her, saying he was like the great Haydn who put on his Sunday best to compose, this action seemed important. More than once he shaved for a second time in the evening, dabbing his cheeks with perfume. He could barely understand what was happening and, though he did not exclude sexual attraction, he did not see himself as in love with the girl. He was grateful that this had happened even when it betrayed his devotion to Gillian's memory.

Alison remarked on his sartorial smartness.

'You were always neatly turned out,' she admitted, 'but I expected you to fall from grace.' She used these old-fashioned terms to him with an ironical courtesy which he found attractive. Sharp as she was, she would not criticize him too fiercely. 'Not like Fred Greene.'

'I always think of him as a natty dresser.'

'He was. But he can't be bothered now. And he drops bits of food on his clothes.'

'Poor old chap.'

'Poor old nothing. He could do better if he put himself out.'

'Perhaps he hasn't the energy. He's eighty.'

'Don't you let him take you in. He does just what he wants to do. And he's as capable now as he was at fifty, as he's quick to warn me when some legal matter crops up.'

'You're not telling me that he could eat less messily.'

'That's exactly what I am telling you. He just does not try, or think, when he's on his own.'

'You must be in trouble with us two old men to keep in order.'

'Not yet.' Alison's face assumed jokey seriousness. 'And shouldn't you include Geoffrey amongst the old brigade?'

Job Turner's daughters pleased him. They came up to visit him in the weeks after their mother's death, and held conferences on his welfare over the telephone. Their conclusions and questions were reported to him by Alison; they took comfort, it seemed, that he had not gone to pieces, that he was still capable, that he wasn't beyond advice. Congratulations buzzed when he moved to the Lodge.

70

'It means,' he told Phyllis, a medico, 'that if you have any more children, I shan't be able to put you up.'

'Never mind,' she said. 'Martin's in for a registrar's post up here. He says he won't get it, but if he does you'll have me round your neck as well as Ally.'

All three of them had something of their mother about them. Hilary, a biochemist, now teaching at London University, sent him copies of her scientific papers which he filed when he had failed to understand their drift. He listened when she took part in a discussion on Radio Three and sounded, not only very sure of herself, but exactly like her mother.

' "My monstrous regiment of women",' he called them to Alison, 'are keeping their beady eyes on me.'

'You should be so lucky.'

He saw from the way she looked at him that she had not thought he could continue his life so amenably without Gillian. He guessed she'd expected rebellion from him, shown up in shabby clothes, or in choosing to live with some colourful young miss from his staff, or, worst of all, retiring into his home, refusing to be sociable, acquiring some eccentricity which would draw attention unfavourably to himself and his status. But here he was, tractable, decent, decorous, a credit to them all.

Job never tested his theory out by putting a blunt question to his daughters. He cleaned his shoes, carried his grief under a respectable waistcoat and walked about an uncaring world with his blue eyes wide open.

# 9

Frederick Greene asked Turner over for Saturday lunch.

Job was not keen to accept, because he occupied the whole of Saturday morning at the county music school with piano lessons and a choir rehearsal.

'I shan't be able to make it before one-thirty,' he warned.

'Excellent. Gives the fatted calf another half hour of life.' Greene sounded strong, almost youthful. 'I look forward to your visit.'

'How's Elgar?'

'You seem, Turner, to have formed some odd opinion about my interest in Elgar. It's an interest, you know, not an obsession.' He coughed. 'But I suppose once people have made up their minds nothing as straightforward as factual evidence will serve to change them.'

As soon as Job Turner arrived, ten minutes late, old man Greene resumed the subject.

'There was one thing I wanted to ask you,' he began. This afternoon he was carefully dressed without a hint of the slovenly. 'Would you say that Elgar's success depended on his wife? Given his musical talent and all that?'

Job tried to marshal evidence one way or the other, adding a rider on the complexity of human motivation and behaviour. His host listened, tilting his wine glass away from himself, nodding, frowning as though Turner's scattered observations were beyond his grasp.

'The reason I asked,' Greene said in the end, 'was that my wife occupied no such place in such success, or otherwise, I made of my life. And I'd have thought that wasn't unusual.'

'Your wife cooked and washed and mended for you, looked after your house and Geoffrey, made things easy for you. That seems a considerable contribution to me. Elgar's different, of course, in that he worked at home where his wife ruled the

72

staves for his day's stint, and encouraged, praised and pushed him. He was thin-skinned; he needed her.'

'As I didn't need Cecilia.'

'I spoke without my book, but I was just suggesting that you did, whether you noticed it or not.'

'I noticed when the house needed dusting.'

'Did it ever?'

At this moment the door opened and a well set-up woman, in young middle age announced that lunch was ready. Greene led Job to the dining room where three places were laid at the large table. The woman wheeled in the food, began to serve, lamb, peas, carrots, new potatoes, and then sat down on the third chair to eat with them.

At first Greene made no introductions, but carefully spooned mint sauce over all the food on his plate. He stabbed a small potato and thrust it into his mouth, pulled it immediately out again, still on the fork.

'That's damned hot.'

'What do you expect?' the woman asked pleasantly. 'You'd complain if it was cold.'

Greene did his best with a smile.

'This is Mrs Harper,' he said to Job. 'Sandra Harper.'

'Glad to meet you.' Job put down his cutlery but did not stand, could not shake hands. Mrs Harper graciously bowed from the neck upwards, a regal movement that consorted badly with her voice. The three returned with relief to their plates.

Sandra Harper was plainly dressed but wore a prettily flowered pinafore. When they had completed the first course, she collected, carted off the plates and returned with the pudding.

'What is it?' Greene, rudely.

'Gooseberry fool.'

'No reflection,' Greene cackled, 'on the visitor.' The other two tried to register recognition of the witticism, failed signally.

'Did you ever hear the expression "playing gooseberry"?'

'Yes,' Job answered.

'It means burdening a courting couple with your unwanted company.'

Nobody offered comment. Mrs Harper served Greene, then Turner, then herself.

'Has it, do you put real cream in it?' Greene.

'Yes,' she replied, 'but tinned gooseberries.'

'As boys we called them goosegogs.' Greene seemed to have little idea of acceptable social behaviour. Job Turner, concentrating on his dish, complimented the cook, who shrugged in embarrassment. Greene added not a word, slurping and scraping until he demanded a second helping. At the end of the meal, Mrs Harper cleared the table, Greene prohibiting Job from helping with the dishes.

'Let her get on with it. She insisted on being here. It would have been salad and cold meat otherwise. She says her husband's on overtime. I don't know what to make of her.'

'I see.'

Greene had now lit a thin cigar, awkwardly, gesturing with it.

'I've slipped again.' He lowered his voice, pointed towards the kitchen, puffed. 'With her.'

Now he twisted his face, wagging his head in the caricature of an oriental trader.

'The reason I asked you up was to get you to do something for me. As you might have guessed.' His voice was normal, cultured, unforced. 'Don't you worry. It's nothing difficult or out of the way.' He glanced towards the door which led to the kitchen, but out of mischief. 'I want you to play a duet or two with me. On the piano. I want to be up to standard with your Susan girl. We'll wait till she's brought the coffee in.' He grimaced, blew smoke. 'One round of giddy pleasure, isn't it?'

Greene talked on until Mrs Harper appeared, when he checked himself in the middle of the sentence that in no way concerned her. She poured out the coffee, formally.

'Make sure you drink yours today.' She spoke as to a child and received no answer. 'That's it, then. Some of us have work to do.'

Greene looked helplessly at the cigar in his fingers, put it delicately smoking into his ashtray.

When Job Turner had drunk his second cup his host invited him to the piano. Greene carried out his untouched coffee which he perched on a low table by his side.

'I've had a bit of work done on it,' he grumbled. 'Costs a fortune these days.' He opened an arrangement of Bach's Second Brandenberg Concerto.

'Which side do you want me?' Job asked.

'You take the top for a start.'

They settled but Frederick Greene seemed loth to turn over from the title page. 'Brandenburgische Konzerte von J. S. Bach für Pianoforte zu vier Händen bearbeitet von Max Reger.'

'Sounds more serious,' he said, 'in German.'

Job Turner rudely flipped the page over.

'Non legato,' he read out. 'Volles Orchester. Italian and German. I'll give you four in.'

They played through the first movement at a good pace. At the end Greene sat badly out of breath. Recovering he said, 'Thank God I was playing the lower part.'

'Allegro. Cheerful. Merry. Lively.'

'I'm eighty.' In actuality he had played with considerable skill. 'We'll do it again in a minute.'

'Which part do you play with Susan?'

'We're supposed to do either. I pick the lower. It's easier.'

'And you don't do it so quickly?'

'No. She's been only the once so far. I enjoyed it. Gave me a taste for duets. That's why I asked you up.'

Job turned back to pages 2 and 3, began to count. They set off at a sharp, rhythmical pace, banging at full orchestra, fastidiously picking out the solo voices. At the conclusion of the movement Greene took a sip of his coffee and laughed out loud.

'Were you sight-reading that?'

'Yes. It's not very difficult once you're used to the idea. Right, let's do the slow movement,' he bullied Greene. They played, then repeated.

'That's value for money,' Job said. 'One side each.'

'I played it for Susan on the music centre.'

'I still call it a gramophone.'

Job flicked through the pages of the Finale, trying out some running thirds and sixths.

'I hope Reger's kinder to you than to me.'

They played the movement without disaster.

'You've got a good pair of hands,' Greene said admiringly.

'Not as good as Susan's.'

'Ah, she defers to me, slows down if I'm in trouble.'

'That's bad. I shall instruct her to. . .'

'Let's sit in the comfortable chairs.' Again he moved his coffee. Crumpled in his seat, Greene appeared exhausted, or half alive, licking his lips. He took another sip from his cup. Mrs Harper appeared, breezily.

'Have you gentlemen finished with the tray? I see you haven't.' She stressed the second pronoun. 'Don't hurry. I'll come back. Shall I pour you another cup, sir?' to Turner.

'No, thank you. It was delicious.'

'We always drink instant at home,' the woman said.

'We can tell.' Greene, grumpily. She laughed at him, expecting something of the sort.

'I enjoyed the music. Very nice indeed. It was both of you, wasn't it? Together, like. I thought it wasn't Mr Greene on his own.'

'I'm not Horowitz.'

'Don't let it worry you.'

She swept out smiling broadly at Job Turner.

'What do you think of her, then?' Greene demanded.

'Cheerful. Smart. And it was an excellent meal.'

' "The way to a man's heart . . . " ' Greene stubbed the cigar, almost viciously. 'She has her points. You think I'm disgusting, don't you? Don't you bother to deny it.' He looked sorry for himself. 'Tomorrow evening I'm taking Susan to the Tchaikovsky concert at the Royal Concert Hall. You're not going, are you?'

'I'm afraid not.'

'Neither are Geoffrey and Alison. I thought I might cadge a lift.'

'How will you get there then? And back?'

'Taxi. Expensive, but easy. She's not, that's Susan, heard the First Piano Concerto live. Did you know that? And they're doing the Fourth Symphony.'

Greene looked sleepy so that they did not play again and Job Turner made his excuses. Frederick opened his eyes long enough to whisper,

'You're leaving me in the clutches of that woman, are you?' He sat up and shouted to Mrs Harper to show the visitor to the door. She appeared in the hallway wiping her hands on a small tea towel.

'He'll have enjoyed playing the piano,' she said. Job shook her hand, nodding.

'He seems well, considering his age,' he offered.

'Yes. Yes. He is.'

The air outside seemed less oppressive, fresh, untrammelled. On Tuesday he had arranged to give Susan Smith her first lesson on the Hall piano. She emerged from a distant door with her father, who carried a bunch of keys.

'How was Tchaikovsky?' he asked.

Susan's enthusiasm was matched by her father's. 'We're all going to the opera,' Smith said. '*Carmen*. She's talked us into it.'

He led them in again through the empty storerooms, up the uncarpeted stairs, and into the cool foyer. After he had unlocked the door to the drawing room, he touched Turner on the arm, detaining him.

'How's she getting on?'

'Very well.'

'We're pleased. Especially her mother.'

'Good. She works hard.'

'We try to encourage her. She's conscientious.'

'And talented.'

'Her mother will be pleased to hear that. Mrs Waters didn't say much. When I asked her once she just answered, "Her examination results speak for themselves." That's all right, but we like to hear it in plain words. We, and Sue herself, have invested a lot of money in her music.'

'You could invest it very much worse.'

From inside a rippling scale from the piano interrupted them.

'She's off,' Smith said, delight on his face. 'She doesn't waste much time.'

'No. Any more news of the Hall here? Are they selling it or what?'

'There was talk of making it into a hotel at one time. But I've heard nothing recently. They've been hanging about long enough, God knows. I'll sit down out here and listen to you.'

'Why don't you come in?'

'Susan doesn't like it. "I don't want spectators, Dad," she says. I can understand that. She's not giving a performance, she's getting something right.'

Job Turner, impressed, went in to his duty and pleasure.

More than an hour later, with the lesson over, he found Smith standing. Susan had remained at the piano.

'It sounded well,' Smith asserted. 'Would you like a look round?' He led along the foyer to the huge stained-glass window. 'You should see that first thing in a morning with the sun behind. It's something, that is.'

'How do you keep the place clean?'

'You can't. But I have a system. I divide it into sections, and each section gets a going-over once a fortnight.'

'Do you have help?'

'No. Run on a shoestring. Still, I can't complain. Lucky to have a job. Ran my own business, but had cash-flow problems. Had to give up. Didn't go bankrupt. But a chap I know on the council used his influence for this lark. Great long list of applications for the job as you can imagine these days. But he put a word in. Handy-man, you see. Did my apprentice-ship with him as a joiner.'

'And you like it up here?'

'Yes. We had to move in; we lived in a council house before. Buying it. It was a struggle to make my mind up. On my own, I seemed to be working weeks on end for nothing. People don't pay on the nail. You send your bills off, I used to spend every Sunday morning making 'em out, doing the books, estimating and so on, and what's the result? You lose the price of a second-class stamp or two.' He paused before the sweep of the staircase. 'Up here.' They began to ascend; below Susan practised brilliantly still. 'But as I say, I was in two minds. I worked hard enough, gave satisfaction on my own, and I broke even on the whole, and always looked forward to a good profit. But it was a constant worry.' They stood on the upstairs landing while Smith picked out a key, led into a further drawing room, with shrouded furniture, dark eighteenth-century portraits, presumably of the family, an Adam fireplace not out of balance with the Victorian proportions of the room. 'Lady Staton's room. Her bower, you could say. A lot of the stuff's been taken out.'

'I was thinking how crowded it was.'

'They had different ideas then.' Smith extended a hand towards the cluttered mantelpiece, lifted the cover from a small table to demonstrate the plenitude of bric-à-brac. 'As I was saying, I didn't know what to do. It was easier because Shirley had a job. She's assistant school sec'etary at the Raleigh Comprehensive. We shouldn't starve; not that the education committee pays very well, any more than the council here.' He ushered Turner out of Lady Staton's dim magnificence. 'But we have fuel and a roof over my 'ead and a telephone for nothing. But there are drawbacks. We were buying our house from the council, and we'd got it in nice order. Garden an' all. And this is a long way out if you haven't got transport. And it's like the Army, on duty twenty-four hours a day. But there.'

Now he had opened a bedroom, with a towering four-poster, dressing tables, mahogany wardrobes, small unfashionable prints. Smith opened a further door.

'The dressing room,' he said. 'Edward VII had this room more than once. And we know what he was like.' He pointed to another door. 'They had a bathroom put in later.'

'What happens if the council sells the place?'

'They might give me a job on the estate. Mark you, they might not, and then I'll be out.'

'They won't provide you with a house?'

'No, because I've kept up my payments on my own. My brother-in-law and family rent it from us. Whether I'd get him out is another matter. It's all very tricky for some of us.

Perhaps you can see now why I want Susan to get on, not do anything daft.'

They stood again on the landing looking down into the gloom of the foyer.

'I often wonder,' Smith began, 'what it must have been like to own a house this size. I mean you can only occupy so much space, sit on one chair at a time. But imagine all this, blazing with lights, the music playing.' A Brahms intermezzo sounded from Susan below. 'You could cram a lot of people in here. And this is a small affair compared with some of the great houses.'

'What's it like to live here?'

'Lonely in winter. We're not too distant from civilization, if you think about it, but it's far enough to keep people away in the cold weather.'

'What about the people who work on the estate?'

'They all come from outside. Come in their cars.'

'What about the other lodges?'

'There's only the one, West Lodge, the big main place and they use that for offices, and storage and garaging the estate vehicles. Nobody lives there. They say they're going to sell off the stables, privately, for reconversion. It's a nice spot.'

'And the estate cottages?'

'Like your place, sold off already. There weren't many really. The majority of the land was worked by tenant farmers. It was a hunting lodge.' Smith sighed, oddly, a plump, solid man, identifying himself with the gentry. 'I would have liked to have seen it in its heyday.' Smith opened no more doors, made for the staircase. 'I'll show you round some time in the daylight.'

'Don't you get broken into or vandalized?'

'A certain amount. But though it's out of the way, it's difficult for burglars. And I've made it harder. They'd need a van to cart the stuff away.'

'And it's not worth their while?'

'Depends, I suppose. The silver and jewellery are all gone, and the more valuable pictures. And a lot of the furniture. The family have two other estates. I made a bit of a study of it since I've been here.' He spoke modestly. 'It's easy enough if you know where to look. The library'll order books for you. And one chap down there has published a little, well, it's a pamphlet about the Statons.'

'They were here for a long time?'

'Yes, and no. They sold it off and then bought it back. In Victorian times, 1880s.'

'Why?'

'Spare cash. They owned valuable industrial and commercial property. And perhaps the place was going cheap. And perhaps they had a sentimental attachment. I'll find out one of these days.' They stood together downstairs. 'I'll see if Sue wants to stay. She often practises until gone eleven. One of the advantages. Disturbs nobody. I'll leave her the keys.' He marched away.

Job Turner looked about him, at the shadowed heights, the uncouth shapes in a half-darkness. Two small bulbs feebly glimmered by the door; a hand torch would have been as efficient. He felt the comforting coolness of a wooden arm of an ornate chair, more like a stage prop than a piece of domestic furniture. He squinted at the back and what seemed a carved coat-of-arms. The air smelt fusty, undisturbed.

Smith emerged from the drawing room whistling. There had been hardly a break in the piano playing.

'She'll lock up, she says.'

The two men walked shoulder to shoulder through the ill-lit store rooms.

'I'll leave this switched on for her.'

Outside Smith accompanied Turner as far as the main, arched gateway. There they stared out together towards the darkening woods as if unwilling to part.

'I shall have to go.'

'Come up one weekend, and I'll show you round the whole place. Funny to think kings and queens came here. Mark you, they'd go in by the entrance on the other side. But they might well walk out this way to the stables. Now it's just you and me.'

' "Oh, what a falling-off was there." '

'If you say so.' Smith laughed deep in his belly. 'Thank

you for coming up. You'll see your way back. I'll close the gates.'

Job Turner heard the final clang of wrought iron from a hundred yards down the road. Soon he would see the light over his own porch.

# 10

The day after his school broke up for the summer holiday
Job Turner drove to Cambridge to attend a further conference
on the teaching of music. Hot, airless weather suited and
rested him; the lectures and demonstrations were good. He
met again Dr Mackenzie, the Scottish lecturer from Liverpool, and the pair walked round the courts and gardens of
the colleges.

'Is this the best place to learn anything?' he asked
Mackenzie.

'I don't think it matters. Or not to me. Tradition or scenery
doesn't mean a thing while I'm studying or writing.'

'I like to think of Orlando Gibbons here,' Turner said. They
stood staring up the scaffolding on King's College Chapel.

'I like to think of you here. Or anybody. Except perhaps
a terrorist with a bomb. This place is supremely beautiful,
but it has no connection with or influence on the music I
compose.'

'That doesn't seem right to me.'

'You're a romantic.' Mackenzie's 'r's rattled with irony.
They walked round the botanical gardens where the younger
man demonstrated an ignorance of flower names so abysmal
that Job Turner felt morally bound to begin to instruct him.
'This is the wrong place. We have too much and too many.
Some clothhead's front garden with one or two plants from
the market stall.'

'Did you not have a garden at home?' Turner asked.

'Oh, yes. Quite large. All I did was to dribble a tennis ball
about.'

They admired Henry Moore's statue in Emmanuel College
before switching their attention to the ducks strutting towards
them.

'Moore's nothing compared with,' Mackenzie pointed at

coloured wing feathers, 'that chap. Both are simple, but the bird's simplicity immediately suggests complexity.'

'And that's good?'

'Aesthetically, yes. I admire the complicated, especially when it gives the appearance of straightforwardness. Or has an easily grasped structure.'

'Doesn't that depend on the prejudices of the graspers?'

'Oh, yes, yes, yes. I mean we don't find Bach's florid, instrumental arias or those Mozart art-songs very memorable. We won't be bothered. I won't. It concerns me.'

The Doric pronunciation of 'consairn' added seriousness.

They listened to a piano recital of works by Busoni.

'What the hell has the "Fantasia Contrapuntistica" to do with teaching kids in school?' A grey, cropped-headed teacher rattled his coffee-cup, within earshot. Job listened.

'Widens your horizons.' Man in velvet jacket.

'I can neither like it nor play it.'

'For all you know that's just as acceptable or easy to young children as Beethoven is to you.'

'I can see you've been nowhere near a junior school lately.'

Mackenzie gave an interesting hour on a string-quartet he was composing. The talk was low-key, brilliant in organization, convincing. He dealt with the first movement, ten minutes long, from the initial scribbles in his notebooks to its completion three months ago. When he had finished, four students from the Royal Northern College played it through. They had, it appeared, been offered no coaching by the composer who said that though there might be difficulties, both of performing or interpretation, there was nothing either permissive or unusual about the notation. 'What I put down on the paper is to be played as written. Of course there'll be argument but if they can play the notes in the time I indicate they'll be well on to a performance.'

The students played. The music moved with a bustle of speed, was discordant, struck the listener about the ears with a fighting energy. Though contrapuntal and, on first hearing, uneasily overbearing, there was nothing dry about it.

'Not one memorable bar.' The crop-headed man, in the interval.

'I think I must agree,' Velvet jacket.

'I wonder if he can hear what he's put down,' the teacher continued.

'To the extent of correcting wrong notes, you mean?'

'And these chunks of rests get on my tits. The classical composers don't keep stopping for no bloody reason you can make out.'

'But it's a method, a means.' A young pale man, obviously a subordinate of crop-head, with an old-fashioned open collar over a faded tweed jacket.

'I'll give you that. But so would be sticking the music stand up your arse.'

After the interval Mackenzie rehearsed the quartet, courteously, without bombast, but insisting on intonation, pointing out mistakes, linking passage to passage, part to part. The students, talented young men, then played the movement through, were vigorously applauded.

'Worse than bloody Busoni.' Crop-head's conclusion.

'There's real musical, creative energy there.' The pale man, bravely.

'Some of you will hear anything in anything. To me that was from the start, and remained so, unpleasant noise. Random noise. And, John, don't give me any cock-and-bull about people not understanding Beethoven or Schubert. This is different in kind.'

Crop-head, Job Turner found by inquiry, was the influential headmaster of a school which had recently won a national and an international award for music. On the strength of these he had been persuaded by his music staff to attend the conference. Velvet-jacket headed the department. The pale young man directed the prize-winning orchestra. Crop-head, Job saw, was fond of both, was liked in return, but felt he had to throw his philistine weight about.

'He's like all headmasters,' the pale assistant answered Turner's query without hesitation, 'in that he doesn't get contradicted often enough. It's an occupational hazard.'

'Before you go on I'd better tell you I'm a head.'

'You're in a good position, then, to judge whether I'm right or not. But I'll say this for Georgie-boy, he does support us.'

'Is he interested in music?'

'Oh, yes. He sings in one of our choirs. He finds money for us, and that's something these days. We need our patrons.'

The week passed quickly. The place, the company, the lectures and demonstrations satisfied, livened and soothed. He invited Mackenzie to visit him. The grit of the summer term was washed off; he rose at six, read for a couple of hours before breakfast, and was still sharp at midnight. A glance in his shaving mirror showed the worn face but inside he was a young energetic man, capable of radical change. He warned himself to be careful.

When Job Turner returned home, he cleared a backlog of letters and set about his garden. He shopped, practised the piano, drew up a syllabus, wrote a report on the conference and all with zest, as if he'd not long to live. A short note from Ian Mackenzie confessed a similar vigour; in the hot weather when he usually felt listless he had completed the slow movement and sketched the scherzo of his quartet all inside a week. Turner's spirits bubbled. 'And Doctor Mackenzie/ Wrote it out in a frenzy,' he chanted to himself as he hoed and chopped.

Alison and her family were away in Bournemouth; he received a picture postcard. 'We're all brown as berries and bursting with ice cream and lemonade.' From Frederick Greene he heard nothing; it was unlikely that the old man had gone off for a holiday. He would have lowered his Venetian blinds against the sunshine and kept indoors in the sultry heat, making himself miserable.

Job saw nothing of Susan Smith. She and her family were spending a fortnight on the Costa del Sol at the beginning of August, and he would be away at the end of the month so that Susan would not attend for a lesson until the first Tuesday in September. She would benefit from the break, he considered. He had sent her two postcards from Cambridge, one of mediaeval music, the other of the courtyard of Trinity; she kept a scrapbook of holiday cards, she had told him.

Out of mischief or superabundance of energy he telephoned Frederick Greene who groused about heat, prices, the state of the world, but invited him round for coffee next morning. Mrs Harper let Job in.

'Do you know, he's still in his bath?'

'Perhaps he'd forgotten I was coming.'

'It's written on his memoryboard. In his own writing.' She walked the length of the passage, inviting Turner over her shoulder to sit down in the living room. A moment later she thumped violently on the bathroom door. 'Mr Turner's arrived,' she announced, without panache. The visitor heard no reply. 'I've put the kettle on,' she said, appearing again. 'Do you take milk and sugar?'

'Are you sure it's no trouble? I can easily go back. Just milk, please.'

'I'm having a cup, and ne' mind what he does. He's forgetful sometimes. He's a remarkable man.'

'I'm sure.'

'In more ways than I can tell you.' Her face indicated no innuendo. 'It makes me wonder.' She did not elucidate the sentence, but marched out. When she returned with a tray, Greene had still not shown up. 'He's a real tortoise.' She banged out, along the corridor again, shouting, 'Have you dropped off there?'

Greene arrived, red-faced, thin clean hair uncombed, trousers held up by old-fashioned braces on buttons. Mrs Harper looked him over. 'For God's sake get your jacket on, man. What will Mr Turner think?'

'He'll think what he likes.'

'And look at them slippers. You're treading the backs down. I s'll have to come in and dress you next.'

Greene waited for the reprimand to end and the woman to quit the room. His expression demonstrated self-satisfaction.

'She seems fond of you,' Job ventured.

'I wouldn't be surprised.'

Job Turner gave some account of the conference at Cambridge, and Greene recalled that he and his wife used to visit Geoffrey when he was a student there thirty years ago.

'I don't suppose it's changed much.'

'Did Geoffrey enjoy his time there?'

'Enjoy? Don't know if that's the word. He worked hard

enough. Always did. A good student. He went into subjects I knew nothing about. When I qualified as a solicitor it was through a kind of apprenticeship. We were trained to look after property or solve legal difficulties. I don't say it was all rule of thumb. And we had to pass exams. There was plenty of rote-learning, but I don't think there was any idea of educating us. We had to do that on the side. Of course you soon learned to read carefully. And think about what people wanted, but Roman law and that sort of stuff. . . . No, what they call strictly vocational. Whereas Geoffrey was educated, as it were, through the law. Later he had to learn the ins and outs, the tricks of the trade just as I did for his Law Society exams, but I think. . . I don't know. I'm only guessing.'

'Is he a better lawyer than you?'

'In the day to day work, no, I shouldn't think so. We don't have too many novelties in our humdrum profession. One has to be careful and have a good grasp of the rules or conventions. Geoffrey's manner is, let's say, more polished than mine and that will suit one sort of client. But I felt his time at Cambridge wasn't wasted. He could drop in somewhere for a lunch-time concert pretty well every day of the week during term, and, for instance, he attended some lectures on philosophy. Nothing to do with his course. Did it off his own bat. And he was up against some clever people.'

'You regret that . . . ?'

'Regret, regret.' Greene did not allow the visitor to complete the question. 'Yes. Just as my father regretted,' he grated on the word, 'that he didn't attend the secondary school as it was called then. We had books at home, I was encouraged to visit the library, and I was made to learn the piano, so I can't complain. And I went to Sunday School. I suppose my father did. And there we learnt about Urim and Thummim as well as the love of God. Do you know what they are?'

'Does anybody?'

Greene cackled, but offered no explanation. His hand shook. He wiped his mouth with a clean handkerchief. He dropped his voice.

'Would you say that my sense of deprivation, of educational deficit led to my pursuit of women?'

'No.'

Greene waited, mouth open, hand trembling.

'Go on, man,' he said. 'You can't stop there.'

'I think it may be a contributory cause. I don't know. I'm not very ready to attribute characteristic traits to single traumatic causes. We're highly complex, er, congeries of instincts and experiences. . . .'

'Congeries. Good word,' Greene mocked.

'Aggregation.'

'Thank you. Thank you.' Greene laughed and in good spirits told how he'd taken Susan Smith to a concert of the St Cecilia Choir when they had heard 'Jesu, Priceless Treasure'.

'What did she think?'

'Baffled for a start. I don't think she knew much about four- and five-part singing. They did some madrigals. That thing about "and running in and out, and running in and out". She giggled. I don't think she'd realized either that music can be both clever and funny. I played her a record of the Badinerie from the "Flute Suite" to show her that even old sober-sides could raise a titter.'

'Good for you.'

'It's got me out of the house. The harpy there doesn't approve when I tell her about it. She thinks I'm out for one thing only with women.'

'And Susan. What does she have to say?'

'Not much, when it comes to actually saying anything. But she's possessed with a wonderful musical memory, and is so quick. It's a treat to expose her to these works; she points things out to me the first time she's heard something that it would take me years or dozens of performances to notice. It's a pity she didn't start earlier.'

'There's music on the radio in the home, but her father's an odd fish. Believes in keeping himself to himself. Doesn't want charity.'

'Wouldn't you think the school would have noticed her talent? That's what you're supposed to be there for, isn't it?'

'Susan,' Job Turner answered, 'would be one of these very

89

quiet, hard-working little girls, never pushing herself forward, never making a nuisance of herself. I bet the music teacher was surprised that she gained the top grade in 'O' level Music. Oh, he'd expect her to pass, but I doubt if he'd ever heard her play the piano. She'd never volunteer.'

'He should have kept his eyes skinned. She's outstanding.'

'It's easy enough to blame him. I shouldn't be surprised if he didn't have to teach his 'O' level pupils in his lunch hour. No provision on the timetable proper.'

Greene squinted at his visitor who noticed that there was no show of eccentricity now about the man. His voice sounded level, cultured, reasonable. He wanted the facts of the case; he plastered down his newly washed hair with his hands to add to the image. He drank his coffee, did not smoke, sat without restlessness. He seemed as interested in the deficiencies of the state system of education as in Susan's unusual gifts. They talked with ease.

Turner was, therefore, surprised when, as the grandfather clock struck twelve, Greene stood and dismissed him with 'I must prepare myself for lunch now. Can you let yourself out?' Presumably he had curtailed conferences in his office with this homely, polite firmness. Mrs Harper, who had been on the qui vive, dashed along from the kitchen to see the guest off the premises.

'He'll have enjoyed your company. "Job Turner", if you'll excuse me, he says "is nobody's fool. It's a pleasure to hold a conversation with him." '

He shook her hand. It was scrubbed clean as a surgeon's, with beautifully shaped, oval nails. Her eyes were light blue, and large.

'His health is better,' she submitted.

'I'm pleased to hear it.'

'I tell him he'll live to be a hundred.'

'Does he look forward to that?'

'He makes out he doesn't. But all men like complaining. My husband has aches and pains galore.'

'Are they real?'

Mrs Harper considered that, gnawing at her lower lip.

'He thinks they are. But he's a big baby. Now Mr Greene he's different; he's grown up at one time or the other.'

'Why is that, do you think?'

'Well, he's an educated man. And dealing with other people's troubles, going into court, or writing out wills must make you think.' She paused, wrung her hands, breathed a deep lungful in. 'What about this young girl, Mr Turner?'

'You mean Susan Smith?'

'Yes. He takes her out to concerts. And she's been up here to play the piano with him.'

'It's good for him. Gives him something to anticipate. When you are old, you tend to allow yourself to be cooped up. You don't venture out. It's all too much trouble.'

'Is it good for her, though?'

'You're not suggesting . . . ?'

'I'm not suggestin' anything.'

Her mouth clamped; she rattled the door handle. Her expression ordered him off the premises. As soon as he had crossed the threshold, she slammed the door shut behind him.

The day before he set off for his holiday, Job Turner met Susan Smith's father. Both men were tramping through the woods on the estate in the evening. Turner had been into his school, but found it unwelcoming. The caretakers were cleaning and polishing; chairs were piled on tables, the walls bare. His secretary had worked with him on the few items that needed attention; outside his office, raucous, ill-tuned portable sets thrashed Radio 1. The cleaning ladies smiled and greeted him, but as a stranger. In the smell of disinfectant and floor polish he was afflicted with alienation, a feeling that his influence here was as ephemeral as these ablutionary exercises. The chief caretaker, hair Brylcreemed upwards like a Ted's, sidled in with his report. Work of purification went well; no break-ins, and no vandalism apart from some chalking on the top-yard wall.

'I've 'ad it weshed off for you.'

Turner thanked the man who on his way out made his effort at social communication.

'This is how schools ought to be all the time,' he said. 'Wi' no kids rip-roaring about 'em.'

'I see what you mean.'

Now in the evening, at the end of a hot day, he walked fast but aimlessly about in the woods to rid himself of depression. He had scrubbed his hands and face, but he fancied that the stink of disinfectant hung about his clothes. Smith's face, he noticed, shone tanned to a ruddy mahogany; he looked ready and pleased to bandy a word or two with Turner.

The holiday had been just what they needed; sunshine all day, reasonable rooms, eatable meals. Sue was well, had started practising again.

'She missed her piano. One little place we went in had one. Wasn't much good. Bit honky-tonk, but she sat down there, and played Chopin and Schubert. And then that Mozart "Alla Turca" Sonata. Got quite an audience. Not that she noticed until they clapped, and she blushed bright red, though she was the colour of a lobster to start wi'. They liked it. The landlord, proprietor, whatever you call him wouldn't let us buy any more drinks. On the 'ouse.'

'Did he invite her back?'

'No, he didn't. Perhaps they have to have a licence for music, like our pubs. And I don't know if she'd have gone. She's got a young man, you know. Had to write a letter to him every day. Don't know what she found to talk about. I mean all we did was sit there in the sunshine, and walk a hundred yards to the hotel for a meal or a splash in the swimming pool.'

'Did she receive any in return?'

'One or two. But the post's crazy. Don't know if it's us or them.'

'And do you approve of him?'

'The young fellow? We haven't seen him yet. He's working in her office. He went to London University and then the Poly here for a year. He's passed all his exams but he had to do another two years to qualify. This is the second, and then he might have to go somewhere else to find a job.'

'Is he from these parts?'

'No. Well, not that far. His dad's a railwayman in Chester-field. As far as I know he's all right, but I don't know how serious they are. He's twenty-three or four, and she's nearly eighteen. They've got their way to make.'

'Is this the first?'

'The first she's told us about. We don't know what goes on in their heads.'

'What does her mother think?'

'She wittles. "Our Susan's sensible, in't she?" she keeps saying to me, but as if she doesn't believe it. I tell her. "It happens to all of us".' Smith considered. 'I tell her, "Your feyther didn't think you'd made much of a catch in me, did he now?" and she answers, "Well, I know that." I sometimes think women aren't blessed much by way of imagination.'

'If he's a decent young man, I'd think it was good news. One of my sons-in-law is a solicitor.'

'This one's a sort of a Labour man, from the bits she lets drop. Worrying his head about starvation or South Africa or "nukes" as she calls them.'

'Don't we all?'

'To be honest, Mr Turner, no, I don't. I've got enough on my plate. How long's my job here goin' to last? What's goin' to happen to my sister's lad who's serving in Northern Ireland? What'll my wife's mother do when she gets incapable of lookin' after herself? My old father in hospital? I've plenty on my mind wi'out carrying the whole world's burdens. I can see you think I'm selfish, and probably I am. Charity begins at home, in my view. It's only them who has the time and the money to spare who can afford to waste it on Africans and hippies. And as to these lesbian women camping out protesting about the nuclear deterrent, I'd lock 'em up. You don't agree wi' one word of this, d'you, Mr Turner?'

'No.'

'Look after your own, I say.'

'But some people won't do that. So their dependants have to be cared for.'

'That's why we pay taxes. Or to some extent.'

'And we'll all be wiped out in a nuclear war, taxpayers, women's libbers, babies, child abusers, the lot.'

'If the bomb's got my number on it, that'll be that.'

'We shall all die, and those who are wiped out at once will be the lucky ones.'

'So what? There's nothing I can do about it. Nor you, if it comes to that.' Smith looked fatter, more aggressive, his face bloodier. 'Oh, I know. I should protest and vote and march. No, thank you. Let them as wants to get on wi' it.'

'You said you'd lock them up.'

'If they break the law of the land, yes. You should see the damage some on 'em do in these woods. Swinging on young branches, pulling saplings up, dropping litter everywhere. They don't act like human beings, and I tell you, Mr Turner, if it were up to me I wouldn't treat 'em like humans. They're no better than animals. Worse. They need corporal and capital punishment. It's the only language they understand.'

Now Smith had lost his fire, and spoke glumly, as if repeating something everybody had known and long accepted. Job Turner's spirits drooped; he wanted his world filled with decent people loving their neighbours.

'I'm no sort of politician,' Smith continued, 'as you can see. But there's something sadly and badly wrong somewhere.'

'Original sin?' Turner, jibing.

'What's that mean?' Surly again.

'All humans are born sinners. It's inbred. We don't have to learn to do wrong.'

Smith shrugged, rejecting or refusing to consider such academic nonsense.

'Wrong varies according to time and place,' the man answered. 'They give you medals in wartime for doing what they call murder in civvy life.'

Job Turner shifted from foot to foot. He felt lifted; Smith was thinking again. He wondered from the phraseology whether Smith had done army service at one time.

'It's funny when you think about it.' Smith had immense, solid weight about him, as if made of stone or cast-iron. 'Here I was walking in these woods, happy as a lark, enjoying every minute, and congratulating myself on living on a job where I can do this every day of my life, if I wanted to, and I meet you, and we start talking about politics and inside two minutes my blood's boiling. I mean, you're an educated man, so I ought to see it as a privilege to exchange a few words with you, but no, not me. I'm blowing my top before we know where we are. I wonder why this is. Can you tell me?'

'No. I wouldn't even try to guess.'

'I can't make it out myself. Perhaps there's something basically wrong with me, so that I can only bother about me and mine, and lose my rag when I'm told to do otherwise. Is that possible?'

'I suppose so. Was your father like you in this way?'

'Yes. Now you come to mention it.' Smith beamed, hummed, as if light had dawned. 'He was. He was a Conservative working man when that was rarer than it is now. He'd argue and fist the table, didn't matter where he was, or with who. My mother used to laugh at him and call him '"Itler". She was a different cup o' tea altogether. Are you just having a walk? Do you mind if I stroll round with you for half an hour? Are you sure, now? Just say if you don't want me.'

As soon as they began to move Smith became a different man. He led Turner off the beaten track and deep in the woods, pointed out a badger's set. 'We don't say too much about it, or the bloody hooligans'll be up here, with their dogs and their sticks.' Back on the path he led to the main lodge, where they peered through the windows.

'They use this as the headquarters for the foresters.'

'Nobody lives here?'

'No. They're making a tremendous difference to these grounds, as you can see. They were neglected for years. Now they're making the effort, and people are coming out here and enjoying themselves. But, once you get that, you get wrong 'uns.' This time he laughed as if perambulation settled or contained his fears. 'I used to like it when I first came up here, when the paths were overgrown, and undergrowth was wild, and there were dead trees. Why's that?'

'It's like our love of ruins. It excites certain types of imagination. They used to build ruins in the eighteenth century, you know.'

'I can understand that.'

Smith talked at length as they walked, about friends who had made for themselves objects they admired. He numbered amongst his acquaintance a violin-maker, a model-steamtrain builder and a man who designed and fashioned grottoes, stone arches, and Japanese sculpture for his back garden, All wanted for themselves what could not be bought in the supermarket.

'I've joined a band again,' he continued, dodging amongst desires. 'I put it down to you. Since Susan started with you, I took my old instrument out of its case, and gave it a blow. By God, I was rusty. But up here you can play to your heart's content and there's no neighbours to complain, that's the beauty. I auditioned for the Bagthorpe Colliery last week, I was good at one time, played solos for Readon & Turle's, and I just scraped in. They're a bit short of players, I reckon. Wouldn't have got in at one time. But I did, and I'm going to enjoy it. Mark you, it's the summer break now, and it's giving me a bit of a chance to get myself up to standard.'

'That's good. Do you play with Susan?'

'Now and again. We did the Haydn Trumpet Concerto last night. And the wife's pleased. Best thing I could have done, she says. We'll see though.' He speeded up his progress, surprisingly, powerfully for one of his weight.

'It's coming back. The skill. The lip. I'll master it if it kills me.'

He laughed out loud, like a child, and slapped his fat thigh.

'I was good at one time, though I say it myself. I could play.'

# 11

Job Turner found to his surprise that his holiday suited him.

The weather was hot and sea mists burnt away early on Alderney. He walked round the island, clambered in the old forts, lounged in heather, ate huge meals, prepared himself physically for the next term, wrote a few letters and a dozen postcards. He struck up a casual friendship with two ladies in the first week and missed their hearty vigour in the second. Both held responsible positions in London, one with a fruit importing firm, the other with a publisher. They knew a great deal about literature, literary figures and music, kept him amused with anecdotes. The two women rose later than he, but they sat with him for dinner and, as the talk prospered, went out together for a drink to top up the bottle of wine the three shared. He felt young with them; they were in their thirties, and lovers, he guessed, but they flattered him, pulled his leg, set him tricky quiz questions about musicians. At the end of their time – they had already spent a week ahead of him – he carried their bags to the taxi for the airport, kissed them with a pang after they had exchanged addresses and promises to write. The second week, hotter and headier than the first, seemed dull without their questions, and their replacements, a middle-aged couple with two girls young enough to be grandchildren, passed the time of day with him, but settled once the children were in bed to read novels over an iced glass of lager and lime. He would, he knew, never see June and Michelle again, but their absence wore powerfully down on him for two or three days. By the end of the holiday he had recovered his equipoise, but he surprised himself by the strength of attraction to these clever, lively young women. They were his sort, grown up, intelligently funny; they made the wary, chary widower into a human being again.

97

On his return to Beechnall, he heard from the estate agent
in charge of the letting of his house that the family who had
taken it had returned home a month earlier than expected
and this gave an opportunity for repairs and decoration if
Turner felt they were needed. He arranged to visit the place.

The young man from the agent's arrived ten minutes late.

'Toby Hardwick,' he introduced himself. 'From Wenham,
Hinde. We've not met before.' He shook hands with Job
Turner who had stood patiently in the front garden marvelling
at the profusion of the roses there and the untidiness of weeds
which Gillian wouldn't have countenanced. He had, though
he had keys, not let himself in, nor opened the gate to go
through into the back garden, but stood quietly at the foot
of the steps leading up to the ornate front door, and then,
growing impatient, walked the ten yards of curved path to
the old iron gate, heavy with layers of black paint.

He had forgotten the quietness of the short cul-de-sac on
which Oak Villa stood; it seemed as free from noise as his
present house; the sound of mild movement in the branches
of summer trees was remarkably similar. No front doors
opened, no cars set out or returned; hedges grew high enough
here to mask lower storeys; if curtains were edged aside to
allow observation they would have to be those on second- and
third-floor windows. The houses, the shrubs, the streetlamps
were set in a warm and comfortable immobility. The arrival
of Hardwick's Cortina had a vulgarity about it, interrupting
the sabbath calm of this first Thursday in September.

'I think you'll find it in good order,' Hardwick said,
weaving his fingers amongst the keys. 'Very good tenants, the
de Boys, very good. Away as much as he was here. He
respected the place, though. "This is the sort of house I was
brought up in," he said to me, "in Hampstead. Big and solid
and respectable." And he'd rub his hand up and down the
woodwork. Looked after the place. And the children were
the same.' Now he had opened the stained-glass door into the
unlit long corridor with the white staircase at the end. 'He
was in television, Mr de Boys, you know, and I expected his
children to be ravers, in the drug scene, God knows what,
but nothing of the sort. All quiet, getting on with their home-

work, so to speak. And he was a bit strict.' Hardwick slightly straightened a print in the hall, looked again, head on one side, made a further readjustment.

The house smelt, as it had during the occupation of the Turners, of furniture polish, but looked bare because the houseplants, monstera, aralia, tradescantia, with which Gillian had crowded every room, had disappeared. The place was lighter than his present dwelling, and with its high ceilings and ornamental cornices, seemed spacious. He looked at the carpets, the furniture, the baby grand on which he struck a chord, and found badly out of tune. 'We need to see to that,' he instructed the bland Hardwick, who made a note. Job Turner ran his hand along the dining-room table where they had sat together, the five of them, the air rich with one of Gillian's beef casseroles, and argued and laughed or conducted their mild family quarrels. The breakfast room, his study, formerly a butler's pantry, lacked life; his bookshelves stood empty; his desk, too large for the lodge, had a few loose papers in the main drawer. There were pieces of arithmetic, the titles of three Virago novels set out with ISBN numbers formally to fill a whole page, the beginning from a letter, with a printed address, Oak Villa, 7 Magdala Close, and heading 'From Edward de Boys', beginning; 'My dear Charles, We had hoped . . .' There it stopped, on uncreased cream paper in biro. Turner flicked open the small side drawers and found nothing.

'No fivers,' said Mr Hardwick genially. 'You'd be amazed what people leave behind.'

The upstairs rooms were ready for use, with beds made up, but lacked the litter of life, the hundred and one bits on the dressing table, the magazines or clothes dropped to the floor. Job Turner had hardly ventured into his daughters' rooms, except with a morning cup of tea; these spaces had seemed then exploding with hanging dresses and bright belongings, sweet with unguents, neat but full as a barrack square on a WRAC parade. He smiled at his simile; his daughters had nothing in common with the military, except an energetic accuracy of fire. Now everything froze tidy; wide unoccupied surfaces wanted movement.

99

'The place is in very good order,' Hardwick affirmed. 'We have a Mrs Gillot in, two mornings a week, even when there are no tenants. She's very conscientious.'

Job Turner remembered Mrs Gillot, a sturdy woman, whom Gillian had engaged. Those two energetic women had appreciated each other. Wendy Gillot had belonged to some Pentecostal church and had gone about her work singing. In the holidays he had heard and enjoyed her strong voice, free of harmonics or vibrato, slap in the middle of the notes:

'Blessed assurance, Jesus is mine;
O what a foretaste of glory divine.
Heir of salvation, purchased of God,
Born of His spirit, washed in His blood.'

'Who wrote that?' he had once chaffed her.

'I don't know, Mr Turner. Do you know?' She was shrewd.

'Some Victorian lady, Van something or other. Or was she American? I'll look it up and tell you.'

She smiled, and bustled on, lugging the vacuum cleaner, condemning him, he was sure, for his typical concentration on the feeble conduit through which the promises were conveyed rather than on the power and pure strength of God's abounding grace. In the period after his wife's death Wendy had continued working here, and he had recommended her to the estate agents, but he was surprised that she was still in attendance. He had felt, perhaps wrongly, that she did her stint here neither for the money nor love of the house but to demonstrate her attachment to Gillian.

He had not seen her since he left the place, but she had turned up twice weekly with her Moody and Sankey setting all straight, leaving behind the whiff of polish. Job Turner would have liked to shake hands with her, though he knew he'd do no such thing even if it were possible. Hardwick outlined the cost of redecorating the two main rooms and the kitchen, claimed it was worth the money in that they could charge a higher rent. The house-agent stroked his chin. 'The more spick and span the place is the better it's treated.' He was sure Mrs Gillot would see to the preparation. 'On the whole, nowadays, you don't need to clear rooms for painters and decorators to work in. They make less mess with new paints.' Turner gave his agreement to his proposal to refurbish. 'We'll give you a full account of the money we spend and deduct it from your account.' He exuded cheerful confidence.

Job Turner remarked on the closed-up smell of the rooms.

'Nobody has lived here for nearly a month,' Hardwick answered. 'And one would be unwise to leave windows open. Mark you, it's nothing to some of the places I have to go in. There's mould growing up the walls. How the hell people expect me to sell for 'em I just can't imagine. But there it is. One of life's mysteries.' Turner decided the man had his series of clichés for each situation.

'And what do you tell the prospective buyers then?' Turner asked sharply.

'Put the best face on it I can. Not always easy. House purchase is a slow process here compared with London and the south-east. People have time and leisure to look round. And change their minds.'

Turner switched his attention to the pictures in the drawing room. Three signed and numbered prints by Ken Longcake, an Athena *Bridge at Nantes* dignified over the fireplace in a wood and silver frame, three small batiks of running horses, two Victorian oils in ornate gold frames, black as soot, which he'd bought to his wife's unconcealed derision at an auction, a large Selwyn Hughes taming the wildness of the Orkneys, and two American watercolours by Jane Furney. Gillian could never be content with the placement of her pictures.

'We've something like a hundred altogether around the house. I must shift them about; never allow them to become mere background.'

'But they leave marks on the wall in different places,' he had objected.

'Nothing that a paint brush or Flash and hot water won't move.'

They had hung there undisturbed since her death. That vigorous woman, Gill or Mummy at home, Mrs Turner in the street, Dr Turner at the university, had no idea when she rearranged her 'art' that it would be for the last time. Doubtless she had delivered a lecture on techniques of seeing or judging to any bystander, had laughed and dashed, had issued her orders. Now, the pictures, unmoved and unmoving, seemed nailed to the wall. Job Turner bit his finger in chagrin.

'Keeps the glass clean.' Hardwick. 'I'll say that for her.' He tapped a Longcake broken branch with his fingernail.

'Who?'

Hardwick glanced down at a paper he held in his hand.

'Mrs Gillot,' he said, relieved by his notes. The agent then renamed the new client, his date of entry, outlined the agreed improvements and the form of their notification to the owner. He asked politely for additional questions, and when Turner hinted that all seemed clear, said he'd have to be on his way for his next appointment.

'I'll leave you here,' he commanded now. 'You have your own keys to lock up. Go over the house again, and check everything in your own time. Then, if you decide on further alterations, give me a ring. I'll fix it. Glad to have met you. Lovely place you have.' He shook hands, like the captain of a football team, and was out of the front door inside seconds.

Turner had wanted to spend some time on his own in the house, but had been diffident about asking, fearing that the fly Hardwick would have suspected some attempt at mild chicanery on his part. A sentence from his Latin 'O' level Virgil knocked in his head. 'What the gods themselves dared not promise, the rolling day has brought unasked.' He sat down in an armchair with that ragged remnant of his education. He could not recall the Latin, and wondered if he had an *Æneid* amongst his books either here or in the Lodge. The drawing room was washed in a greenish light, windows shaded by the rowans in the front garden from the morning sun, very still, not yet warm, uncomfortable in its promise of comfort. It needed talk, music to complement beauty of shape. Turner rose, walked the walls. 'Don't leave anything movable or valuable,' the house agents had warned. 'People are not honest.' The pictures were still where they had hung them; he had sold off or given away on his move hundreds of the books he and Gillian had collected. The bookcases, tall and glass-fronted here, were empty; he noticed no cigarette burns on carpet or woodwork. As he left the room he found he could not remember either the fabric, colour or design of the curtains; he turned back. Gillian must have made the choice, but he could not recall the occasion.

Saddened, he opened the floor-to-ceiling wall-cupboard in the breakfast room. Brilliant white outside, its interior was dark blue, the colour of oriental night skies in illustrations in a child's *Arabian Nights*. Gillian had decorated this room in their last summer holiday together. 'If I don't do this and the pantry now,' she had said, when he had told her to take it easy, 'I shall never do it.' She had spoken the truth. The paintwork was as fresh, as unchipped as on the day it was completed. The kitchen cupboards were bare, though Gillian's saucepans, with one or two additions, held their place. No grease stains disfigured the stove; the grill, what his wife had called 'eye-level for dwarfs', shone bright silver still. The mop and dishcloth lay stiffly dry; a dripping tap had splashed a brown stain in the sink; the calendar on the wall was two months out of date with a red circle round the last Tuesday of July and the word 'home' neatly underneath in felt tip, in a childish hand. The electric clock continued its spurious ticking, plain as ever; windows, ceilings, floor were clean. A few ants crossed the draining board. Carefully, so as not to make a noise, Job Turner unbolted the back door.

The dustbins were empty, the garage padlocked.

He walked the flagged path finding the garden more over-grown than he expected; 'Little Dorrit' spilled. Bedding plants, nemesia chiefly, ageratum prospered, but Gill had always refused to grow such. 'This is not a municipal park,' she had pronounced. The lawn looked parched, but short, except in the shadow of surrounding shrubs, where the grass straggled long and green. Roses dominated still and nothing of autumn touched the trees. He sat on the garden seat which he had bought Gill for a birthday present. He remembered her pleasure, and its tempering 'I nearly bought one myself last week. Good job I didn't. It wasn't nearly as good as this.' The paintwork on his house was bright; north wind and rain did less damage than the sun. He could see above the weeping willow the bedroom windows of his neighbours' property, but

103

heard nothing of their well-modulated, old-fashioned voices in the garden. The Misses Banham would be up and about, and keeping a discreet eye on the comings and goings next door; he wondered how they had fared with his tenants. Maiden-ladylike they might be, but they could fight their corner, with sharp notes or solicitor's letters. He left the seat; the apple trees were heavy with fruit. A ripple of wind disturbed every leaf in the sunlight. Job Turner found this a good place. He returned to the yard by the second path Gillian had designed and built to cope with a slight incline and to wind amongst taller shrubs and sturdy cherry trees behind. Back at the foot of the stairs he realized he had not made a second tour of the bedrooms. He decided against it. The house exposed itself in deadness or insensibility, too immobile to move him, inhuman as masonry and furnishings should be.

He checked the back door and let himself out at the front, standing for a moment in the porch. No noise disturbed the street and the morning sun played amongst the leafage. There was no oak tree in the street garden in spite of the name of the house; next door two huge lime trees occupied the sky. At the end of the summer term he used to smell the lime flowers as he returned home; they had announced the proximity of the holidays. His heart had lifted for joy.

The door in the next house clicked. Miss Dorothea Banham appeared.

'Good morning.' Job Turner lifted his Dutchman's cap.

'Oh, good morning.' Miss Banham expressed spurious surprise. 'I haven't seen you recently.' More than two years. They inquired after health and family. Miss Banham carried a trug and secateurs, perhaps to account for her presence. 'You are not moving back, are you?'

'No, just looking the premises over.'

'Not too much damage, I hope?'

'No, surprisingly intact.'

'There will be new people in soon, I presume?'

'Yes. We're arranging some redecoration, and at the beginning of October. . .'

'A family?'

'I believe so. American academics again. The last lot were television moguls.'

'So I understand. They seemed friendly enough, when they were here. Entertained rather frequently. Out in the garden if the weather was fine. The whole air smelt of alcohol. And people talked and laughed at the tops of their voices.'

'I hope it didn't disturb you.'

'We have double glazing. But Hetty and I walked down the garden. To listen. It does one good to realize that our kind of life is not the only sort. We're not such old fogeys as all that, you know, Mr Turner.'

'You weren't invited?'

'They had asked us in. But not for that particular event. It must have been a kind of farewell party. It's odd that a family lives so close for nearly twelve months and then disappears. We shall never see them again.'

'But you'd like to?'

'I did not say that, Mr Turner. Their ways were not ours, and we should not have wished to associate too closely with them. And vice versa I imagine. The de Boys would have looked on us as survivals, would have found nothing but amusement in us. But they were not a nuisance, no. They did not presume to. . .' She broke off. 'They gave us a glimpse of a different world. It reminded me of the time when as a child we drove to evensong. We lived in the Park then. And as we passed by the centre of the city we could hear the Salvation Army band playing in the open air. I liked that very much. So did my father, I think.' Mr Banham had added to his considerable fortune during the First World War. 'We had no connection with them, of course, except that my father made an annual contribution to their funds. And perhaps on closer inspection I should not have liked what I found. But the sound of their music, and the uniforms and silver instruments attracted me greatly so that I remember them with enormous pleasure to this day.'

'You don't hear them nowadays.'

'No. I suppose not. The television has replaced them, as it has supplanted so much.' Miss Banham spoke like an 'O' level essay, he thought. 'So perhaps it is not inappropriate to equate Mr de Boys with the Salvation Army.'

The two laughed, she more strongly.

'I saw Alison the other day,' Miss Banham began. She seemed determined not to let him escape too easily. 'I had occasion to call in at the offices of Boyce, Greene and Hardy. I used to deal with old Mr Greene, but now he has retired Alison conducted the business. She was very efficient and pointed out all sorts of interesting legal niceties. Mr Greene never did that; his view was "Leave it to me, ladies. I'll do the best for you." I don't think he thought we were capable of either understanding the law or making up our minds.'

'Which method do you prefer?'

'Both have their advantages. But I understood exactly what Alison was telling me; she made it absolutely clear. And so I felt quite pleased with myself when I could go home and explain it all to Hetty. Not that she was interested.' Miss Banham looked about her. 'I can remember Mr Greene as a boy. I went with my father to the Greenes' works; my father had his printing done there, and he took me there with him one day. It was unusual. Perhaps that's why I can remember it. But Frederick Greene was about, perhaps assisting his father. He was about my age and wore a wide, white collar.'

'Was he good-looking?'

'I can't remember.' She laughed that curtly off. 'He married a girl who was in Hetty's class at school, Cecilia Kingsley. It was thought by some that he was keen on Hetty, but it came to nothing. We had some degree of freedom in the 1920s, you know, though nothing like that enjoyed, or should I say, "abused", by young people today.' She sniffed. 'My father would not have stood in their way. He was no snob. Perhaps Hetty changed her mind or Mr Greene did. She would never go down to his office; that always fell to me, but as I was the elder, the more businesslike, it may have had nothing to do with their former attachment. Hetty never discussed the matter with me.'

Miss Banham talked on about old Mr Boyce and her father's charitable concerns and their present difficulties with the garden. 'We dare not venture out, Mr Turner, unless the weather is temperate.' He gave her a brief description of Frederick Greene's position. 'I'll tell Hetty,' Miss Banham said. 'She's sure to be interested.'

Job Turner slipped away when Miss Dorothea's verbal energy seemed momentarily to flag. She wished him a polite but formal goodbye as if his departure had no importance for her, and trotted towards her weeds. He had satisfactorily occupied a few minutes of her spare time this morning. At the paint-plastered gate he paused; there had been matching railings but they had been taken away for the war effort; the sawn-off stumps of the uprights could be seen still on the top of the wall, at the foot of the laurel hedge. The swollen thickness of the paint had altered the pattern of the gate, like arthritis on knuckles. Ugly, he thought. 'Mr Turner. Mr Turner.' Dorothea Banham was calling him back.

She stood again by the hedge between the gardens.

'Alison is a clever girl,' she announced. 'I always thought so when she was young. She never appeared childish to me, always neat, always ready with a sensible reply.'

'Yes.'

'I don't think such behaviour is much in evidence these days, and not much appreciated when it is. But I don't expect you to agree.'

She had lost interest, and was already turning away. He wished her good morning and made off with speed. In the street he could hear her snipping. The trees blocked out all distance in the summer; in winter one could see the skyscraper office-buildings in the centre of town through branches. He wondered why Miss Banham had called him back to make the comment she had; perhaps she hinted a criticism of his upbringing of the child or his present performance as a head-teacher. He would never know.

Job Turner drove down to his school where some of his staff were in preparing their rooms for the new term. They seemed pleased to meet him again, raised their problems briefly, but mainly pushed on with their work, as he wished them to. The secretary offered him coffee, but neither lingered over it. He had no sooner settled to his correspondence than his deputy arrived. 'Has Bruce Ferguson rung again? He

107

said he would when I told him I guessed you'd be in.' Ferguson was the area education officer. 'When you've done your letters, I'll come back. There are one or two little matters I'd like to discuss.' Turner began to dictate answers, almost unthinkingly, finding nothing of interest. The phone interrupted his ennui.

'Ah, you're there.' Bruce Ferguson. 'Can you come down to see me this afternoon? Two-thirty? Don't be late. No, I don't want to explain now. It won't take long. It won't. . . No, I'll say no more. Two-thirty.' Phone recradled.

Ferguson did not usually dabble in mysteries. Job Turner was intrigued, turning over possibilities. Somebody had bequeathed money for music in the schools, and they wanted his advice. They were to be forced by government economies to merge the four music schools into three, two, one. How could this be done? He returned, slightly enlivened, to his mail and his secretary.

# 12

Ferguson kept Job Turner waiting the statutory ten minutes amongst the civilized chatter of electric typewriters. The two shook hands, formally. A smile ephemerally replaced Ferguson's habitual expression of anxiety. A small man, glasses always in the wrong position on his nose, his suit rumpled, he seemed harried by his work, his desk haphazardly thick with papers. He poked a hand in the direction of a chair as if both might jack-in-the-box away. Before he had time to say anything his phone rang and while he answered the creased face assumed lively interest.

'Curse 'em,' he said, putting down the telephone, and writing a note. 'You've heard of this Gordon Miller business, I assume.'

Miller was the headmaster with whom Job Turner had quarrelled before he took on his present post. He did not answer.

'Miller's been in trouble these last few years. Eccentric. Neurotic.' Turner knew of the rumours, but remembered the man twenty years ago, ambitious, clever, unscrupulous. 'We've tried to help him, but he wasn't the sort to be . . . interfered with.' A bark of critical laughter. 'The school has been going down. Last Friday he came in with his resignation.'

'Will he be sixty?'

'On the day he came in.'

'But he'll need to give notice?'

'Unless we come to some accommodation. Job, we've talked this over, the director, the chairman of the education committee, the chairman of the governors and we want you to take the school on.' He pulled his lips in. 'Now just listen to me.' Turner had no intention of doing otherwise. 'You're fifty-seven and you always talk of retirement at sixty. So you have three years in the place.'

'What if it drives me cracked, and I decide to soldier on for sixty-five?'

'We'll risk it. You're a headmaster of twenty odd years' standing. I know what you're going to say. In the primary sector. But you trained for and did your class-teaching as a secondary man. And you've kept in touch with secondary pupils at the music schools. Moreover, you know the Acton Comprehensive.'

'Twenty years ago.'

'You know what can be done there. It's a good neighbourhood. Your choirs and operas aren't forgotten. Miller's let it drift. Bluntly, we want a good caretaker who'll put it back where it belongs, and then we'll eventually appoint a go-ahead young man. Woman.' He groaned with his face. 'It's not as bad as all that. You'll straighten it out in three years because the parents will back you. We need an old hand.'

'Aren't there any secondary heads available?'

'Sometimes, Job, I suspect that you people in the front line think that we admin-wallahs are utterly brainless. We looked round. Carefully. I did. The director did. The inspectors. And you're the man.'

'You'll have to advertise the job. The unions. . .'

'No, they won't. They know I can get round it by making you acting. But the situation's unusual. . . .'

'What?' Job asked. 'A headmaster who's lost interest?'

'None of your cynicism. The union will be fighting for a decent retirement package for Gordon Miller.'

'And the staff?'

'Will be pleased to serve under somebody who's doing the job properly. Teachers have been having it rough enough, but the Acton Comprehensive more than most, courtesy of G. Miller. No, they'll be pleased to consolidate, and get on with new exams, and build the music department up again, and the sports, and have somebody there who supports them, and who gives the appearance of being moderately sane.'

'And my school?'

'Deputy takes over as acting head. Job advertised in due

course. He can put in for it if he wishes. You can tell me whether or not he's fit to get it. They'll do all right. Gives young Friend what you say he's always hankering after, the chance to run the choir without your telling him how to do it.' Ferguson shut his eyes as if to close the subject. 'Makes your last three years interesting for you. You should jump at the chance. Agreed?'

Ferguson tucked his hands together mock-prayerfully and grinned.

'Well. . .' Turner nodded back.

'There we are then. I don't need to mention increased salary and, subsequently, pension. There are still some perks for those who undertake responsibility. I'm not saying it will be easy. It won't. Miller really got across the staff. During these recent strikes he antagonized everybody, teachers, parents, children, kitchen staff, even the director.'

'He wasn't without talent when I knew him.'

Ferguson shrugged.

'You didn't like him much, they reckon. But he went to pieces towards the end. No moral fibre. He was a good starter, full of ideas, right or wrong. But he couldn't keep up with the interminable dullness of the daily round. He should have changed jobs every five years. And recently, he might have been ill, physically. Looks it. And there was family trouble. And then with all this strike business he lost his judgement completely, saw himself as the last of the defenders of culture and society and learning against fractious kids, illiterate teachers, uncaring parents, educational theorists, drug pushers, God knows what. He's been on the edge of a break-down long enough. He's done the right thing by retiring, but he's left Acton in a mess. It's a school I like. My daughter was there. It ought to be one of our best, and isn't. Over to you, Job.'

'When do I start?'

'First day of term. Thursday. I'll pass the word round. Tell your deputy, will you? Frighten him to death.' Ferguson stood, stuck his hand out. The pair shook. Then the education officer waved his hands over the paper on his desk. 'Some-times I think I know how Gordon Miller felt.'

'You'll cope.'

Ferguson nodded, ruefully in control of himself.

'Thanks, Job. You're the man for this. I feel, for once, I've done a bit of good today.'

Turner sat for half an hour in the main square of the city watching the dull play of the fountains, the passers-by, the children, pigeons, drunks, the line of taxis. Elated and surprised he hugged his new knowledge to himself, and then walked purposefully the two streets to the offices of Boyce, Greene and Hardy, Solicitors, Commissioners for Oaths. He read the list, white on new metal; heading eight other names were those of G. F. Greene, MA and A. F. L. Greene, MA, LL B. Job Turner, hesitating, decided not to call; he would telephone his news to Alison. He picked up his car and drove back to school, but it was now past four and deputy, secretary, teachers had gone home. The caretaker had not yet appeared. Turner did not let himself in, but stood in the playground gratified with the ways of the world.

The next fortnight flew past, full. His telephone rang incessantly at home and at the Acton Comprehensive School. He seemed to be running two establishments; his former deputy questioned him at least twice a day over matters which common sense should have settled. Even Jeffrey Friend rang about the choir; the man realized now that if his charges did not do well he would have to carry the blame. Job's new secretary, a middle-aged woman, was knowledgeable and helpful; she had admired Miller, had grieved over his decline, but did not hold it against the new head. The three deputies set out to impress him; without cynicism he observed their methods. One railed against the attitudes of the children. The second brought in two written schemes for the improvement of standards in the lower streams and one about career counselling; the woman gave a dull factual account of her work with the senior girls in and out of the classroom. None, he noticed with pleasure, voiced explicit criticism of the previous headmaster.

Pressure groups did their best. The PE department needed expensive equipment; Chemistry, Physics and Art had enjoyed no major replacement of stock for three years. The

112

senior mathematics master was seriously considering a return from modern to traditional, but this meant new books. The head of music, already well known to Turner, looking for miraculous change, outlined the festivals and concerts he hoped to manage, and the purchase of music this would entail. To all of them Turner's answer was the same: 'Write down and cost what is absolutely necessary this year; put in with it a second list of what you will want next year. Bear in mind how much money we shall have.' He named the sum, and the bonus awarded to a new headmaster. 'Don't forget, either, that I can do arithmetic.'

Another clique, two young men and a ferocious girl, called on him to do away with morning assembly. He listened, said he had no intention of breaking the law in spite of the strength of their arguments, but asked them for a written outline of what they would do with the twenty minutes to half an hour they saved each morning. Certainly there seemed no lack of interest in education. He listened cagily. He let no interview run on longer than a quarter of an hour, however sensible; he could form no idea what the effect of this curtness had on his senior staff. He arranged longer meetings in the lunch hour with departments about examination results. He compared their successes and failures with those of other local schools, and of the private schools. At a staff meeting he announced himself as an examinations man. 'O and A and CSE and now GCSE are not the be-all and end-all of education, but they earn jobs and impress parents. At the end of this year or the beginning of next I shall ask for, and doubtless get, a full-scale inspection, to see what outside experts think of our standards.' He invited younger members of staff to visit him. 'You'll get a quarter of an hour of my time, if not satisfaction. It won't do your case any harm if you write it down so that I can read what it is you want.' One morning he pointed out to a young geographer that there were two spelling errors in a notice he had pinned up. The man blushed deeply, then asked if the head had taken the offending paper down. 'No. Nor have I mentioned it to anyone else. But I expect you to correct it.' The young teacher spread the story, though in what form Turner did not know, but two of

113

his deputies attempted to congratulate the head. He sharply reminded the junior assembly that this new broom expected a more robust attempt to sing the morning hymn. Now and then he walked the corridors of the senior block in which he had his office to judge what happened at changeover bell or break. He learned more from the school secretary than from any other source.

All this occupied him constantly both in and out of school. He was not displeased by the Acton Comprehensive; if it was the disaster area he had been led to expect then he had lost his powers of judgement, but he was determined to give value for money. Gordon Miller, the ex-headmaster, called in one morning to collect some belongings: Turner allowed him a polite fifteen minutes and then dismissed him. Miller seemed thunderstruck that this former subordinate did not set store by his advice.

At home in the Lodge he slept well, worn out physically but waking excitedly. He almost forgot that Susan Smith was due for a lesson on the Tuesday of his first full week at Acton. During the summer she had attended on Noelle Waters regularly, and was well-advanced with her preparation for the winter Grade 8. Noelle had clearly taken over again.

'She hasn't the exact dates for the exam,' Susan said, 'but it will be late November/early December. She's doing the entry.'

He gave Susan over an hour, enjoying every minute. At the end when she was about to leave, she drew on her light mac and faced him by the front door.

'There's something, Mr Turner, I want to say to you.'

'Go ahead.'

'I don't think you'll like it much.'

Neither fear nor irony tinged the voice. She spoke in the same efficient way that she rippled up a scale or arpeggio.

'You might be disappointed in me,' she continued.

Now he felt uneasy. This girl could move him as his day-time staff and pupils could not. Even as the tremor touched him, he condemned his scale of morality.

'Let's hear it,' he said, cheerfully.

114

'I've decided that when I've done Grade 8 I shan't have any more piano lessons.'

'Is there any good reason for this?'

'You might not think so.' She spoke as to an exact equal. 'I've got a young man. We're going to be engaged. His name is Douglas Middleton, and he works in our office. At the end of this year he becomes a fully qualified solicitor, and it's possible that he'll be taken on permanently. Mr West wants to retire, and Mr Sibley will be leaving soon to go into local government. We shall be married, and I shan't have the time to spend on my diploma.'

'You'll continue to work?'

'Oh, yes.'

'Your father and mother know all about this?'

'Yes.' Susan frowned. She looked angry, obstinate.

'How old are you, Susan?'

'I shall be eighteen at Christmas.'

'And when you're married?'

They stood, awkwardly silent.

'It's a pity,' Job Turner said in the end. 'You've made such rapid progress in these few months I've known you.'

'I have. And I have to thank you for it. You're a remarkable teacher.' The girl had recovered her poise, and spoke her sentences as if she had learnt them by heart. 'But Douglas will be looking round for a house shortly, and we shall have to spend time and money on it. We've only the money we earn or save.'

'You're very young.'

'If I'm old enough to take a diploma, I'm old enough to marry.' He was reminded of the arguments amongst sixth-formers years back: if I'm old enough to die for my country, I'm old enough to vote. 'I must go now.' She looked at her watch.

'Are you seeing Douglas?'

'Tonight? No. He knew I had this lesson. Besides, he had to take some work home with him.'

She smiled, mitigating her rebuke, and skipped away, sturdily, swinging her music case.

Job Turner sat down on the chair by the piano stool,

contemplating the keyboard. His disappointment grew heavier by the minute. The house, lit only by the lamp near the piano, seemed small, damp, gloomy, shadow-packed. Change, transhumance, smarted.

His black day had begun well.

The music inspector had visited him with good news. He had come across a cache, his word, of orchestral instruments and proposed handing them over *in toto* to the Acton Comprehensive. He, moreover, was proposing more lessons by peripatetic music teachers in the school. Job Turner liked Guy Woodhouse, the inspector, knew him as a hard-working young man with ideas. Obviously he had been instructed by Bruce Ferguson to give assistance to the new headmaster; equally clearly, it suited his purpose to do so.

Gordon Miller towards the end of his tenure had not allowed the inspectors into any of his classrooms. He had announced this as a principle to his staff. 'You are professional men and women; you do not need outsiders, non-participants interfering with your teaching techniques. If you require assistance you have heads of department who are not only paid to sort out your problems but who ultimately carry the responsibility for the success or failure of your work.' This might have been popular had Miller's other pronouncements and behaviour been less eccentric, or even consistent. If a teacher needed help from an inspector, Miller's rudeness saw to it that none was forthcoming. Stanton, the music specialist, regarded by Miller as a wrecker of the timetable to prepare for ego-trips of speech day or concert, had suffered most. Stanton's face, when Turner had carried his news to the music room in the lunch hour, had reddened in ineffable delight.

Susan's announcement demonstrated to Turner how vulnerably he stood. He had been congratulating himself on his coolness, his distance from emotion during his first days at the strange school, his ability to make up his mind, to accept or reject without tearing apart the fabric of life. He had slept well, kept worry at bay, eaten heartily, thought clearly, been neither friend nor enemy. He had made his authority patent, but easily, without clumsiness. And now a girl of seventeen had thrown him down. He looked at the keys, the reiterated

116

ebony patterns of two and three. They meant nothing untouched there, mocked aspiration.

He had not argued with Susan, not put up a reasonable case, nor even asked the right questions. 'Had she told Mrs Waters? Was it only a case of money? Had she lost interest in music?' During these next few months he had determined to put her through it so that her distinction at Grade 8 would lead to a scholarship to one of the royal schools. He had prepared to pull strings. And now quietly she had brushed him aside, disregarded her outstanding promise, shown herself ungrateful for his care, acted uncouthly.

He pictured her again walking from his door, jaunty, relieved that she had made the unwelcome announcement, swinging her music-case in celebration. Her back had been broad, womanly, and firmly turned against him. Unwillingly he recalled her father's obstinacy, his selfishness; unfair as the consideration was he drew satisfaction from the comparison. The sins of the father were visited upon this daughter. And yet she had phrased her Beethoven sonata with great beauty, serenity even; her scales had run perfectly, her sight-reading, as always, immaculate, musicianly. Disappointment spread, coloured the decisions in school. He found himself snapping at the secretary, needlessly, but had the grace to apologize.

That evening he rang Noelle Waters who knew already, it appeared, of Susan's decision.

Mrs Waters showed, at first, neither surprise nor great emotion. When you, Mr Turner, and she seemed to speak of him as a young man, had taught as many pupils as she then he would learn how often this happened. Yes, Susan was gifted, no doubt of it, would have won a scholarship to the Academy, or if she had not wanted that, successfully taken her diploma in a year. But young people knew their minds. The earlier periods of youthful affluence followed by industrial depression and unemployment had made teenagers independent.

'Mr Turner, when I was her age, I listened to my teachers, followed their advice. That took me to the Royal Academy and some professional engagements. But then, I called a halt.

I decided to marry, and though I knew that meant the end of me as a concert pianist I can't remember any great struggle.'

'Do you regret it now?'

'I'm an old woman, Mr Turner. I shall never know whether or not I would have made a full career as a soloist. I probably ended in the place where I was most fitted, as a piano teacher in a provincial city. I've taught too many people, but I made something of a name and could refuse, oh, for the past thirty years anybody I did not want. At my best, my life depended on the success of my pupils. Whether that was the fittest way to occupy myself I do not know to this day. It's what I did, and there's no going back on it. When my husband had to retire early on account of illness, it meant I could support him financially. We never had children. I regret that now. The casual if intense relationships with my students had to take the place of a family.'

Noelle Waters went on to congratulate him on the difference he had made to Susan Smith's musicianship.

'It's remarkable in so short a time. I wish we had worked in tandem before. I am no more than a trainer, a coach. I cram them for exams. Of course I tried to broaden their minds musically speaking, but my reputation depended on success. And success as a teacher, as you know, comes by doing only those things that are necessary. I hear people talking of the educational value of this course or that, but I found that people excelled in exams by doing only what they were examined in, and never mind the rest.

'I'm a bit of an examination-man myself,' he confessed.

'I've nothing against them. They are useful. But they are limited.'

Mrs Waters talked on. She was lonely; she was intelligent. Since her retirement she had spent time examining or adjudicating her performance in life, and was not happy about it. He could not, therefore, expect from her an outright condemnation of Susan. The girl, her experience told her, probably acted sensibly in marrying her boyfriend. Mrs Douglas Middleton carried more clout than Miss Susan Smith, LRAM.

'But she could maange both,' he objected.

'Oh, yes. But it would entail difficulty. She's decided against that.'

'Why?'

'Temperament. Family outlook. Her father's a bit of a slave-driver. And hasn't a lot of time for continuing education for women. Not really.'

Turner let her talk. Noelle Waters at seventy found the world an unsatisfactory place. Perhaps increasing bodily aches or weaknesses made her consider her life a failure. He listened to the precise, old-fashioned voice condemning at length, as in an eccentric judicial summing up, all she had represented or accomplished in nearly half a century of teaching. It saddened him, even as he praised her work, her outstanding list of successes. She laughed, slyly.

'I would have been disappointed if you hadn't said that, Mr Turner.'

She did not stop there, but wandered on. It amazed him that in spite of the maziness of her utterance her meaning was so clear. Yes, she had tried to instil musicianship, to make sure that each group of a pupil's examination pieces had variation of style or period as well as technical difficulty, but, but, but, but. . .

'You didn't realize, then, that while you were teaching you were merely coaching people to jump through hoops rather than educating them musically?' he asked.

'I suspected it, I expect. But the exhilaration of success, and the fact that I had so many to cope with at a time, and all of them good in their different ways, gave me a sufficiency of satisfaction.'

'So it was not until you retired. . . ?'

'That is so. I can stand back now.'

'And now you realize this, are you depressed or angry about it?'

'Sometimes. Sometimes. But I am almost certain that given what and who I am, I'd just do the same all over again if I were given a second chance. We can't escape from these minds and bodies of ours, nor can Sue Smith.'

Job Turner sat down at the other side of the room from the telephone, disheartened and yet exhilarated at the old woman's independence of mind. He had not, in spite of prompting, forced her to admit that Susan Smith had been her outstanding pupil. That disappointed him but Noelle Waters, a formidable woman, stood as little nonsense from herself as from her pupils.

At the end of the week he rang Frederick Greene. The old man had heard nothing of Susan's decision; she had been to his house something like a fortnight ago and they had spent a very good evening playing duets.

'That was probably before her Douglas proposed.'

'Probably, possibly, yes, yes, yes.' Greene sounded jaunty as if his friend's defeat had pleased him.

'It's a shame. A waste.'

Frederick Greene repeated the nouns in a quavering parody, and continued,

'Yes, I suppose it is, if it's final. But from what you say you've from now until December to make her see the light. If your lessons are really interesting she might change her mind.'

'I don't think that's likely.'

'Why not? She's only a child, really. Young for her years. You should be able to influence her. After all, you're an educationalist.'

'Do you think I should try?'

'What I think is not of very much importance. I'd like to see her do well, but if she's not having any, then she's not having any, do or say what you will. You'll try, being you, but whether you'll get anywhere is another matter.'

'She's so gifted.'

'Yes. But when I look at these Young Musician competitions on the telly, competitors are marvellous. All with Grade 8 distinctions, I understand. But they won't end up as professional musicians, even of a moderate sort. I know some of them don't want that, but. . .'

'The opportunity should be given to all those who have the talent. If, later, they lack the temperament, or strength, or luck to be really outstanding, at least they've had the chance.'

'There are more talented people about than you imagine.

120

Just because you don't come across too many in your school you shouldn't get it out of perspective.'

'What's your advice, then?' Job Turner ground the question between his teeth.

'Oh, what you always intended to do. Teach her and niggle at her and persuade her to go on.'

'And will you help?'

'How can I? She'll pay as much attention to me as to the lamppost outside my house. I'll encourage her to attend concerts or play duets if she thinks fit, but beyond that I can do nothing. I'm a pragmatist. I'd like to see her do well. But even if she does all you want of her, she'll probably end up sitting in her front parlour every evening listening to children plinking through "The Merry Peasant" or "Für Elise".'

'At least she'll be trained to pick out the outstandingly good pupils.'

'Well, yes. If that's any comfort to you.' Greene laughed, without mirth. 'Or her.' The old man put the phone down as if no more words remained to be said.

On Sunday Job Turner was invited to Alison's home for lunch. The meal was excellent and he enjoyed his play with the children. His daughter wanted to question him about his new job and its implications. She didn't waste time, brought out his attitudes or hers into the open, made him weigh advantages against disadvantages, forced him to justify his decision. Her husband sat smilingly through the inquisition, but the au pair girl threw him glances of sympathy. Job Turner enjoyed his daughter's performance, and his own; it did him good to think out where he stood and what he wanted in the swirl of action that made up his weekday work.

'Has the school real possibilities?' Alison wanted to know.

'Yes. I think so. I'd like to think that you'd not be unduly worried if you had to send Sarah and James there when they are old enough.'

Alison grimaced, tartly.

'You're concentrating on middle-class children, are you?'

'The majority are because of the catchment area. That doesn't mean they're all academic by any manner of means.

121

But I have a feeling that in the last few years we've neglected the really bright on spurious grounds of equality.'

'That's élitist talk from an old socialist, isn't it?'

Geoffrey Greene laughed out loud at his wife's jibe, hugged his knees. Sarah, on the hearthrug with a toy hospital, looked up delighted at her father.

'The sort of equality I want,' grandfather Turner said, 'will allow anyone to develop his, her abilities as far as possible.'

'Idealism.'

'Of course. One doesn't always receive justice from the law courts. But the principle stands.'

'What's wrong with the school?'

'It's slack. There have been strikes and disruption in the past year. That meant a real effort by everybody concerned to keep things standing still, not getting worse. The effort wasn't forthcoming. The headmaster antagonized his staff, both his friends as well as his enemies. When people made a real attempt to initiate or improve or even compromise sensibly he got in the way and, as far as I can gather, unpleasantly at that. A saint would have been in trouble last year, but he was a neurotic.'

'Are some of the staff inefficient? Or antagonistic?'

'Of course. On the whole, though, they're decent, hard-working people who'll do their best. I wonder sometimes whether schools will ever be the same again. When I started teaching, in a grammar school, teachers gave up their lunch hours and Saturday afternoons to run societies and umpire cricket and rugby matches. That won't happen again. The government, and rate- and taxpayers have let it be seen only too clearly what they think of the teaching profession.'

'Attitudes might change.'

'It will take time. No clever sixth-formers will consider teaching as a career these days. But I can't alter that. What I have to do is settle seething feelings, cool it, as they say, make it possible for my staff to do their best according to their abilities.'

'Is a headmaster important?' Alison asked. 'I remember Miss Renwick at school was always telling us when we were in the sixth what a fool the headmistress was.'

'She was cracked. Renwick.'

'Oh, yes, but clever. Knew a hawk from a handsaw.'

Job Turner explained his own intentions, or pretensions, but without enthusiasm as yet. He could not be sure. This school was large, spread about; responsibility was delegated. At the importunity of Stanton, the music king, he had taken over the junior choir who would give their first public performance in the City Musical Festival.

'Will they win?' Alison asked.

'They'll do well, I'll tell you. But I'm not sure whether I want them actually to win. They're working hard, turning up twice a week in their own time, and that's good.'

'You're a saint, Job,' Geoffrey Greene interrupted. 'The one you were talking about.'

'Why do you say that?' Alison asked, very quietly.

'Your father's putting the good of the community before his self-interest.'

'I think he likes playing God, interfering with other people's lives. And he's very competitive. Aren't you, Pa?'

His daughter spoke softly, laughing, without malice. She had not sorted him out, he concluded, and thought it not unwise to goad him into action or self-awareness from time to time. Job loved his eldest girl for her liveliness, her mental athleticism, in which she resembled her mother. He settled back in his chair to convey to her Dorothea Banham's encomium of her methods.

'She's a sharp old blade,' Alison assured him. 'I wouldn't try to hide much from her.' She hid her face. 'When we were young we used to call them Miss Salt and Miss Vinegar.'

'And Dorothea was Miss V?' Job.

'Certainly. Hetty would allow you to fetch the ball you'd thrown over. Not big sister.'

'She seemed to have a soft spot for your father,' Job told Geoffrey.

'Birds of a feather.'

'What's that, Daddy? Birds and feathers?' Sarah from the hearthrug. Geoffrey explained in his mildest legal manner. Alison listened, then added her own gloss. Susan repeated the aphorism in a grown-up voice. The au pair tried it with her

123

Belgian accent. 'Ils sont du même accabit,' Alison translated. 'Good God,' Job thought, 'is there anything that woman doesn't know?' He'd given her her chance in life. Or Gillian had. Or she had taken it for herself. Maxima cum laude.

He stayed with enjoyment till four, but when they begged him to share high tea, he refused.

'Families must have time to themselves,' he admonished.

'You're family.' The affable Geoffrey.

'He's Grandpa,' said Sarah. 'Not my brother, but my Grandpa.'

' "Standing in the need of prayer." Now you'll have to explain that.'

As he left, the whole group clustered at the front door to wave, call, blow kisses. Pleased with himself for once, he drove round to the park where he had played as a boy and, sitting in his car, watched the antics of children in the autumn sunshine. The morrow at Acton seemed close but manageable.

# 13

'My father-in-law was praising you,' Alison, sprightly over the telephone.

'Beyond my deserts?'

It was a fortnight later when Job Turner lounged listening to his daughter. She had just returned from a week in the Cotswolds, with all her family and Michelle, and was reporting back to her father. The weather had been heavenly, Sarah perfect, James adorable, while she and Geoffrey had relaxed without a worry. The dizzy au pair had proved a treasure. Job suspected that the modicum of praise coming his way resulted from holiday euphoria. Alison hoped he had not been overdoing it. She often, he considered, spoke to him with the same tone and lexis she employed to the three-year-old Sarah: a quiet rationality that anticipated, perhaps even hoped for, some unexpectedness of reply, or attitude.

He had been exerting himself, he said, and enjoying every minute. The school demanded, and received, his time from eight-thirty until six. The awkwardnesses and grievances, and they abounded, he took without apparent difficulty; the pleasurable moments more than compensated for hassle. The choir which Stanton had handed over was good, but in the month under his tuition had shown signs of becoming a virtuoso instrument for him to play on. His staff had settled to work; his deputies approved and supported, insofar as he could tell. Work prospered, not to be snuffed out. He matched Alison in cheerfulness.

His lessons with Susan Smith had gone without a hitch. She had practised hard, and he pressed her towards perfection, but without any further mention from either side of her retreat from music. Job Turner had decided to teach her with all his care and power, and leave it at that for the present. He would not come short on account of her desertion. Susan on her part seemed subdued except insofar as fingers and ears eloquently demonstrated concern and skill. Ten or a dozen lessons remained; he'd concentrate on her musical ability not her conscience. His subterfuge, he saw it as such, comforted him.

Job Turner was ready then to bandy pleasantries with his daughter.

'Don't stop there,' he encouraged. 'I'm hanging on to your every word of praise. What did he say?'

'We were talking about what was to be had from life at his age. That's usually his text for incessant complaints. But this afternoon he was quite different. He spoke positively, with no whingeing.'

'Good for him.'

'And he attributed this in some measure to you. "Job Turner has put ideas into my head so that I'm never short," he said. For example, Elgar. He'd listened to a great deal on your recommendation and learnt from it. "Your father always comes here with something interesting," he told me, "so that if nowadays anything untoward crops up I find myself arguing it out in my head against him." '

'How does he know what my views would be?'

'Ah, now. I asked him that. He said he didn't know, but when he put the contrary of his first opinion on any subject, it always seemed to emerge in your voice, and in his imagination with your mannerisms. I pressed him to find out why this was so, and he said it had surprised him. "It's only recently that I've come to appreciate Job," he said. "I'd always thought he was a bit of a grey, quiet figure, touching his forelock, a typical teacher, and much under the influence of his wife, but now I've found this is not so. He's ideas of his own, and so I've come to use him as my devil's advocate." He said it was very odd he did this in your guise. It had never happened before. He had always had to put the two sides of a case, but he'd always done it for himself. He asked *me* why it was.'

'And what did you say?'

'I'd no idea. I wondered if it were lack of practice on his part so that he had to dramatize the arguments now. I've gathered he was good as a lawyer, clever and sensible, but quite different from the Fred Greene of his private life.'

'A split personality?'

'He always maintained, according to Geoffrey, that a good solicitor had to be a hypocrite, an accomplished actor, never too personally involved.'

'That can't be right, can it?' Job Turner.

'I don't know. There's something in it. Some cases I deal with appeal to me strongly as a human being. But I'd give equally sound legal advice to somebody who was about to try something I didn't altogether approve of. It's beside the point. You've made a deep impression on Father Greene, and that's quite a feat. Mark you,' and Alison laughed, 'it might, this liveliness of his, be put down to the better weather, and his improved health since last winter. He's fewer aches and pains and fears. Still, it's interesting that his recovery should take the form it does. You've inserted yourself into his life.'

'Is that good?'

'I don't know what tomfool opinions he ascribes to you. But he certainly seems better. I thought last January–February that he was on the way out, or at least edging towards it.'

'There may be other reasons.'

'Certainly. Still, Geoffrey's pleased. The old man's always been a nuisance, but if he began to lose his marbles altogether. . .'

Something of the energy of Alison's goodwill transferred itself to him. He settled to his piano which he had neglected since his time at the Acton Comprehensive; practised the first movement of the 'Hammerklavier' with enthusiasm. He wished he could play with the ease of Susan Smith.

Next morning he received a postcard, Cheltenham Art Gallery & Museum, the *Dowdeswell Pike* (1896), from Frederick Greene inviting him to telephone and fix the time of a visit. He did so, found the old man surly and unenthusiastic, but arranged to call at five-thirty on Saturday evening.

'That'll suit,' Greene agreed. 'There's nothing on the telly.'

The garden of his bungalow blazed with autumn dahlias,

127

though leaves on the limes and fruit trees were still thickly green.

'The apples are nearly ready for picking,' the host said cheerfully. 'I'll have to talk to the gardener.'

'Don't you usually?'

'No. He pleases himself. As long as there are flowers and no weeds and I see him about at work he knows he'll be paid.'

'How are you keeping?'

'When the weather's passable, I survive. But nights are really drawing in now, and that means winter. I hate the cold.'

'Do you go out much?'

'I have been on a bus-trip or two. One. To the Cotswolds. That's where I got that ridiculous picture I sent you. I looked about for the sort of cards I wouldn't want to receive and brought them home to dispatch to my friends at strategic intervals.'

'Was that when Alison was there?'

'No. Before she went. It was a week's coach tour. Mrs Harper recommended it. Her mother had been on a similar affair.'

'Did she go with you?'

'Who? Sandra? Or her mother? Don't be so bloody silly.'

'Did you make any friends?'

'No, I did not.'

He sounded disgusted, but had taken to his favourite chair where he sat alertly enough, glasses on the end of his nose.

'You've changed jobs, Alison tells me.'

Turner gave a succinct account of the circumstances, and the old man stroked his chin.

'So you were invited, were you? I thought that only happened at the ancient seats of learning. Don't they have to advertise? What's happened to the unions?'

Job did his best with the hoarse questions. When the cross-examination was complete, the old man stared at his shoes, then hoisted himself straighter by the arms of his chair.

'The director of education must think highly of you.'

'He hardly knows me. He'd take advice from the area officer and the inspectors.'

128

'And they'd know what they were talking about, would they?'

'Modesty forbids. . .'

'I see. I always found it better to arrange things according to convention. Caused less trouble in the long run.'

'They were in a hurry. My predecessor caught them out with his resignation.'

'But they could have made him serve his full term. Three months, four, is it? They must have been glad to be rid of him, and they must have been pretty certain of you.' Greene waited for the visitor's nod of approval. 'They must have had confidence in you. You'd like that.'

'Wouldn't you?'

'Of course.' The old man scratched his face noisily. 'I can't remember it happening to me. Not as blatantly, anyhow.' He peered. 'You inspire their trust.'

'Wrongly, do you think?'

'Who am I to say?'

Old Greene had enjoyed the exchange and, standing now by his desk, searched for his cigar box. He opened it once he had his hands on it, but almost immediately clicked it shut and turned away.

'I'm trying to cut down.' He sighed, breathily, then wheezed shufflingly back to his chair. He had aged twenty years in those two or three minutes. 'You know, Turner, I have this same sort of confidence in you. You're a solid citizen; it makes me feel safe to have you around.'

'You've not asked me to do anything for you.'

'No. And I hope I shan't have to. But my trouble is old age. I find myself, for instance, reading something that at one time I could have skimmed through and understood without trouble, and now I can't make head or tail of it. Nor do I particularly want to. And yet there's loss of temper; I'm angry, raw about my lack of concentration. I oughtn't to be. Apathy would be more appropriate, but it isn't. I fume at myself and curse.' His face assumed a series of wrinkled masks, all equally unintelligible to the visitor. 'Now you. When you're here, I seem to rise to the occasion, gather my wits.'

'I don't come often.'

'No. But I use you. I argue with an imaginary Job Turner, or exchange ideas with him. Barter, banter. And that means you must have had some effect on me. When you're not here I talk to you. It's a new development with me, but I'm sane enough. You're my whetstone.'

'And is the air-drawn figure more useful than the real one?'

'You're like that daughter of yours. Thinks everybody's a bloody fool but her. No, I'm grateful for what you've done for me. You've marked out a few ley lines or lifelines and I've followed them. To my advantage.'

'It's good of you to say so,' Job answered soberly.

Frederick Greene shrugged himself straighter in his chair, cleared his throat fiercely.

'None of your humble-pie stuff, or I shall begin to wish I'd said nothing to you. I'm cooped up here in this bungalow. It doesn't matter that you're in that dog kennel of yours because you can get out. This place is convenient, they all tell me; that means it's boring.'

'It isn't small.'

'No, but it hasn't got the clutter of years. I know where everything is.'

'You had to search for those cigars.'

'I do my best for myself. But Mrs Harper, Sandra, she straightens it whether I want it or not.' He blubbered out his lower lip. 'She doesn't make head or tail of me.' He squinted. 'Yes, we're still at it from time to time. But she said only yesterday, "You don't act like an educated man sometimes. You're worse than my husband." '

'What did she mean?'

'I think she equates education with order, knowing what you're doing, and ability to put it into words.'

'Not a bad definition.'

'It fits the lawyer's office. But my life's full of holes that no amount of talking or arranging or tidying or preparing for will fill. The pits gape where you don't expect them. And my hackles rise. I shout for no reason. Or because I'm helpless to set things right. My curbing mechanism's gone. So she never knows when the next explosion's coming, or why.

Keeps her up to the mark. But she thinks educated people don't raise their voices, can put their complaints into grammatical sentences once they've thought it out.'

'I see.'

The two men paused, Greene to regarner his strength, Turner to allow him the opportunity. The old man, after a minute's silence, dashed himself upright, made for the desk, found the cigar box at once, opened it, clashed it immediately shut.

'Shit,' he spat.

He stumbled back to his chair, his face as unhappy as his posture.

'Have you seen anything of Susan Smith?' Job Turner spoke very slowly.

'No.'

They were locked in uncomfortable silence which Greene broke in the end.

'Is she still coming for lessons?'

'Yes. And doing just as well as ever.'

'She'll pass her exam?'

'She'll walk it.'

'Have you said anything more to her about this idea of giving up her music?'

'No. I just teach her as if she were still intent on making a career of it.'

'That's deliberate, is it? On your part?'

'I suppose it is. I don't know what else to do, really.' Job Turner sounded defeated.

'You hope success will change her mind for her?'

'I doubt it. But, yes, that's about the length and breadth of it.'

Again the silence, so barbed with trouble that Turner almost begged Greene to light up and succour them both.

'Were you a prodigy in your time?' Greene, wheezily.

'Yes, in my very small way. I was doing academic work as well. I don't think I was nearly as talented as Susan Smith.'

'Do you ever regret that you never made it as a concert pianist or conductor?'

'Vaguely. Occasionally. I lacked the push as well as the

131

opportunity. A virtuoso's life has its drawbacks. No, I've done about as well as I could. They don't often make musicians headmasters. Music's very marginal in English education, a nuisance or an optional extra. I tell you what I do regret, though God knows what I could have done about it, and that's stopping my wife's progress in the educational world. She was right out of my class.'

'Um. But she died. We're unusual, Turner. We're widowers. It's usually the other way about. Was your wife older than you?'

'Younger. She was killed in a car accident.'

'Yes. I'm sorry. I'd forgotten that, just for the minute, just while I asked the question. That's age for you. Cecilia was two years older than I was. She came from higher up the social scale than I did, though I doubt if her father was any richer than mine. But she was used to travel, had relatives who were important civil servants, consultant physicians, a bishop, that sort of thing. It seemed to matter at the time.' He smirked as if clearing his teeth. 'Not that she was an intellectual, really. Nor am I, come to that. I don't read as much as I might. I wish I did.'

'You wouldn't have liked to follow an academic career?'

'No. Law's a useful set of rules society's acquired one way or the other. It has its interesting holes and corners, I'm sure. Not that too many of them came my way. But if you go beyond that, it's no longer law you're studying, but philosophy or morality or religion or politics.' Greene's voice sounded strongly, as he poked his right index finger into the palm of his other hand. His rheumy eyes glistened. Muscular control seemed re-established. 'If I'd come from a higher social stratum I might have been a barrister and made more money, or ended as a judge. I don't know. Anyhow, what are you going to do about this Susan Smith of yours?'

'As I'm doing now.'

'And not take to arguing with her?'

'I might. It's a pity she should throw everything away.'

'Not everything.' Greene looked cunning. 'She's going to marry a decent man with a respectable profession. That's something. She'll bring up a family.'

'We don't know that she has any gift for that. And even if she had, society doesn't offer its big rewards to talented mothers. No, I'd like her to have another year or two under tuition as a pianist. She's plenty of time for marriage and children.'

'Nobody knows how much time he has. Your wife, mine. They're gone. But your wife left you an Alison, and I understand your other daughters are clever. And Cecilia provided me with Geoffrey, my successor. He's a better man than his father.'

Greene appeared fatigued, drooping, and when Turner suggested that the visit should end, the host made no demur.

'That's our success, then?' Turner asked.

'Do you never feel or think in terms of failure?' Oblique. The old man peered.

'I know that there are things that are beyond me, so I don't take them on. I had a dream the other night and in it I found myself committed to writing the music for an opera. It was about King Arthur. I seemed to be a lot younger than I am, perhaps even a schoolboy still, and I didn't feel unduly troubled. In fact I had the first two chords of the overture ready. They were the first chords of "Zadok the Priest". I knew they weren't exactly original. Yet under all this was the certainty that I was incapable of writing the opera. It was uncomfortable. I'd been conned somehow into it and everybody else appeared confident of my abilities.'

'It isn't an account in dream-language of your uncertainty about your new job?'

'I've considered that, and I don't think so. Odd, isn't it? Basic insecurity about my whole life perhaps.' Job Turner smiled. 'I've outstayed my welcome, so I'll leave you.' Greene did not deny it, but accompanied him to the front door where they shook hands, rather sheepishly.

'I'll speak to that Susan Smith for you,' Greene said, off-handedly. 'That is if she gives me the chance.'

That pleased both, and they shook hands again, like boys over a bargain.

# 14

Phyllis Stockton, Turner's middle daughter, the following weekend dashed up the motorway to see him, accompanied by her husband and three-year-old son, Thomas. She and her husband now held junior appointments in a London hospital, though Martin had forged slightly ahead because of her short break from business, she grumbled, while she was giving birth. They stayed with Alison for three days, but appeared on both Saturday and Sunday to have a meal with him.

'It's a real doll's house,' Phyllis declared of the Lodge, which she had not seen before. Martin had grinned nervously as if he'd expected a defensive outburst from his father-in-law at the criticism. Phyllis looked over her husband with good-humoured condescension.

Job Turner had never quite come to terms with this daughter, or rather with his idea of her. She had always seemed dreamy compared with the efficient Alison, untidy, engaged in some other world. As a child she had read a great deal, played on her own without trouble, been less competitive than her elder sister, less noisy than her younger. Job remembered still the excellent little essays she had been writing at the age of twelve. All three had written well.

'We've bred a poet there,' he'd told Gillian.

'Do you approve of that?' she'd answered him.

And yet Phyllis had opted to do science at school, medicine at university, with great success. As soon as she had finished her preregistration year she had married Martin Stockton, the only son of a Methodist minister, an exact contemporary. They occupied junior posts in hospitals, now together, now apart, and were buying an expensive flat and paying heavily for their son to be cared for.

Thomas had been born just before Gillian's death.

Turner had wondered if they acted sensibly having the

child at this time, had voiced his fears to his wife, who had put it to their daughter bluntly, as he would not. 'She understands English, I'll give her that,' Gill had said when he demurred. Phyllis had apparently looked vaguely at her mother and had said that all was well, she'd manage. When asked if the birth were an accident, she'd told Gillian that it was the exact opposite, that she and Martin had decided it was exactly what they both needed at this stage. Now, this year, Martin hoped to take his Fellowship of the Royal College of Surgeons. 'Or, at least, my first shot at it.'

'Do you have to work hard?' Job Turner asked his son-in-law.

'You'll never find him doing anything else,' Phyllis answered for him. 'He's the nonconformist conscience personified.'

'It's all very well for her to talk,' Martin answered, sparely enough. 'She was easily the cleverest student of our year. Some of us have to slog.'

They laughed with each other, as if in agreement. Phyllis, still dreamy-eyed, handled the child with marvellous competence, talking to him with a grown-up brevity of love. Grandfather stood impressed.

'We don't have too much time together, the three of us. We make the most of it. You think I should give up my job for a time, don't you?'

'I didn't say so.'

'You don't have to. Even Madame Alison considers we're not doing it properly.'

'She works.'

'Yes, but she names her hours which is more than I can.'

Phyllis was an anaesthetist, well thought of in high places, so Martin confided in ten minutes he had on his own with his father-in-law. 'That's the way to get on.'

'You don't begrudge her . . . ?'

'No. She'll forge ahead of me, in the next year or two. After that it's luck or influence, being in the right place at the right time.'

'And you're better than she is at that?'

'No. Not at all. She's diplomatic, and clever with it. I'm a plodder, academically and otherwise. But a decent carpenter.'

Their visit cheered Turner. Here were young people of talent getting, as far as he could make out, their deserts and on their own terms. Justice seemed to exist in their world as it did not elsewhere, and his spurious surprise delighted him. Alison, in her cool way, agreed.

'Oh, Phyl's always seen what corners to cut. She knows what she wants and she'll grab it, wherever it's possible. A smart operator, our Phyllis.'

'Don't you like her?'

'Yes. Very much. I'm praising her.'

'She always seemed so quiet as a girl, not like you and Hilary. You two were like your mother, efficient and. . .'

'Bossy? Come, come. She knows her way round, always has. And without talking.'

Geoffrey listened to this conversation amiably, bouncing Sarah on his knee, quietly lilting her to 'This is the way the ladies ride'. He winked at his father-in-law behind his wife's back.

One evening in October Job Turner, returning late from school, picked up by chance Susan Smith who was waiting at a bus stop, and drove her home. She chattered about a crisis at her office caused by the breakdown of a photocopying machine. A day's rage by the senior partner, Mr Frogmore, had winkled out some 'expert' who had repaired the machine, but she had then had to stay to copy some forms the firm had promised to important clients. 'Or that was his story,' Susan said, laughing.

'Don't you believe him?'

'There was no hurry. It could have been done tomorrow. But Mr Frogmore doesn't like being contradicted, even by machines. And he'd made up his mind these things were to be finished today and so I had to wait for the man to fix the machine, then print them off, and put them in the envelopes that I'd already addressed.'

'Did he stay behind with you?'

'Oh, no. I wouldn't expect him to. He'd have been in the way or finding me other work.'

'You don't mind having to stay on your own?'

136

'No. I lock up quite often now. There are usually other people around, cleaners and so on, even when I'm late.'

The girl looked fresh, as if she'd just stepped from the bath, and cheerful at the end of the day. She explained how her mother would put back the evening meal, and how she'd still manage two hours on the piano as well as some ironing and a 'little typing job for Douglas' she didn't like to do in the office. She seemed lively, in good spirits and yet contained, in control.

'Mr Greene rang me up,' Susan announced at a traffic light. 'I'm going up there on Saturday to play my exam pieces to him. He asked me to. Douglas is away this weekend. He's going to his grandma's in Doncaster. I didn't want to go.'

'I see. Good. Does Mr Greene make any comments on how you play?'

'Not really. I mean, I've never taken all my exam pieces up there before. But he listens. And sometimes he asks me to play something again because he's enjoyed it so much. Or that's what he says.' She paused, looked at him, and spoke simply. 'He said I shouldn't stop having lessons, that I should go on with my diploma.'

'That's what I think.'

'I know. He wants to pay for my lessons.'

'What did you say?'

'I thanked him. I didn't know what. . . He told me to talk it over with my father.'

'And you've done so?'

'Not yet. But I shall.'

They were driving past Turner's home now, then through the dark avenue of trees, and up to the Hall.

'Is money an important consideration?' he asked her.

'It's not the only one, but we shall need all the money we can make. Douglas won't be earning all that much more than he is now. He'll be working his way towards a partnership. The Frogmores think very highly of him. And I shan't have a piano. We can't afford one. Not yet.'

'So you won't play.'

'I can't if there's no piano, can I?'

'It's a pity.'

'And then there's the time factor.' They sat in the car under the single electric standard outside the gates of the Hall. She spoke steadily, expecting attention, copying perhaps Mr Frogmore or her Douglas. 'We shall want to get the house straight, and I shall still carry on with my job.'

'So you won't have the time?'

She paused, clutched at the bag on her knee.

'I suppose I could. If I wanted to. I don't want my marriage to be the second thing. To the music.'

'When is it you're getting married?'

'Oh, the date's not fixed yet. Next summer perhaps. When Douglas's immediate future is settled.' The legal voice sounded again. 'Say in about a year.'

She sat comfortably. The brickwork of the wall and arched gate was picked up by the single electric light. The Hall heaped itself beyond in darkness, more imagination than shape, and the trees both left and right played odd disappearing tricks with the eye. The wind, subdued now, was strong enough to shake close, illuminated leaves.

'It's lonely here,' he said.

'Suppose so. My dad loves it. It'll break his heart when he has to leave.'

'Have you spoken to Douglas about continuing lessons?'

'Oh yes. We often talk over things. My mam and dad never do. I told him about Mr Greene's offer to,' she coughed, 'subsidize my lessons.'

'What did he say?' Job Turner wanted to hurry her, but she sat motionless, hands on bag on knee.

'He said it was very kind of him. Just as it was good of you to spend so much of your time. You both must have a very high opinion of me.' She looked away, lifting a hand to her face. 'I don't know whether I dare tell you what he said next.' Susan laughed, gently, to herself, dispelling seriousness. 'He said it was strange that two people like you and Mr Greene in these days of unemployment at home and starvation abroad should want to spend your money, time and talents on teaching one girl to play the piano. He thinks, you see, that there are more important targets for charity than me.'

Her speech was deliberate, clear and adult, as if coming

from a middle-aged woman not a pretty girl. Job Turner felt a flushing of anger.

'What does he think I do all day? Except prepare people to qualify for jobs? And organize schemes and collections and concerts for African relief?'

'I know. I told him that. He's quite steamed up sometimes, but I think that's because he's chosen to be in a profession that serves the well-to-do. He feels guilty about it.'

'There's no need. Plenty of working-class people buy houses and get divorced and need solicitors these days. You do some legal-aid work, don't you?'

'Oh, yes. Both Mr Frogmore and Mr Sibley defended some miners in the strike just recently. And Mr Frogmore's a Conservative if ever there was one. He told Douglas that it might lose him custom elsewhere, with some of his usual clients. Especially as he was so successful.'

'Will it?'

'Douglas doesn't think so. He says Frogmore's as crafty as a barrow-load of monkeys. He knows exactly which side his bread's buttered. Douglas admires him; they get on ever so well together. And his wife. And yet he can't stand his politics.'

'Does Douglas fear he'll end up himself as a true-blue Tory?'

'Oh, no. Not Douglas. He's serious and worried, though. About unemployment.'

'Does he go to political meetings and so forth?'

'He's joined the Labour Party.'

'Does Mr Frogmore know?'

'I think so. Douglas would go out of his way to tell him. Being him.'

'Isn't his political work the equivalent of your studying music? Has he never thought of that?'

'He wouldn't spend so much time on it as I'd have to. Two or three hours every night and more at the weekend. We'll see.'

She closed the conversation cheerfully, thanked him for the lift and had the door open, long legs out in no time. She raised a hand and was gone. Job Turner watched her to the

139

iron gate which she swung open a foot or two, slipped through into the darkness, closing it without a sound. Leaves moved; he turned on engine and headlights, disturbing the air. In the swift half-mile back to the Lodge he felt encouraged.

He tried to imagine what Susan would be like in twenty-odd years when she approached forty. That was unfair, saddling her with thicker hips and cruder responsibilities, but necessary. Would she be radically different if she continued her piano studies for the next year or two? It was clear to him now, he was outside the car opening his own white gate and garage door, that she would not try for a scholarship to one of the music schools nor pursue her career in London. To marry Douglas was her premier objective. At least there would be a piano in the house. Her acceptance of the lack of instrument, at least for the present, had shaken him; she could listen, of course, but those powerful, delicate fingers would never be the same. Job Turner angrily clanged down the garage door, shut the gate, went indoors.

A letter from Phyllis thanked him for his hospitality. She apologized for her delay in writing, but they were up to the eyes in work. Tom had a bad cold; she had suffered three visits to the dentist, Martin slaved day and night but they had nothing to complain about. Alison had kept her in touch by letter, but it was great to see them all so that they mustn't leave it so long next time, though he knew what it was like. She described a spare Sunday they had spent at some sort of outdoor pop entertainment for charity in Hyde Park and thoroughly enjoyed themselves. The beautifully observed and noted couple of pages reminded him of Phyllis's compositions in the first form. He wondered, carrying the letter to the kitchen and kettle, what part he had played in his daughter's life. She never touched the piano now, though she had shown considerable skill, had passed her examinations without difficulty until she had announced in the sixth that she wanted no more music lessons. He had argued, but Gillian had come down, to his surprise and annoyance, on his daughter's side.

'I hope she'll come back to it some day,' his wife had tried to pacify him.

'Hope's no bloody use,' he snapped, out of character. 'She

140

could continue her music without any depredation of her other work.'

'Depredation.' Gillian mocked his word. She understood how his anger and embarrassment presented him with this façade of objective language.

Job Turner prepared himself a sandwich, sat down with plate on his knee.

'Bread and scrape,' he said out loud, looking at his meal. His mother would have disapproved.

It had been a poor day at school. A dull assembly had preluded a string of callers in his office, staff, deputies, a demented traveller in photocopying machines, two pupils for minor disciplinary offences, a parent, the police about a boy concerned in a local robbery. All had, in their own opinions, some serious point or excuse to make; none seemed to him of any importance. He had polished his trousers' behind while the real responsibilities of education had happened, had been delegated elsewhere. On such days he wished he had stayed in the classroom or at the primary school where he could at least have made some impression. When he was not listening to earnest voices, he filled in boring forms, or signed returns made out by somebody else.

'I'm a high-class clerk,' he told his senior deputy.

'Well paid, though.' Cheerful north-country sense. 'For a teacher.'

Throat dry, he took to helping himself to cups of water, he'd drudged away, tired himself out and achieved nothing. Meeting Susan Smith had broken the tension; Phyllis's letter had continued the process. An attempt to play the piano brought back his depression but, determined not to slump and sleep in front of the television set, he'd written to Phyllis a letter describing himself as a catalyst. The metaphor caught his fancy so that he finished his epistle cheerfully, pulled on his shoes and went out in the darkness to the postbox.

On his return he'd barely removed his raincoat when the telephone rang.

Mr Smith was investigating Greene's offer to pay for Susan's lessons.

'She told us tonight. I've been talking to her mother since

she went off to practise in the Hall. And her mother says, "Ring Mr Turner. He'll know what it's about." We've great respect for your judgement, y'know.'

More dependents.

'What's the problem?'

'It hardly seems right to me. Why should he want to spend his money on her? He's got a son and grandchildren of his own. I wonder if there isn't something else behind it all.'

'A catch, you mean? Of what sort?'

'I mean when she mentioned about carrying on with music after she's married, we said straight away she could have our piano. It's maybe nothing to write home about, but it's in tune. It suited her until I got the one in the Hall done up. But we're not well-to-do. We're lucky we've both got jobs these days, but the wedding will set us back a few quid.'

Job Turner explained why Susan should continue with instruction, and why Greene thought it worth his while to support her endeavours. Smith chipped in, rudely. His objections were two: he could not believe that Greene would splash his money about without advantage to himself, and he grudged his own inability to continue as a patron of his daughter's progress. Twenty minutes later he rang off, unpersuaded, arguing still, punctuating his certainties with a refrain, 'I don't know. I don't know.' By the time Smith had finished he had convinced Turner that he could well pay for his daughter's tuition himself, though he'd no intention of doing so.

Susan said little at her next lesson, but claimed that the visit to Greene had been a great success. She had played well, and Greene had lent her a book on Beethoven's piano sonatas. Moreover she had been invited to take Douglas to tea there on the following Saturday. The old chap had cackled, she said, smiling bleakly. 'You can play the piano, and he can talk to an old pro. About soliciting.' Turner wondered if she understood the double entendre, but capped it with a notice he'd seen in the front window of an American house: No solicitors. 'It meant no hawkers.' Susan smiled in the same wooden, unamused manner, humouring him, giving nothing away, her father's daughter.

142

'Did you play duets?' Job asked.

'No. Just the pieces. And then I got him to name scales for me. I don't stay too long. He soon tires.'

As she went out into the night, she said,

'My Dad seemed angry about Mr Greene. He's a funny man, sometimes.'

'Have you made your mind up what you're going to do?'

'Not yet. We're still talking about it.'

She refused his offer to accompany her along the dark paths.

'I shall be all right. I can run. And my Dad will probably walk his dog this road. He knows what time we finish.'

Smith immediately appeared: he had obviously been standing hidden, waiting.

The rest of the week had been more productive. A well-attended parents' evening, an excellent meeting of the Parent–Teacher Committee which made it possible to fund a lavish Shakespeare production at Christmas, and some breath-taking singing from his choir made Job Turner feel he was not wasting his time. Ferguson, the education officer, turned up one morning and stayed to sample the school dinner.

'How are things, then?'

'Quiet. That's what I wanted for a start. Children attending and being attended to.'

Ferguson poked his nose in, stalking the senior science block unaccompanied, spending an hour in a preparation room with the Head of Science, asking questions, guardedly promising new equipment. When he left the school he stood with Turner by his car.

'Better than I expected, Job. Really.'

'The threat of inspection has smartened one or two up. But I think they're quite pleased, the majority, to get back into the classroom to teach, with no half-days or days off.'

'They don't make you out yet. Fletcher, the Head of Science, said, "He's not like a musician. I expected some airy-fairy body. Turner listens to you, makes you write it down and keep a copy, then explains why he can or can't give you what you want. He's a civil servant. But good at it." '

'He's conscientious is Fletcher. He doesn't altogether see sense yet, but my predecessor had been grossly unfair to him.'

'Your predecessor. . .' Ferguson debarred himself from profanity. 'This will be a good school again before long. As it should be.'

'I hope you'll come now and again to keep us up to the mark. I tell you, Bruce, the thing that terrifies me is that I don't know a half of what's going on. This school's too big.'

'If that frightens you, what about me, then? God knows what some of them are up to. And I've neither means nor time to find out. It comforts me to think of you here instead of that madman, Miller.'

They shook hands in the car park in full view of the senior school.

No sooner had Ferguson driven out than Job Turner noticed two smallish boys strolling across the playground in leisurely conversation.

'Where are you going?' He had descended half a dozen steps towards them.

'We're taking a message for Mr Pearce, sir.' One of the art teachers.

'Oral or written?' They looked at him suspiciously. Fear grew. He stood too still.

'Mr Pearce wants some wood shavings from the craft room.'

'For what?'

'I don't know, sir.'

'Why two of you?'

'He wasn't sure where it was, sir.'

Both children were white-faced.

'Get a move on,' he barked. They ran.

He puzzled why Pearce needed wood shavings. To do a Holman Hunt? More likely it was for some private purpose. Unless he had wanted to rid his lesson of two troublemakers. They had looked harmless enough.

His senior deputy joined him, a sheaf of papers in his hand.

'May I. . . ? I saw you were with Mr Ferguson.'

'What does Pearce do with wood shavings?'

144

The man knitted his brow. He prided himself on being able to answer his senior's questions. This one baffled him.

'Come on in.' Turner used the same tone as to the errant errand boys. But he ushered his subordinate first through the double doors.

# 15

In October the two Acton School choirs and the senior orchestra won first places at the Musical Festival. Stanton, the head of music, walked on air. The junior choir conducted by Turner performed like angels to score 95, the highest mark awarded during the whole proceedings.

'Back on course,' Stanton pronounced.

Job Turner shook eager hands with teachers from the music school, with parents, with George Wrangel, the professor at the Academy, who was adjudicating instrumental classes. Miller, Job's predecessor, resplendent in a herringbone grey suit, advanced to congratulate Turner. The man used exactly chosen words, neither underplaying nor overdoing, to express his pleasure at the success of his old school. Last year, according to Stanton, he had refused point-blank to allow any musical group from Acton to enter the festival, on the grounds that the timetable was sufficiently disrupted by strikes and go-slows. Immediately he had felicitated Job, Miller made for Stanton, shook his hand, slapped his shoulder, braying compliments that could be heard yards away. The stupefied music teacher, escaping, ran to Turner and whispered that it was the first time Miller had ever been seen at this function. The head led his subordinate out for a ten-minute lunch of lager and pork pie, and confessed that he found the behaviour of half his colleagues incredible. Stanton, not quite protected by his euphoria, backed away.

His choir shone again at the concluding grand concert, and it was half past ten by the time that Job Turner, exhausted and famished, arrived home. He had taken his first gigantic bite from a cheese sandwich when the telephone interrupted him.

'I've been trying to get you all evening.' Alison.

'I've been at the festival.'

'Oh, yes.' Her voice was lifeless. 'I see. I'd forgotten about that.' She sucked air in. 'I'm afraid I've bad news for you.'

He waited, beaten down already. The pause stretched; pain creaked through his weary arms. Gillian died again.

'It's my father-in-law. Frederick.'

Again the hiatus, dictated perhaps by her concern.

'He died this evening with a heart attack.'

'At what time?' He'd asked the question before his mind or social sense had begun to work.

'Soon after six. Your pupil Susan Smith and her fiancé were there with him. They rang for an ambulance, and then told us. Geoffrey went straight over, but they'd taken him off. He was dead when he arrived at the hospital. Probably before.'

'I'm sorry. Was it unexpected? I mean, has he been ill this last week or two? I've been so busy. . .'

'No more than usual. He had angina. And arthritis. Bronchitis. But no. He had seemed a lot better to me. I think I told you so.'

'Yes.'

'The young people had waited for Geoffrey, and they went with him to the hospital. But it was all over.'

'I am sorry. Is Geoffrey back?'

'Yes. He took the young people home. The young man is staying the night at Susan's. It was sudden. They'd had their tea, and they were clearing things away when he just groaned and collapsed over his chair.'

'It's a good way to go.'

'Except for those who saw it. They were very shocked, as you can imagine. So is Geoffrey, for that matter. We had thought of going out, but we had cancelled the babysitter because Geoff had a bit of a cold. We looked forward to a quiet evening. And then this happens. Douglas, the fiancé, was very helpful, Geoffrey said. Seems a sensible boy.'

'Is there anything I can do?'

'No. I don't think so, thanks. I'll be in touch tomorrow, and I'll let you know the details.'

'Give my condolences to Geoffrey. I'm really sorry. I was becoming quite fond of the old man.' He concluded lamely.

'I'll ring off now. You'll be tired.'

147

He thought the efficient Alison might inquire about festival results, but she did not. She spoke from flat fatigue. Perhaps she hoarded her reserves to handle her husband. Job Turner stared at the circular bite in his sandwich. His hunger returned.

When Susan Smith arrived for her next lesson, she seemed composed, said she was well, and played as beautifully as ever. She suggested, and this without prompting from him, that she might take a week or two off from her examination pieces, and asked for replacements. He complied at once.

Only when she was about to leave did he mention Frederick Greene's death. She said it was sad, awful. Yes, she would go to the funeral. Then twisting suddenly she blurted out, 'Will you walk back with me? My dad can't come tonight and meet me.'

As they walked towards the Hall she began to talk.

'You know we were there, don't you? When he died?'

'Alison, my daughter, told me. She said how helpful you were.'

'It was awful and unbelievable. I mean, he was just the same as usual, and cheerful for him. And he'd got us a lovely tea, or Mrs Harper had. We, Douglas and I, said we'd clear away, and while we were doing it, we'd only just started, he gave a kind of gargle or groan and tipped over across his chair. We put him straight, and rang 999, and the ambulance came quickly. But Douglas said he must have been dead. We tried to give him a drop of whisky to revive him, but it was no good, he didn't move.'

'Yes.'

'I've never seen anybody dead before. It didn't seem right. He was alive and talking and laughing just a minute before. He didn't say anything about pain, or feeling ill, or anything.'

'He hadn't complained about being out of sorts earlier?'

'Not really. He always complained about something. But he didn't look any worse, or sound it. He just. . . I was in the kitchen. I heard this sound and Douglas called out to me, and I ran back in and we picked him up and put him upright in the chair.'

'He didn't say anything?'

148

'He didn't make a sound. Douglas rubbed his chest and tried him with a spoonful of whisky, but we didn't know what to do. He sent me to ring the ambulance. And then later to get hold of Geoffrey Greene. He said he'd come straight over. We waited for him after the ambulance had gone. That took less than five minutes before he arrived. We went with him up to the hospital. I don't know why. We couldn't do anything. But we went. He seemed pleased we'd offered. I rang my mother from the hospital so she wouldn't worry where we'd got to.'

Susan narrated with clarity, voice strong but quiet under the dark trees of the avenue. They had, Job Turner noticed, quickened their pace, and she held his arm. When she had completed the story, she asked busy questions about funeral services, cremations, how long they lasted, what mourners wore, what he thought about it.

'Why make such a fuss?' she asked. 'Wouldn't it be better just to pay something to get rid of the body?' Her father's opinion, he guessed.

'The undertakers take the body away now. When my grandfather died, they kept him in the front parlour with the coffin on black trestles. They dowsed the place with eucalyptus. I was only seven or eight at the time but they took me in to see him.'

'Weren't you frightened?'

'Yes, I was. The front door led straight from the pavement outside. And people crept in to pay their last respects. My grandparents hardly ever used the front door. But the neighbours banged the knocker, and stepped in and stood there and said their piece. On the day of the funeral friends brought flowers, wreaths with black-edged cards. And afterwards they had a big meal, high tea with ham, and the minister attended. And relatives. And they laughed a lot, out loud. And my grandma didn't seem to mind. I noticed that, small as I was.'

'Did you have horses?'

'No. Cars. Though I seem to recall horses at some time but I can't remember black plumes.'

'It must have cost money.'

'Yes. Working people saved in clubs for funerals, then.'

149

'That doesn't seem . . .' Susan searched for the word, 'necessary, does it?'

'I think psychologists believe that one should make an attempt at some sort of show. And to spend on the funeral or the gravestone.'

'Now, you mean. Or then?'

'Oh, nowadays.'

'To impress the neighbours? That hardly seems sensible.' Susan's sentences were awkward, put forward against superstition, placing logic against the cold shudder in the spine. Here spoke her father's girl.

'They say that holding some sort of ceremony and erecting a memorial seems to draw a black, concluding line under the dead person's life. Then the bereaved can accept that he's gone and come to terms with it.'

'Is that true?' she asked.

'It sounds reasonable. We held a religious service for my wife at the crematorium, though neither of us held strong Christian views or went to church.'

'Are you an atheist?'

'No. I don't think so. Gillian was, perhaps, more so than I was. Am.'

'And did it help you to come to terms?' The voice harried him naively.

'One can never come to terms with anything as tragic, or stupid, as that. Hardly a day passes but it pains, harries, worries me again. But I can bear it, just about.'

Susan squeezed his arm so strongly that they stopped. She kissed him full on the mouth.

'Thank you,' he said.

'I'm sorry.' They had spoken together. He recovered first. 'You're a good girl.'

They set off again, stepping smartly. After a hundred yards she spoke out, plucking up courage, stopping him again.

'If the corporation develop this estate there'll be lights all the way along here.'

'And you won't like that?'

'It will be sensible, with all these horrible things you read about in the paper. But I love it wild and dark and weird.'

150

'These trees were planted by humans, you know. By whoever laid out the estate.'

'There wasn't any chance of electricity then. I like the dark.'

'You've never been frightened of it?'

'No. Sometimes when I practise in the Hall, I don't switch on the drawing-room lights. I can't see to read the music. And it is creepy, scary, but I enjoy it.'

After another minute's sharp progress in silence, he began to thank her for looking after Mr Greene in his last moments. Her replies were off-hand.

'We couldn't do anything. We didn't know how to. Kiss-of-life . . . or . . . Douglas says that in hospital they thump them quite hard, even old men.'

'Well, yes. But Fred had been enjoying himself. He didn't know what was coming. He looked forward to hearing some music and talking to your young man. And without too much pain, it all was over and done with. That's better than a long-drawn-out illness.'

'Do you ever think of dying, Mr Turner?'

'Not really.' He remembered Frederick Greene's identical question. 'When Gillian was killed, I wished I'd have gone with her. But one emerges. Even from all that grief. I thought I wouldn't, at one time. I wanted to die. But my daughters were very good, and my friends. Now, I never think much about death. Or rarely. Or rarely of mine. At my age friends and relatives die. I've come to expect it. If I had my choice of exit, it would be like Fred Greene's. A quick heart attack.'

'I've thought about death. Quite often.'

'Have you?'

'I told my dad once. I felt absolutely awful. He just said, "Don't be so bloody morbid." That's typical of him, though. He's always in the right. He always knows what you should say or think or what you shouldn't.'

'Don't you get on with him very well?'

'Not too bad. He loses his temper and shouts. And he talks to my mam as if she's a slave. But she won't answer him back. "It's wasting my breath," she says. But I think he feels

151

very depressed, sometimes. He knows he could have done more with his life than he has.'

'Is that right?'

'Yes. He was bursting to leave school and get a job and earn money. "I knew damn-all then, and there was nobody to tell me otherwise." ' She imitated cleverly. They had stopped again.

'I said to him, "You wouldn't have listened." He wouldn't. "That's right, my gel, I don't suppose I would, but I just wish now that there had been somebody knocking about to give me another point of view, some schoolteacher or parent or somebody." '

'His father didn't help?'

' "My dad was a clown, a bloody clown," he says. He's still alive you know, but Dad won't go to see him. He lives in a hospital ward in Newark. He's blind, and out of his mind. He sits there and twiddles his thumbs like a baby. We. . .'

'Do you visit him?'

'Never.' She thrust her arm, linked with his, deeper. 'It's no use. He wouldn't know me. We've never had much to do with him even when he was all right. And he's been like this for years now. My dad wouldn't take him in. We hadn't the room, he said. I think he meant inclination.' They walked.

'Does your father hit it off with Douglas?'

'Well.' She laughed; Job saw the quick whiteness of teeth. 'He's cagey. Waiting to catch him out. He asks Douglas all sorts of questions about the law, oh, trespass, and burglary. Doug is very good, and makes a lot of points my dad hasn't thought of. That narks him. But he enjoys it; I bet he boasts about his knowledge down at the Deerstalker.'

'Does he go there often?'

'No. On Sundays when they make a thing of it. Dress up. Otherwise he might drop in on somebody's birthday. He walks about a lot in the grounds. "I'm as good as lord of the manor," he says. My mam has to get him books out of the library on wildlife. It's made a great difference to him.'

They stood now on the asphalt triangle of roads before the main gates.

'Thank you for bringing me home,' Susan said, unhooking her arm.

'A pleasure.'

Susan lurched forward towards him, kissing him on the mouth, clumsily. Jerking back, she paused, then repeated the kiss. He held her to him and she made no attempt to withdraw. Job Turner bent his head to lay his mouth on hers, but briefly if with warmth. She fastened on to him, greedily, pulling him into her, but though her lips opened, she clutched and kissed awkwardly, bungling, without the experience to express sexuality. When she withdrew she breathed rapidly. He caught the whiff of face powder or cheap scent.

'Thank you, Susan,' he said solemnly, priest at prayer.

'I wish you were my dad,' she said. Sexually aroused, he felt the pang of disappointment.

'Yes. My daughters probably wanted someone different.' Cooler now, he could keep from making a fool of himself, but he despised his caution. He should have caught the child up in his arms, displayed his passion. She would have been terrified. He doubted that. That searching inexpert mouth had been explicit enough.

She was gasping still, unviolently robbed of air.

'Sometimes you seem like a young man,' she said.

'But I'm not. Fifty-seven.'

They stood a yard apart, in shadow, under the high wall, off the road.

'Sometimes when you'd given me a lesson I wanted to kiss you.' She spoke very thinly, hiding the words from resonance.

'That's nice.'

'No, I don't mean like that. I wanted to kiss you as I did just now. A dirty kiss.'

'Dirty? Yes, I see what you mean.'

'Is it wrong?' There was nothing childish about the voice.

'No. But you have to consider Douglas. He'd be angry, wouldn't he? You're going to marry him.'

'Oh, I know that. Douglas is all right. We shall make a good married couple. I like him. He's sexy, and handsome. We haven't gone all the way. Not yet.'

153

They heard footsteps crossing the yard inside the Hall gates; both listened. Susan put a hand in apprehension on his chest.

'Who's that?' he asked.

'It'll be my dad. Perhaps he came home earlier.'

The gate, pulled widely, creaked. Smith emerged, and Susan called out.

'I wondered where you'd got to.'

'We were talking.' The girl's voice did not waver.

'Oh, hello, Mr Turner. Thanks for bringing her back. Woods can be dangerous places these days.'

'We didn't meet a soul.'

'No. I don't often at this time of night. But it only needs one. I always carry a stick up here after dark-hour.'

'I thought you were going to be late tonight.' Susan, accusatory.

'Fellow didn't turn up. No message, no excuse, no nothing. Just not there. Wi' some of these people you wouldn't know the telephone had been invented. Still, he's the loser, and I've been able to put my feet up. Your mam started to wittle, though, once it got past nine o'clock. "Where's our Sue?" You know what she's like. So I put my boots on, and came out. You'd better be getting in. I'll walk back with you, Mr Turner. Return the compliment, eh?'

Susan thanked her teacher, slipped past the two men who watched her cross the long courtyard. A door gleamed open, was closed.

'The wind's getting up,' Smith said, setting off. 'I'm glad you could come back with her. She's been a bit nervy since old man Greene died. It was a good job Douglas was there.'

'She's sensible. She's often left in charge of the office from what she tells me.'

'Yeh. She wouldn't have panicked. But it must have been a shock for her. She's only eighteen, when all's said and done. I know some of these young bitches are as hard-boiled as o'd whores these days. But she isn't. She's sensitive. Doesn't say a lot. But she feels it.'

'What's her young man like?'

'Oh, suits her.' Smith smashed at brambles with his stick.

'But not you?'

154

'I didn't say that. Tall youth he is. Wi' glasses. Quite a good cricketer. He's very polite and studious. Doesn't half know the law.'

'But he's not exactly your choice?'

'Oh, I'm not saying that. He'll do. He's got a good job. He's well in with the principal and he'll work. No, they'll be well suited.'

'I can't help thinking you're not exactly satisfied.'

'That's in your mind then, Mr Turner, not mine. Nobody on earth is good enough for a man's daughter. You've got three. You ought to know that.'

They said no more, treading the road under the trees, Smith still hacking at the long grass in the border. When the man spoke again his tone was different, sullen.

'I suppose Mr Greene's death's put an end to this idea of paying for her music?'

'Unless his will. . .'

They stamped on in silence until they reached the lodge.

'Is she getting on all right? With the music?'

'Marvellously. She's very gifted.'

'Ye'. She works at it, I'll give her that. Better than wastin' her time on this everlasting pop stuff.'

A few more words were exchanged, of thanks, of parting, and Job Turner let himself in, glad to be alone. He shivered; night air hung thin.

Meticulously straightening the sleeves, he hung up his coat, and sat down in his armchair without switching on the light. Shivers pleated his back.

He felt again that warm, awkward mouth on his. 'Dirty' she had called it. He was amazed, even impressed, by her innocence, her inexperience. Some of the thirteen-year-olds in his school flaunted a more obvious sexuality. A sudden pain and he discovered he was biting at a finger. Out there, at the gate, he had felt carnal desire for the girl, and she for him.

About six months after Gillian's death he remembered Alison's teasing him in her driest lawyer's voice. It was, he guessed, her acknowledgement that he was beginning to recover.

'Do you ever think of marrying again?' she had asked.

'No.' He had felt a surge of bitterness at her question, his wound re-bled, but she did not notice.

'I was afraid you would be announcing your engagement to one of those pretty little dollies on your staff.'

'Do me a favour.' He covered his gall.

'I'm glad you haven't. It wouldn't have worked out.'

'Why not, pray?'

'Quite apart from the difference of age, your whole cast of mind is different.'

'Go on.' He spoke his imperative to staunch her flow; he failed.

'Oh, you're Authorized Version and Wordsworth and no consecutive perfect fifths. You think the Beatles are up to date. And you've convinced yourself that those pert bottoms of yours have never consulted a decent dictionary or a proper book of reference in their lives. They can't spell. They don't know what a full stop is for. They don't study Latin. They've never heard of a passacaglia or an oxymoron or a tort. . . .' She laughed at herself.

'Steady on, now. Why should I be in such a hurry to marry such dunderheads, then?'

'Sex. They flap their false eyelashes at you and you're floundering. It's happened before.'

'Not to me.'

'Watch it. Don't boast too soon.'

He had wondered at the time whether her flippancy had masked a real warning. He had been eyeing a pretty probationary teacher with more than fatherly interest. She had a BA degree in languages, and fluffy fair hair, and an eloquent bosom. Her eyelashes dipped before him. But no; he had not been serious. An old man can dream his dreams, but he was shrewd enough, he told himself, to recognize the boundaries of reality.

And now he had kissed an eighteen-year-old in the trees like a schoolboy, and he was afire. He rose from his chair, and paced round the unlit room touching furniture, talismans of his virtue or sagacity. From the mantelshelf he picked up the photograph of Gillian and himself taken for their twenty-

156

fifth wedding anniversary. His fingers played on the frame, on the coolness of the glass, on the sharpness of the corners. In the dark it had weight, solidity, strength, but lacked the important quality: it could not be seen.

Job Turner returned the photograph to its place, and stepped across to turn on the light. He retraced the short steps to the photograph. Gillian smiled at the world, easy as always, confident; he stared ahead, neat, a swarthy man with a white collar and subfusc suit, but wary, lacking trust.

He ran his hand down his face. Susan must have found it rough.

# 16

In his will Frederick Greene had made provision for Susan Smith's musical tuition for the next two years. He had added a codicil a few weeks earlier: she was to be taught for her diploma 'under the direction of Noelle Winifred Waters, ARAM etc. and Job T. Turner, B. Mus., ARCM etc.' Geoffrey passed this information on to Turner, together with news of a surprising bequest. His grand piano had been left to Job, and his upright to Susan. Otherwise most of his property and monies, both considerable, went to Geoffrey and family.

'I'm glad he remembered you,' Geoffrey said.

'It's a big piano. I don't know whether I can fit it into my poky place.'

'You can always sell it.'

'I wouldn't do that.'

'You can't keep a piano out in the garden,' Geoffrey chortled. Carroll's word, much employed in the comics of Job's youth, exactly matched the sound.

'Perhaps your father was trying to say something to me.'

'Ah, but what?'

'Get into a bigger bolt hole.'

'Had he advised you to do that? At any time?'

'Not to the best of my remembrance. Have you told Susan yet?'

'No. The bequest starts from the day the result of her next examination appears. I don't know when that is.'

'Just before Christmas. Just after.'

'I see. I don't think there's any objection to your breaking the news to her.'

Turner, pleased and worried about his own bequest, informed Susan of hers at the end of their next lesson. He had looked forward to but had dreaded this meeting. Important tasks at his school had been streaked by his guilt and uncertainty; he did his work no worse, but he could not apply his whole mind. He seemed to be alive elsewhere.

Susan arrived, prompt and undemonstrative as ever, the end of her nose slightly red from the autumn chill. She removed her coat, hanging it on the usual peg, commented favourably on the warmth of his house, and sat down immediately at the piano.

He named a scale. She rattled through it without an error. Another. Equally perfect. Arpeggios, running thirds. She waited on his commands, obeyed, smiled shortly at his word of praise. He listened to her pieces, discussed them; Susan, as always, grasped at once his suggested improvements, tried them in practice, laughed once when she failed to come up to scratch first time, set it right, and then objected in words. She seemed contained, dedicated, wasting no time, making the most of his expertise. Sight-reading, ear-tests followed, filled the hour, expanded it by five minutes, every second occupied. Job sat back, tired, satisfied, as if he had been programming a marvellous robot. The music had brimmed, over-flooding humanity. They knew they had worked.

'Relax,' he said.

She blew out breath, clasped fingers above knees, smiled, shaking her head.

'Would you like a cup of coffee?'

'If you please.'

When he returned with the tray she still sat on the piano stool. He invited her into an armchair, poured and passed, then in a quiet voice outlined Greene's bequest. The girl blushed, then more deeply, embarrassed at embarrassment.

'I don't know what to say.' It took her long enough to come out with that.

'He must have thought very highly of you.'

'He was generous.'

Turner wondered if that were so. He had not asked, nor been told, whether Mrs Harper had been rewarded for her services. Perhaps both were tired, but the news had silenced them, forced a constraint between them. Job made no attempt to break in. The pair sat motionless in the bright little room, electric light glinting on the glass of his prints.

'I shall have to think about it.' She was first. 'And talk it over with Douglas. And with you, or Noelle.' Her face broke into a small, sly smile. 'Would it be possible to accept one part of the bequest and not another? To take the piano and not the lessons?'

'I don't know. I've not seen the exact wording.'

'The lessons have to be from you and Noelle?'

'It said, according to Geoffrey, "under the direction of". I suppose we could recommend someone else if we thought fit. I'm not sure.'

'Could I have a break, say, for six months, after I've finished this exam? And then take my two years' worth?'

'You'll have to discuss that with Geoffrey. I imagine he, or somebody in his office, will administer the trust, if that's what it is. Knowing him, I expect he'll interpret his instructions generously.'

'He won't mind the money going to me?'

'Mr Greene was a rich man. Well, comparatively. Contrasted with you and me. Geoffrey and his family inherit the bulk of the estate.'

'I'm glad. That's good.'

Susan glanced up at the clock, drained her coffee, hitherto untouched, and jumped up.

'Look at the time. My dad'll be waiting outside.'

'Won't he ring the bell?'

'No. He won't interrupt. He'd sooner stand and swear.'

She snatched her coat from the rack, bundled herself into it agilely, fastening the toggles.

'I feel excited,' she said. 'I've never had anything from a will before.'

Susan kissed him strongly, but flat on the cheek, not mouth. At the same time she hugged him, surprising him with her vigour, sheer brute power. Then she had the front door open, she existed in a world of swift physicality quite different from his, and was calling out,

'Hello. Are you there?'

Her father's voice answered from the shadows up the road. Man and dog appeared darkly. Job Turner shouted a greeting, which was rumblingly acknowledged. He heard

160

Sue's cheerful, 'I've got something to tell you' and listened for their footsteps to die away. It took long enough; they disappeared, then sounded again, in a ghostly echo amongst the susurration around. Finally he caught only the noise of twigs and last leaves.

'A good turn out.'

Job Turner heard the phrase three times at Frederick Greene's cremation service. People expressed surprise or begrudged the old man this last tribute of attendance. Turner hardly knew a soul there; here was a large congregation of professional people drawn from the town where he had lived for the past thirty years, and yet apart from Alison and Geoffrey, Job could put a name to barely half a dozen. His own solicitor was absent or unseen. Susan Smith, face white and wooden, sat two rows in front of him. On the way out he noticed Mrs Harper dressed to the nines accompanied by a man in a baggy navy-blue suit, presumably her cuckold-husband. The two whispered together, their lugubrious expressions unburdened and unsuitable.

The clergyman, who admired Fred Greene, spoke of the old man's full and 'substantially successful' life, as a lawyer, a business tycoon, a reader of the classics; Greene apparently studied and enjoyed, so Job Turner learnt, Virgil, Dante and Jane Austen, had relished the countryside, the 'brightness of gardens', the 'turn of the seasons'. His love of the piano won its mention. 'After a day spent on the intricacies of the law, or investment, he liked nothing better than to relax with the "Pathétique" Sonata or "Les Adieux".' He faced the infirmities of age with a 'wry stoicism' as he had borne the vagaries of his life. A gap in nature, in society, had been opened.

Turner bussed Alison, shook hands with Geoffrey, drove Susan Smith to her office on his way back to work. He had been invited to the buffet lunch at the house of the younger Greenes, but had declined to attend pleading that he had to visit his old school that afternoon to present prizes and wanted an hour at his desk. In the car, in the sunny October late morning, warm as August, he and Susan sat uncomfortably;

161

three times he introduced light, quizzical sentences, and though she answered politely it was clear she preferred to sit unspeaking with her hands clasped together between her legs. She wore gloves at her mother's instigation, he guessed. The solemnity not so much of the occasion but of what it represented had silenced her; he felt much the same. Something important had happened in that newish, smart brick chapel on the city boundary, had been recognized or symbolized. The expression 'the bosom of his Father and his God' latched in his mind. He could not place it; it did not seem appropriate to Greene; he remembered having to set it to music in a college examination. His solution had long been forgotten, but not the words. He must look it up. The faint scent he had noticed the other night hung in the car after Susan had left him; his memory of that was perfect.

Whatever had happened at the Broxtowe Crematorium, it had no more effect on the Acton Comprehensive School at the other side of the city than the headmaster's absence. The sunny yards were stylishly empty; a large double class did PE out on the playing field; the classrooms buzzed; from one of the music rooms he heard the opening of Elgar's 'Enigma Variations'. Not unsuitably, he thought; not 'Nimrod', that would have been overdoing it. The organist had not played it, either, nor had the parson mentioned Greene's interest in the composer. One cannot have or know everything. His secretary with a sheaf of papers for signature or attention frustrated his intention of consulting the Oxford Dictionary of Quotations in the senior library. Mrs Bexon smiled her admiration of his dark suit, white shirt, black shoes. He looked like the headmaster of a public school on television. He did his best for an hour, then left at noon to join his old school at their juvenile lunch.

He sat with John Duncan, the acting head, and Bruce Ferguson, the education officer, all doing their best to look festive. The children carried and attacked plates of chips and gravy; small voices shrilled; teachers supervised in sober, often beautiful dresses; collages and displays of silk, vases of chrysanthemums, lively staggering pictures, daubs of passionate paint adorned the hall. The building was newish, almost contemporaneous with the Acton Comprehensive, but it shone, was lively, togged up, colourful, a disciplined riot compared with his present bare walls and few silver-framed watercolours. Some of the classes filed into the hall, 'War March of the Priests', where parents already occupied the back quarter on small chairs. A young Pakistani mother, beautiful in trousers, ushered in two preschool children with shining hair. Occasional saris livened the sobersided rows, poppy-scarlet. All clapped as Turner, Ferguson and Duncan made their appearance. A hundred eyes turned.

The acting headmaster welcomed his visitors, outlined the school's progress. The choir sang a Mendelssohn duet, a Britten folk-song arrangement, a version of a pop song, and Turner, suitably complimentary, handed over the cup the school had won at the Music Festival. This was collected by a boy and a girl, both of whom he recognized but could not name. He presented books, shaking hands with children who had, to judge from their performances, never shaken hands before in their lives. Duncan then introduced him, saying he needed no introduction. Turner spent five minutes praising everybody in sight, extolling education, encouraging them all to read, move and sing more, then sat down. The teachers expecting a longer homily led the clapping; three cheers were given for Mr Turner; the National Anthem was sung with two verses. Ferguson, Duncan and Turner sipped instant coffee in the acting headmaster's room.

Outside in the street the education officer consulted his watch and complimented Turner on his brevity.

'One thing I like about you, Job, is you don't hang around.'

'I thought Peter Duncan spoke well.'

'Yes, he did. But he won't get the job, you know.'

'When is it coming up?'

'Next week. A much sought after plum.' Ferguson grimaced at his own expression. 'At least four existing heads have applied for it.'

'Who'll they appoint?'

'Christ knows. Doesn't much matter. But it won't be Duncan.'

'Ever?'

Ferguson groaned comically, though whether at Duncan's failure to reach the standard or at the inequities of the world Turner could not guess. They shook hands, two similar men, middle sized, broad, dark hair beginning to whiten, red faced. Put them in overalls, Turner thought, they would have looked exactly at home behind a window cleaner's handcart. His last man, nobody would come out as far as the Lodge, did his rounds in a Ford Cortina. Turner waved as he drove off; Ferguson seemed to be consulting a notebook or diary over his steering wheel.

Job returned to perch at his desk for an hour before his own school was dismissed. He signed a few more letters, read an unenlightening report on truancy, talked on the phone to the university education department about next term's student-teaching practice. He watched the classrooms clear, the Lowry children stream off over the yards, the staff take to their cars. No one knocked at his door; the secretaries wished him goodnight; he heard the shout and clank of care-taking. Out on the playing fields a rugby squad was coached. He sat at five o'clock in a deserted place, with an empty desk, trying and failing to read a pamphlet on youth employment. In this room he had no access to music, deliberately. A thin shelf of books did not tempt him.

He had looked forward to the visit to his former school where people had seemed genuinely glad to see him, but could not disguise that he was no longer a significant part of their working life. They had trotted away willingly to their own concerns. Deflated, he turned his mind to the crematorium. Fred Greene's body would be cold ashes now. At five to six he heaved himself out of his chair to find the main doors locked for the night, his car single in the park. Standing, he considered his evening meal; it was too late to shop. Bread and scrape again. Unhungry, he patted his belly.

At half past seven Job Turner had not shifted from his armchair. The tea things littered the table; crumbs were scattered unbrushed from his pullover. Forcing himself up, he found himself cold and turned on the central heating before washing the dishes. He lacked energy, but snapped out loud, encouraging himself against inaction, 'Come on, lad.' Having

164

straightened the kitchen, he paused before his records, but could not be bothered to make a choice. He shuffled over to his piano, did not even pull out the stool. Walter Rummel's arrangement of Bach's 'Mortify us by thy goodness', open on the stand, offered no temptation to play. 'Come on, man. Get organized.' Once more he looked towards his chair. There was no one to whom he could decently make a telephone call. He had already from school congratulated Duncan. Alison was out, he knew. The thought of his deputy's future disappointment stirred no emotion, good or ill. Job yielded to the chair, lethargy and silence. Two clocks struck eight.

He heard a click at the gate latch, footsteps bypassing the front door, then nothing. He waited. All still. Certain he had made no mistake, he stood up, listened again. Footsteps, a hiatus before the peal of the bell tore into his silence. He had expected nobody. Cautiously unbolting, he opened the door on its chain.

'Are you busy?' Susan Smith's voice, subdued.

'No.' He let her in. She did not remove her anorak, but walked ahead of him into the main room. 'Are you cold?'

'No. I've cycled down. I've put my bike round the back and locked it.'

'Coffee?'

'If you're having. . .' Her voice tailed off once the point was made.

'Sit down, then. Shan't be a tick.' The electric kettle responded immediately. He reached for mugs, neatly extracted a milk bottle from the fridge. Susan had followed him, hovered. He spooned instant coffee. 'Are you all right?'

She was examining a calendar, October, Trinity College Bridge, Cambridge with hanging willows, a punt. His question went unanswered.

'Biscuit?' he asked.

'No, thanks.' Job ushered her out of the kitchen with his tray.

Susan sat down opposite him, but concentrated on the steam from the mug at her elbow.

'Well?' Cheerfully. 'No practice tonight?'

She jerked at the skirts of her anorak, militarily.

165

'I was on my own. They've gone over to my aunt's in Leicester for two days.'

'And Douglas?'

'He's got a function, a committee.' Her eyes opened wide at him; in this light they seemed dark not blue. 'I couldn't practise properly. I had to do something. I couldn't sit still. I took my bike and rode down here.'

'And if I'd been out?'

'I'd have pedalled back.' She shuddered, crossing her legs with violence. 'It was this morning.'

'The funeral.' Job spoke the uncomfortable words to soothe.

'Yes. It seemed . . . weird.' She spoke so low he had to listen hard. She lifted her head.

'You hadn't been to a funeral before?'

'No.' She smiled at him, winsomely, he thought, wholesome. 'But I knew what to expect. The words. The Lord's Prayer. "The Lord's My Shepherd." And what the vicar said. About Mr Greene.' Susan clutched her hands between her knees, as in the car, and her voice withered into tears. She cried without embarrassment, face uncovered, wet mouth distorted.

For a moment he allowed her to weep before moving across to sit on the arm of her chair. He cradled her to him and she bored into his pullover.

She sat up in the end, mopping at her face.

'That's better,' she said. She felt him. 'Your pullover's quite damp.'

'It'll come to no harm. Drink your coffee.'

She obeyed, and he backed away to his own chair and cup. Susan returned his smile. She straightened her spine.

'It seemed awful,' she began.

'You don't have to talk about it, unless you want to.'

'I know that. But he was so dead. It was final. We shouldn't see him any more. Not even a skeleton. Just something like cigarette ash. Do they burn the coffin as well?'

'Yes, I think so.'

'How can you separate the different sorts of ash?'

'I don't suppose you can.'

Susan had put down her cup, was crying again, not noisily. He made no attempt to interfere. Again she wiped her face, stood, picked up a large cushion, dropped it at his feet and crouching on it clasped his legs. Now she sobbed vehemently as he fondled her hair. On her second recovery she pulled off her anorak, laid her head back on his lap.

'He was an old man,' Job comforted. 'He had done pretty well.'

'But he could still play duets and enjoy music.'

'Yes.'

'Don't stop stroking me. Please, please.'

They occupied a silence, a vacuum together until she suddenly jerked upwards, plumped on to the arm of his chair and pulled his head into her breasts. She hugged, uncomfortably for him, with strength, but he made no attempt to struggle out. They rocked together. She straightened herself, picked up his hand, placed it on her left breast.

'Touch me, touch me.'

Hesitatingly he caressed her. Her nipple hardened. She breathed noisily, sob interspersed in quicker gasps.

'That's beautiful.' She emerged, laid a head on his shoulder.

'Finish your coffee.'

'I'd sooner stay here.' A *sotto voce* giggle reassured him. He kept exactly still. 'You're nice to me.'

Susan weighed heavily into his lap; relaxed, almost abandoned, she kissed his cheek in short, dry pecks, then nuzzled him, moaning in what appeared as coherent sentences in an unknown tongue. His fingers stroked the silk of her hair or cherished the full curve of her breasts. He lost himself in this long discomfort of affection.

'I'll finish my coffee before it's cold,' she said.

She leapt up and away. Job Turner massaged his legs, muttered an excuse, went out to the lavatory. When he returned she was still standing on the short hearthrug between the chairs.

'Hello,' she said. 'I've seen you somewhere before.'

She had never spoken to him like that before, with an insouciant impudence, either innocent or ignorant.

'Coffee soon runs through me.' He did not know why he came out with this; perhaps he was making an appeal.

'You should try something else.'

'I'm a lost soul, Susan.'

'I'm sure you're not.' She spoke with urchin confidence, grinning, shaking her hair loose. He picked up and examined his empty cup. Now she stood, calves back to her chair, facing him at two steps distance. Quickly she pulled her sweat shirt over her head, felt to her back, thumbed off her brassière, dropped this on the other garment at her feet without removing her eyes from his. A fixed smile disfigured her face.

'That's better,' she said.

Susan knelt on the cushion by his chair, her arms reaching out to him. He touched the smooth muscularity of her shoulders.

'Are my hands cold?'

'A bit. It doesn't matter. That's nice.'

He eased her upwards to kiss her mouth, her breasts, to suck at her nipples. Suddenly in the muddled ecstasy, her fingers yanked at his hair with such wrenching, searing violence that he shouted out in pain. She tippled up, and back, and sat down on the carpet arms wide behind her, her legs spread-eagled in their tight jeans.

'I'm sorry,' she laughed, afraid. 'Did I hurt you?'

'It's getting thin enough without your help.' Job brushed it down with his fingertips.

Neither moved. The bare-breasted girl on the floor lounged quite at her ease, resting, confident of her beauty. She wriggled her feet clear of her shoes, comically, examined the effect. He gathered breath, then his wits.

'Put your clothes on,' he ordered.

'Don't you like me?'

'You know I do. Put them on.'

'Douglas asks me to do this. He's a devil. "Let's strip off," he says. We do. There's nothing wrong with it. You see hundreds of women showing their boobs on the beach. We don't go much further, though. We don't have sex. He would if I'd let him.'

'What would he think about your lying here like this?'

She considered, still amused.

'He'd be jealous. But he can't have everything his own way.'

'But what if he went round with other girls?'

'I expect he has.'

More silence, ticking of clocks, creaks in the radiators, the skirting boards.

'You like me like this?'

'Yes.'

That satisfied her, and she stood up, without hurry, flexing her arms in a leisurely PT. She snapped open waist band, then zip and, struggling with the tightness, dragged down jeans and minuscule knickers on to her thighs. Delicately she placed her hands to her waist, arms akimbo, with coquetry, her head on one side like a pretty child. Job Turner did not move. She turned about in a slow circle, as if she had thoroughly rehearsed the movement, returning to hold her first position, less than two yards from him. He knew inexpressible tenderness at the roundness of breasts, dark nipples, the deep navel, shining belly and shoulders, lifted proud face, the pubic tuft, bared tops of thighs above the clutter of clothes. He breathed unsteadily.

'Oh, well,' she said. Knickers quickly replaced, she tugged at her jeans. 'Too much bum.' She flicked up bra and shirt, covered herself with energetic speed. 'There you are. You can look now.' She smiled; he had not withdrawn his eyes. She sat. 'What time is it?'

'Ten to ten.' He pointed at the wall-clock.

'I thought it was later. It seems hours. I'd better be getting back or I shan't be up in the morning.'

'What time are you due at the office?'

'Ten to nine. If I go in earlier I can have a longer lunch break, do my shopping.'

'At what time does Douglas arrive?'

'Same as the others. Just before nine. That's what Mr Frogmore likes about him. He's always punctual. Never a minute late.'

She picked up and donned her anorak, replacing the cushion from the floor to her chair. 'I felt awful when I came

169

here. Really down. I didn't know what to do with myself. It was that funeral. Perhaps I shouldn't have gone, especially as I knew there'd be nobody at home tonight. But he'd been so generous, and I knew you'd be there.' She chattered easily. Turner sat dumb, hawking up his few words. She described the difficulty her mother had in persuading her father to take this short break. 'Every day's a holiday for me up here,' he'd said. Susan's fluency struck him as friendly, back to normality, respectfully excited, sensible.

'I'll walk you home,' he said.

'Yes, please.'

They met no one in the woods. At the iron gates of the hall she unfastened chain and huge padlock.

'Dad says I've to keep this on while he's away. One further obstacle.'

'You're not afraid all alone in this place?'

'No. I quite like it. I'm very careful about locking everything up.'

She slipped inside, replaced padlock and chain, wished him goodnight. Job watched her pushing her cycle across the wide yard; once she turned her head, flicked up a hand, but the movements were quickly over, without meaning. She made her own way.

# 17

Job Turner, energized and baffled, thought frequently of
Susan. He was not, he told himself, obsessed with her, and
this seemed the truth for he forgot her for hours on end when
he was busy at work. He attended many speech days, now in
season, bored and uncertain. Schools spent good money on
public relations, and succeeded in achieving little. 'Headmaster blames society'; 'headmistress slams drug dealers';
'principal appeals for more parent power, or reading matter,
or computers or ethical instruction': the local paper gave them
their small headlines on page six, and hands were shaken and
satisfaction expressed. Music teachers organized second-half
concerts for glassy-eyed councillors, local government
officials and stupefied parents and all claimed to be gratified.
The date of Job's own performance fixed by his predecessor
approached. 'Head calls for normality.' When he expressed
his reservations about these annual jamborees to his deputies
or the senior music master, they shook their wiseacre heads.
'We have to sell ourselves', they said, or 'We can't let X, the
con-man, get away with it', or 'If we don't put on a public
show, people will think we've got something to hide.' 'And
haven't we?' he'd ask them, as they backed away. 'I'd sooner
spend the money on books.' The music master wiped sweat
from his corrugated brow. 'That's what you'll find the office
saying next time you want to purchase musical instruments.
"Stick to basics. Ignore the trimmings. It won't do." ' Job
Turner laughed, admiring the man. 'Funny bugger, Turner,'
opinion ran in the common rooms. 'Sly. No vision. Too clever
by half. Doesn't know his arse from his elbow.' Much the
same would have been said had he taken the opposite line. It
was the head's burden, and he could not feel overconcerned.
He occupied time fully, but he could not claim with profit.

A lesson with Susan passed without incident. She now knew

the date and time of her examination, and looked only to her prowess. Yes, her parents were back, both complaining; Douglas had begun to discuss with Mr Frogmore his status and the scope of his responsibilities in the firm next year. She was to be given a rise from the first of December. The girl seemed attentive, laconic, undemonstrative, concentrating hard on her own concerns, back exactly as before. She made no demands on him except as a musician. The naked woman had vanished, as if he'd only imagined her. As far as he could tell she wore no perfume. Job shuddered.

Alison inquired about Frederick Greene's pianos.

'We can get them out of the way, at least, while the rest of the will's cleared up. Are you having yours here or not?'

'Yes, I am.'

'What are you doing with this?' She tapped the lid of his upright.

'Keeping it.'

'You'll never get everything in.'

'I think so. I've done some measuring up.'

She laughed, began to sing in a masculine voice, chin tucked down: 'Cinque, dieci, venti, trenta'. It surprised him, (Gillian had done it often enough with some antic of hers), that Alison knew the opening of *Le Nozze* in Italian, and could suggest Figaro so musically. He felt ineffably pleased.

'I shall have to try the thing out over weeks, months. I may not like it.'

'I see.'

Alison looked at him as at one adding difficulties to an already fraught situation. 'If it can be done simply, do it,' was her motto. He had a perfectly good upright in the Lodge, and a decent small grand in Oak Villa, so why he needed a third she could not fathom. True, he would probably not be able to sell it at anything like a good price, but money was not all that important to him. Get rid of it; pocket the few hundred and nobody's the worse off. Job knew the way she judged him, but made arrangements for the piano to be collected.

The operation proved epic; a sash window had to be taken out and the size of the instrument rendered the rest of the room useless. One played with back to the wall; the cramped remainder cowered empty in the curve of the piano. Put two dining chairs and a tiny bookcase into the space and it looked like a junk-shop. The piano was in good order, not much affected by the move, but far too powerful in the confined area, with a plangency of tone he disliked already. He closed the lid, sent for the tuner, and shut the door on the bequest.

On one of his few evenings at home, a subjective assessment, Bruce Ferguson called round to see him. The education officer had telephoned during the day, bluff and crafty, to say he'd like a chat, privately out of the way. Job guessed why.

A neighbouring school had featured in the local papers because a pupil had been murdered in the yard, during dinner break, in a stabbing affray. Another child was still in hospital. Both were white fifteen-year-olds, from respectable families, as far as one could tell. The headmaster, 'X the con-man', was pitied by no one at Acton.

'This is where you live then?' Ferguson, dead on time at the front door. He had run his car into the drive according to instructions.

'You found it? No difficulty?'

'No. I used a map.' They settled themselves. Ferguson chose coffee not whisky. 'Very cosy here.'

'Too small.'

'For one man?'

'For this man.' He recounted the story of the piano.

They laughed together, but Ferguson showed no inclination to rise and inspect the prodigy. They sipped companiably.

'First time for years I've been out on my own, on a social visit.' He stretched his legs to demonstrate informality. 'You're one of the few people in the education service I can talk to. I don't admire teachers much these days. Heads even less. But I suppose it's reciprocal. They invariably want something I'm not prepared to give them. You don't believe this, do you?'

'No.'

'You and I, we're of an age. When we started teaching in grammar schools we had at least some common aims. Or

173

élitist, if that's the word. We're creeping back towards it now, bloody and bowed. You've always been that way inclined. And it's not made you popular with some in the political world.'

Ferguson groused on affably while Turner waited to hear his real purpose.

'It's no use you and I, Job, rattling on about education. It's beyond us, friend. You've guessed why I'm here.'

'This business at the Alderman Bernard Brooks School?'

'Yes. I expect you've read the papers. It's a sad affair. It's driving Bertie Moore cracked. Do you know him at all?'

'Slightly. My head of music always refers to him as "Mr X, the con man".'

'Not so far from the truth. While this place was suffering under Miller, Moore tried to take advantage of it. Talked freely of his rival's shortcomings. Tried to poach some of your clever pupils by praising his own academic courses. He wasn't successful; his school draws from two largish council estates, one with a bad reputation. His middle-class children were, and are, more likely to apply to join you here, even in those days of disruption and Miller's lunacy.'

'Doesn't it strike you as remarkable,' Job poked fun, 'that you have appointed two such characters to direct the two largest comprehensive schools in the county?'

'Not I, brother. But, no. Not at all. Both were ambitious. That's the driving force. That's what gets them there. And both were good, at one time, Miller especially. It proved too much for him in the end, and he went off his head in a mild way. Moore is still a competent headmaster for all his slime. But he's got his hands full and he knows it. He's furious that we didn't move him over here when Miller left. One of his favourite topics is our appointment of a junior school incompetent, instead of an experienced man who knows the area.'

'Something in it,' Job answered, with dry relish.

'Well, he's got something now he can use his experience on.'

Ferguson outlined the trouble. The boy in hospital, Terry Hunter, had taken a knife to school and had lunged at and killed a bigger boy who persistently ragged him. His wild

174

stabs had inflicted savage internal injuries on the attacker, but not before the knife had been wrenched from him and he himself been wounded with it.

'There's bullying in all these schools, yours included, if the truth be known. But there are some rough customers at the Bernard Brooks. Two girls were taken to hospital first week of term. Fighting like cats. Lacerations galore. We hushed that up. And it's not the only case. They say violence is endemic in our society. Well. There are certainly some sections of the community where they prefer to slug their differences out with fists and boots rather than in the courts. But this Hunter boy. Let me just fill you in. His father's a collier who continued to work during the miners' strike. Nothing unusual about that, you say; the majority of 'em here kept going. Right again. But Father Hunter was a know-all, mouthy sort; thought nothing of bawling his head off in the pubs and clubs and byways. He wasn't popular even with people whose views coincided with his. And his wife's another such. Shouting the odds at other women in the street. They live up on the Thieves' Wood Estate. Police were called in more than once. Some striking miners' wives scragged Mrs Hunter. And the sins of the fathers, and mothers in this case, are visited on the sons. Now I'm telling you all this because there are two other children, a boy and a girl, thirteen and eleven at Bernard Brooks. And you're going to have them.'

'Thanks.'

'They've got to go somewhere. We can't leave them there. They won't be too bad. The girl, they say, is quite clever and amenable.'

Job Turner nodded, not put out. Ferguson signalled that he had not finished.

'That's not quite the end of the story. The police went in over this Hunter business, and turned up a good deal of other material.' Ferguson's dry cough underlined the litotes. Turner advanced with the coffee pot. 'Kids began to talk. Solvent-sniffing and worse. Drug pedlars at the school gates with the ice-cream van.'

'Where do they get the money from?'

'That's it. Theft for a start. There's been an absolute

outbreak of petty stealing at the school. Moore's been keeping quiet about it. Then from home. And break-ins elsewhere. One thing leads to another. But somebody, the police I guess, leaked this to the press. The director's doing his nut, and there's to be a big anti-drug campaign in the schools, all backed by the newspapers. That's really what I wanted to ask you about. Have you seen any signs in your place?'

'No. But that doesn't mean anything. I was on the lookout. But I'm not sure what to look for. According to Staples there's no glue-sniffing in corners of the playing field.'

'We shall send lecturers round to instruct the staff as well as the pupils.'

He outlined his campaign, listened to Turner's comments. Bruce Ferguson spoke in overdrive; once he began to organize, feet didn't touch. He'd spread the word, and there'd be no excuses. The director had done well to put this man in charge. There'd be action. He and the chief constable were already clashing. 'He and I shout at each other. He's plenty of other problems on his hands and I appreciate that. But when he tells me that half my teachers smoke pot and the other half are gay, well, sparks fly. I tell him that his ignorant constables earn more than my teachers and his thick, fascist inspectors than headmasters. "Make 'em deserve it," I say. We enjoy ourselves, but we get on all right. Basically.'

Ferguson stroked his grinning, wrinkled face.

'I shall be glad to be out of it,' he concluded. 'Really.'

'How long have you to go?'

'Ten years, worse luck. When I came into educational administration, I thought I'd be making it easier for people to teach and learn. Providing books and courses and extra money, not to be wasted. It's nothing like that. Parents have had the stuffing hammered out of them. Good hard-working children these days are not certain to land reasonably paid jobs. Oh, I can remember when young people had more money to spend than was sensible and they blue'd it on clothes and records like idiots. I can even remember some misguided twats trying to sell Mao's *Little Red Book* to the sixth form in a school where I taught. I wonder now if some of 'em

176

would be able to read it. No.' He shook his head. Turner offered him whisky for comfort.

'No, thanks. I'm fine here. I'm having a good grouse and I know it won't pass beyond these four walls. I'm warm; this really is an easy chair. Your coffee tastes of something. You don't smoke. I like your face; I always have. I'm one of the world's bachelors.'

Turner laughed, knowing that Ferguson had five children.

'And since we're talking of domesticity, both Miller and Moore are having trouble with their wives.'

'Why's that?'

'I guess they carry their anxieties home from school too often, and their reception there churns them up. My wife follows me round these damned speech days and sponsored this-that-and-the-others like a lamb. She'd sooner be knitting for the grandchildren. But she's a saint.'

'She's let you out tonight on your own?'

'She's gone to the cinema with a friend. They'll enjoy themselves and she won't be back until midnight. Talk 'emselves silly.'

'Is this a frequent occurrence?'

'Once in six months. I wish she'd do it more often. Anyhow, I want you to let your staff into what we're about with this drugs blitz. We want information from them. The chief constable's convinced that if we can get the schools to come clean we shall be well on the way to succeeding with the larger campaign. So, bags of griff, mate. Pile my desk with bumf, because I think he might be right for once.'

Turner promised to start immediately.

'We don't know where the trouble lies. Some blame the unemployed, but they'll do that for everything. Some say it's the moneyed middle classes, your little lot. The West Indian community, the Pakis, any ethnic minority group, they all come in for suspicion. We want to find out what we can, and put the finger on the wrong-uns. And we start with you, Job. The new broom. Tell us what you can unearth up at Acton.' Ferguson laughed, but his underlying seriousness was apparent. He was trying out his position on Job Turner; if it remained inviolate, a letter would follow tomorrow to all head

177

teachers, but the man didn't want to make a fool of himself, especially with the chief constable and the director breathing down his neck.

Turner put questions, laid on the line what he'd expect from the police and the experts. Ideas clanged between them; Ferguson paid his host the compliment of taking out a notebook and scribbling. A half-hour quick exchange exhausted them.

'Whisky now?' Job tempted.

'No, thanks. If you could brew us another pot of that excellent coffee of yours. . .'

'We'll be up to the hairline with caffeine.'

'And God bless us. That was good. You know, Job, the likes of you and me didn't know if our own children were on drugs, never mind anybody else's. It's so, isn't it? Society's too fragmented for poor old-fashioned schoolmasters like us. We live in a purer, cleaner world.'

'I doubt it.'

'And so do I.' Ferguson rose laughing and, while Turner was in the kitchen, bashed out 'Chopsticks' on the upright. 'We'll tell you what to look for.' He tried loudly and clumsily, the first few bars of Beethoven's Minuet in G.

The two men talked until midnight. Turner, delighted by his friend's comfort, cut beef sandwiches, added mustard. Ferguson knew his way forward from tomorrow and rested secure in that knowledge. They laughed; they were uncouthly frank about colleagues, local politicians, the DES. Ferguson was impulsive, slangy, brusque, hit-or-miss, brutal, relaxed and unguarded, all he could not afford to be in his office. The two men enjoyed themselves unexpectedly.

'You must come up again.'

Bruce Ferguson's face grew grim.

'I came up here to talk business. And I've enjoyed every minute of,' he consulted his watch, 'my four-hours' worth. But I don't think we should tempt providence.'

'Why not?'

'I'm a puritanical Scottish atheist. What could be worse? And we have not sullied our lips with one drop of spirituous liquor.'

The house seemed to contract after Ferguson's departure, wizened into its creaking silence.

'Like angels' visits,' Turner misquoted. 'Short and far between.'

The anti-drug campaign had its successes. The police made some arrests; Job prised out one or two sniffers in his school; letters abounded in the newspapers; a good many people, Turner included, began to learn how the other half lived.

One evening, after a headmasters' meeting for a provisional report from the police, Moore, 'Mr X', stopped Turner on the staircase of the Teachers' Centre. He had obviously been waiting.

'Mr Turner.' He laid a hand on Job's arm. He was a small weasel, with his line of moustache and thinning, black streaks of Brylcreemed hair, the sort of man who'd wear a felt hat in his car. 'Moore's the name. Alderman Bernard Brooks School. I think we've met before.' His voice was surprisingly deep, rich with harmonics. 'Could I beg a word with you?'

Job Turner, not a tall man, looked down.

'I wonder if I could ask a favour of you?' Moore smiled, unwinningly.

'Go on.'

'A bad business this. Have you found much, much . . . oh, evidence . . . in your school?'

'One or two on solvents; some hearsay evidence of cannabis smoking. About what I expected.' He did not know how wise it was to be frank with this man.

'Yes. You've involved the parents?'

'We've laid on meetings, yes. Those so far have been well, very well attended. The PTA's active.'

'You're lucky.'

They began to walk downstairs together.

'And you haven't come across much of significance? As yet?' Moore, again, pressing.

'About what I expected. But it's early days. We'd already been looking. One of my deputies had been on a short course.'

'How did you manage that?'

'Ferguson made the offer. Soon after term started. Somebody had dropped out.'

'So you know what you're looking for?'

'To some extent.'

They reached the bottom of the staircase. Groups of head-masters were exchanging last words before they ventured out into the dark. The occasion seemed both sedate and jaunty.

'This favour?' Job Turner asked. The pair stopped.

'We're holding a small musical festival just before Christmas. I wonder if I can prevail on you to judge one of the singing classes.'

They consulted diaries, made provisional arrangements.

'Thank you. Perhaps you and your wife would like to come to dinner some evening.' Moore flourished his pocket book.

'I'm a widower.'

'I'm sorry.' Moore backed off, as if his face had been slapped. 'I, I, it, er. . .'

'I thought perhaps you knew my wife. Dr Gillian Turner. She was in the university education department.'

'I knew of her, of course. We never met. I never connected you.'

Job Turner did not know what to believe. People like Moore usually had the tittle-tattle of his educational world well recorded for use.

'You'll confirm that in writing, won't you?' Job spoke briskly. 'Goodnight.' And he was through the swing doors. Moore made an attempt at pursuit, but failed.

Job's rapid walk to the municipal parking block worked rancour out of him.

# 18

On the last Tuesday of November Susan Smith took her examination.

Job Turner saw her on the Saturday when she seemed cheerful and confident, though she complained that at this time of year her hands would be cold. There spoke her father's daughter. On the day the weather proved favourable, dry, even bright, he noticed, so that she would be able to manage the ten minutes' stroll from her office without arriving drenched. He imagined she would give herself good time; Noelle Waters would have drummed that in.

At the published time of the examination he was busy and never thought once of the girl. That evening he had a parents' meeting from which he did not return until after ten, and therefore heard nothing. Next morning he rang Mrs Waters for information.

'No. Not a thing from her.' She answered cheerfully. 'I thought she might have phoned you. She'll have done well. She was properly prepared and her temperament's right.'

'Has she said any more about the diploma?'

'No. Not really.'

'We ought to talk about that before long. As we were named together in Frederick Greene's will.'

'What time will you leave school today?'

'About five.'

'Come round here. I have a cup of tea then. I'll give you half an hour, if you're prompt.'

Job liked her sharpness, not masked by the old-fashioned somewhat spinsterish voice, and he reported at her front door at exactly five.

Noelle's husband let him in; he like his wife was small, but more rotund, with a clipped moustache belying an unmilitary

181

manner. A retired accountant, he had been well known in his earlier days as an amateur singer.

'The kettle's boiling,' he said, leading Job in to his wife who sat by a gas fire.

'Are you cold?' she asked.

'No, not at all.'

'Neither am I, but Oliver thinks I am.'

She motioned Job into the armchair opposite, said she had not heard yet from Susan, asked him to begin.

He had no trouble, spoke easily, put the expected case. It would be a shame if anyone as talented as Susan did not complete her diploma. The old lady watched him quite still, as if made of bone china.

'Drink your tea,' she said gently when he had finished. 'Now, Mr Turner, I agree with your general position. Any young person with potential should be encouraged. I shall try to persuade her, use what influence I have. But we ought to see matters straight. At any musical college there'll be a dozen if not a score of students as gifted as Susan. That does not alter your position, I realize. Nor am I altogether accusing you of seeing all your geese as swans. One doesn't know. Energy, temperament, opportunity, luck will all play their part. I was talking to an old friend only yesterday who was at the Royal College exactly contemporaneously with Benjamin Britten. The teachers there did not, according to James, regard the composer as an outstanding genius though we know he wrote some marvellous music as a schoolboy, and we have later evidence from many quarters of the utterly outstanding musicality of the man. And what was the reason? Britten did not want to do what his tutors wanted him to. They regarded him as un-English. Now if professionals can fail to spot what we agree as remarkable genius over a period of three years then . . .' Job remembered Mackenzie, the Scots composer at the conference.

'All the more reason to support any talented student.'

'Certainly.' She drew in her mouth. 'I'm only telling you this irrelevant anecdote to show that we have no idea what the future will make of our pupils. I don't want you to be disappointed, Mr Turner. Susan may consider that there are

182

many more important matters than music in her life. One of the most gifted students of my own time at the Academy, a clarinet player, threw it up and became an accountant, like my husband.'

'But did music play no part in his life?'

'I don't know. But here was a man whom I, and his teachers, considered unusually gifted who called a halt. Others with not half his talent have succeeded as soloists, or conductors, composers, professors. We are not prophets.'

'I don't quite grasp the point,' Turner said, with politeness.

'I am, you may consider, a disappointed old woman. Yes, that is probably so. But one who will, none the less, support you in your efforts to entice,' she stressed the word, glinting across at him, 'Susan to continue with her lessons. But if we fail, it is not the end of music. You must understand that. Accept it.'

'Your argument,' Turner answered on his mettle, 'could easily be taken the other way. What if Britten had turned away in disgust at his teachers' lack of discernment. It might not have been the "end of music", but think of the gap, the loss. And the thing about works of art is that once they're lost, they'll never be exactly replaced. Scientific theory of the highest level will be produced if not by one man, then by another. There may be an important delay, but not a total loss as with works of art.'

Mrs Waters sniffed, a serious sound to him, and ordered him to pass across his cup for a refill.

'I'm glad, Mr Turner,' she had resumed her stillness again, 'that people like you exist in the educational world. You are an idealist. There are not too many. My own training was conspicuously lacking in such people, though I cannot complain that I was badly taught. I myself have been a mere technician of a teacher.' She smiled. 'That has considerable advantages, you know.'

They talked together, suspiciously, appreciatively. Sometimes she dragged out for his inspection a point he had not liked to speak of openly.

'Do you ever think,' Noelle Waters' eyes were black, darting, 'that Susan might do badly, or comparatively so, in

183

this exam she's just taken to put an end to all talk of further lessons?'

'Deliberately, do you mean?'

'Who can say? The unconscious is often as important as the conscious in what we decide.'

'I had thought of it.'

'Good. There's much to be said for facing the bleaker aspects.'

The husband, Oliver Waters, came in quietly.

' "Time to go home",' he sang, breathily. 'I shall have to call this conference to an end, Mr Turner. My wife becomes too excited, and it's not good for her. She forgets she's an old lady.'

'And you're an old woman, Oliver,' she admonished.

'Yes, dear.'

Turner rose, shook hands with Noelle. Her grip was strong.

'I've enjoyed every minute of our talk, Mr Turner. I wish we'd known each other years ago.' She seemed more shrunken than ever, her pallor accentuated by the dark clothes.

'She will not rest,' Oliver Waters confessed at the door. 'It's as though she has some uncertainty or sense of shortcoming, shortfall gnawing at her the whole time. I think she regrets her life. It could have been otherwise.'

'You think she regrets missed opportunities?'

'Most old people, as you'll soon find out, dislike their lot. She more than most.' He sounded undistressed.

'Perhaps that is why she is not as keen as I am to keep Susan Smith on the musical treadmill.'

'Ah, Susan Smith. A good player, that girl, the best Noelle's got. I'm glad she kept her on, when she decided to retire. "I don't want the responsibility," she said. Not that that makes a ha'porth of difference. While ever she teaches somebody, she'll feel responsible.' He laughed and coughed. 'Even when she's sharing with you.' Oliver put a hand on Job's sleeve; he seemed in no hurry to break off the conversation. 'She's a very good pair of hands on her, that Susan Smith. Since I've been at home I've listened to the pupils, especially in winter when I can't get out. And Susan's worth hearing. Good technique, and she plays Beethoven like some old German master.

Schnabel, for instance. I mentioned him to her, but I don't think she'd heard of him.'

'She's very gifted.'

'But odd. I act as a doorman now, show 'em in and out. And she's hardly a word to say for herself. She plays like an angel and then comes out dumb as a rock. There's no animation there. Her face is wooden. As if she's cooped up inside herself. She's not impolite, I don't mean that. But there's no small talk, or idea of the impression she's making. Her face is set in concrete. That's unusual for an eighteen-year-old. I mean some of them are shy, and blush and gush,' he smirked at his rhymes, 'and others are brass-necked as you come, but Susan . . .'

'Have you mentioned this to your wife?'

'Often enough. She thinks the girl's still immersed in the music. But there's more to it than that. Or that's my guess.'

The men shook hands. Turner had not noticed this lack of vivacity in Susan, but whenever he showed her to the door, he was still full of the lesson, their attempts and achievements. He did not understand her, the naked girl, the affianced bride, the father's daughter, the responsible woman in charge at the office. His picture was coloured by her musicianship, her prowess at the keyboard. Job Turner made his way to the East Lodge with his tail between his legs.

Job boiled an egg for his tea, found that he was out of cake and biscuits. This annoyed him since he prided himself on his housekeeping; there were no corner shops within a mile. He consoled himself with a slice of bread and jam. Alison telephoned while he was washing up to inquire if all was well with him; she and Geoffrey were getting ready for the theatre.

'We don't go out often enough,' she stated. 'Geoffrey would stick at home every night of the week with his DIY or a book or some work. I've issued an ultimatum: either he takes me out or I go out on my own.'

'Poor Geoffrey. You sound just like your mother.'

'And a good thing.'

'For whom, though?'

Half an hour later the phone rang again. Pleased to be

interrupted he spoke his name, number. Silence. 'Hello,' he called. Nothing. 'Hello.' This time a sound of indrawn breath.

'Is that Mr Job Turner?' A hesitant female voice. On his reply the caller continued, slowly. 'My name is Sally Moore.'

'Yes.' She seemed to expect recognition.

'I'm the wife of . . . You know my husband. He's the headmaster of the Alderman Bernard Brooks School.'

'Yes.'

Again a long, awkward pause, during which he could hear the rhythm of her breathing.

'I don't know if I'm doing right in ringing you up. Encroaching on your time.' She'd prepared that one. 'My husband greatly admires you and your work. I believe he spoke to you the other evening, asked you to judge some competition, invited you to dine with us. Since then I have heard nothing but praise of you from him. Job Turner this, Job Turner that. I would like to talk to you.'

'About what, Mrs Moore?'

'Yes, that's it. About what. About me.' The phrases were delivered at intervals.

'I see. That's possible.'

'This is awkward, Mr Turner, embarrassing. I don't know you. We don't know each other. My husband and I are . . . well, at loggerheads. We don't hit it off. It's made me quite ill. I've been to the doctor and he's a sympathetic young man, but they haven't much time. "Talk to a friend," he told me, while he was writing the prescription. "It often seems not so bad when you've put it into words." I thought about it, and do you know I haven't a single friend I could confide in. We meet a great number of people at official functions; we dispense a fair amount of hospitality here, or at least we used to, but there's no one, no one I can . . . You see what I mean. And since in these last few days we've had nothing but Job Turner at every verse end I thought I might ring you.' She stopped. 'Now I've done so, I feel silly.'

'Would your husband approve?'

'Why shouldn't he?'

'I'm at a rival establishment.'

'I see. I never thought of that. Ummh. I don't suppose

186

he'd care. Why should he?' She spoke more quickly. 'I was very uncertain, even when I had dialled your number.' A nervous titter. 'I don't know if I've done right.'

'I must leave it to you.'

'You're very reserved, Mr Turner. I thought according to my husband that you'd come out with some remarkable statement. . . .' She broke off.

'That's not very likely, Mrs Moore. I'm a human being, like you and your husband. A widower.'

'Yes. I know. I heard your wife speak once.'

They talked on for another ten minutes, exchanging snippets of information, tentative questions, half-answers. In the end she arranged to visit him on Saturday afternoon when her husband was away at a conference. He carefully gave her directions. She expressed guarded thanks.

During the rest of the week he heard nothing from either Susan Smith or Mrs Waters. Susan cancelled her Thursday lesson by a phone message to the school while he was over in the senior science block. His secretary had made no attempt to contact him until his return, presumably on Susan's instruction. The girl had said nothing, it appeared, about her performance in the examination, nor given any reason for the cancellation. He was momentarily annoyed, but pushed it from his mind.

After spending Saturday morning at the music school he lunched in town at the Hot Potato in company with noisy young couples and their children. At least the self-service was quick, and the meal filling. He ate slowly, pushing his limp salad about his plate; the single child of the family at his table, a boy of four, bounced boisterously up and down and round from his mother's knee. She, poor girl, looked harassed, but did not complain, forking up a heavy mouthful when she could between assaults. The father, pale as death, sat dumb. All uncomfortable.

Turner back at home and closing the gate of his drive jumped out of his skin at the blast of a car horn. Susan's father drove sedately past widely signalling greetings with his left hand but not stopping with news. Job picked up two appeals and a bill that the postman had delivered during the morning. Outside it was dull and the garden needed rain.

Mrs Moore arrived fifteen minutes early.

She was slim, taller than her husband, with a handsome head of iron-grey hair. She wore jeans, a check skirt and a silk handkerchief about her throat. Her figure was youthful, not quite suitable to the hair or the rather severe face. Deeply suntanned, her hands were veined.

She refused refreshment, but sat easily with legs crossed. Thirty years ago, he could see, she had been very pretty. Again she apologized for bothering him, and then paid a restrained compliment or two to his house and furniture. He gave some account of their provenance while she listened with the feigned interest of a provisional buyer. These preliminaries occupied ten minutes, with both parties fluent. Sally Moore finally rapped with her finger-ends on the arm of her chair, calling the meeting to order.

'You don't look as I imagined you, Mr Turner,' she began.

'What did you expect?' He was pleased to keep it light.

'Something like Sir Malcolm Sargent.' He nodded. 'I have never seen you, to the best of my knowledge, though I knew your name. It's rather unusual. Is it a family name?'

'Yes. My paternal grandfather's. He lived at a period when Biblical names were popular. I might well have been Elijah or Habbakuk or Benaiah.'

'I've never heard of him.'

'One of David's soldiers. The man who killed a lion in a pit on a snowy day.'

'Is that in the Bible?'

'I believe so.'

'How ignorant I am.'

She pulled in her lips until they disappeared. Wrinkles disfigured the corners of her eyes.

'My husband and I,' she stopped, perhaps acknowledging the reference, but unsmiling, 'are in trouble. The doctor suggests I should tell someone.'

'And you propose to tell me.' He would prevent it if he could.

'In strict confidentiality.' He agreed with a nod. 'We barely talk to each other now. We can, or I rather, can hardly hear a word from him without taking offence. Whole days pass with nothing but the merest essentials. The tension I feel just to see him is unbearable. I could shriek or kick him or throw things.'

'And yet, Mrs Moore, he had been praising me to you on your own testimony.'

'That's so. It's unusual. I can't explain it.'

'You don't think it's an attempt on his part to reorganize communication between you?'

'I don't think so. He hasn't that much consideration for me. I think he has been impressed by you, finds this agreeable to talk about, unlike the majority of his concerns, and therefore comes out with it.'

'Is it usual for your husband to feel or express hero-worship of this kind?' He smiled to cloak the formality of his question. She stared hen-eyed at him.

'No, it isn't.' She paused. 'And not in this case. Up to a little time ago you were regarded by my husband as an unworthy rival who had done him out of his rightful place as headmaster of the Acton School. He wanted that position. It is only slightly better paid than his present post, I believe, but it has superior status in his eyes, rightly or wrongly. It offered greater opportunity, responsibility, challenge. Or a means of escape. And the committee appoint, if you'll forgive me, "an inexperienced primary school man without so much as an interview." His words. It crowned his many disappointments. Then in the last week or two this miraculous switch.'

'Has he said anything to you about the Hunter case? The boy killed? Or the police investigation into drugs?'

'He can hardly have failed to, can he? Even as we are. It's been in the newspapers.'

'And you've no sympathy for him?'

'Only in an abstract way. As a person I can't bear him now. He's driven me to hate him. I can't bring myself to support him. I know how he must feel, but . . .' The last words cracked into a staccato crescendo.

Sally Moore composed herself, put her hands in her lap, and told how she had met her husband. Thirty-two years ago

189

she, in her first teaching job, had been the junior member of her husband's English department in a London comprehensive school.

'He was superb.' She spoke with sudden warmth. 'He helped me tremendously. He was full of ideas. I remember especially a production of *Henry IV, Part One* he did. I played Kate Percy. It was marvellous. I thought it was a boring play until we acted in it. Not everybody liked him. Some of the boys, and staff, called him Bullshit Ben, from his first initials. His real names are Bertrand Browne.'

For five minutes Sally Moore spoke, with a young woman's enthusiasm, of her early terms in the school. Bertrand left within three years to become deputy head of a larger comprehensive school. Before he went he had proposed to and married Sally and they had honeymooned in France that summer in scorching weather. When she returned she was pregnant. Five years later he had been appointed headmaster of a school in Leicester, and after six years there to his present post. She had not been keen to move but he had insisted. 'B.B. for Bernard Brooks' he had joked. Supporting him she had relinquished the pleasant house in a village, the admirable rural schools where her two sons enjoyed themselves, for life in a town.

'It was a mistake,' her face had not lost its animation. 'Bernard Brooks always had a wild element in it, a constant change-over of staff, more than its fair share of criminals. Oh, he was successful at first. The building was newish, the playing fields were good, the teachers keen. But it beat him in the end. For the last seven or eight years he's been losing heart. He's not given up, but he knows improvement is unlikely.'

'And your boys?' Job Turner asked.

'They're both in America. They're scientists. Alan's an engineer in California, Toby's doing his doctorate in biochemistry in New York.'

'Are they married?'

'Neither.'

They sat in glum silence. Turner asked again if she would like a drink, waited for the rebuff. 'No, thank you. Just hear

190

me out, Mr Turner. I shan't be long. I'm not going to waste very much of your time. But I'm here to speak my little piece.' He indicated compliance, attention. 'I saw how it was going and I tried to help him. The boys were just beginning to be awkward too, at that time. Wanted more of their own way. It terrified their father. He saw too many of his own pupils wasting their chances, and he didn't want it to happen to them. There were constant rows, shouting matches at home. And I was in between. They accused me of siding with him; he called me lukewarm. They were successful in the end; Alan went to Cambridge, Toby to London, where they worked hard, and they both did outstandingly well. I thought at one time they were becoming so antagonized by their father that they'd throw their careers up.'

'He'll be pleased they've succeeded.'

'He's said so, but it was all too late. He lied to me about what was happening at school, and before that he began to deceive himself. I'd hear him boasting to other headmasters, and came to see that they didn't believe him. He had bad luck: there were two proselytizing lesbians, a man who absconded with a holiday fund, some religious lunatic. Vandalism and truancy grew out of all proportion; there were break-ins; the police gave up, wouldn't answer alarm calls. It was awful. But on public occasions he'd be bragging about this advance and that educational experiment. He tried, my God, he tried. I'll give him that. But these last two years he's known he's really beaten, and he's taken it out on me. When we heard that Gordon Miller had suddenly resigned, it seemed like a godsend. He went to see Bruce Ferguson about the post; he even had an interview with the director. But they sent for you. I thought when he told me that he'd hit me. His face was streaky red, clotted, with his veins all dilated. I suppose I wasn't very sympathetic. He raised his fist to me. "You dare," I thought. "Just you bloody dare." And then he burst into tears and rushed out of the room.'

'What did you do?'

'I just sat down, I felt so feeble, and cried myself. It was the end, I knew.'

'And is it?'

191

'I'm still there. I've not left him. Yet.'

'Are you thinking of it?'

'Yes I am. I don't know how I shall manage. I've no pension as yet, and then it won't be much. It'll mean getting a job in a cake shop if they're taking on raddled old battle-axes. If I'd had money I'd have gone long ago. He knows that.'

'And there's no prospect of reconciliation?'

'I see no signs of it.'

'Is he anywhere near retirement? He must be.'

'He's sixty. He could go now, but he won't. He'll work to sixty-five. If there's a substantial pay rise to come it will be worth hanging on, he says.'

'Not at the expense of his health.'

'What else can he do? He's no interests anywhere. He does nothing in the home. When I think of him as a young man, as I first knew him, when he produced plays in and out of school, organized a drama festival, ran a poetry society, served on charitable committees, and did a research degree, I think the educational system that has made him what he is now has something to answer for.'

'Ye'.'

'When I remember how he used to tell me that we were privileged to be allowed to open the eyes of young people to learning, I could weep.'

They sat in angry silence, avoiding glances.

'What do you propose to do, then, Mrs Moore?'

'You give me your advice.'

'I don't know either of you well enough to do that. It will depend on what you feel, what you can put up with. You have looked into it, haven't you? The idea of a cheap flat or bedsitter is not attractive. But it's better than a breakdown. In mind. Or health. There's no prospect of soldiering on, is there? Or going to stay for a time with a relative, a friend?' She shook her head bemusedly. 'If he had been made head of Acton, would it have saved your husband?'

'He thinks so. I don't know. He's too . . . too damaged . . . if that's the word. He believes there would have been rewarding circumstances at your place.'

'There must be dozens, if not hundreds, of decent, well-intentioned pupils at Bernard Brooks.'

'He doesn't see them. He's concerned all the time with the criminal or apathetic element. There's a fifteen-year-old boy up for rape now. And stealing's reached epidemic proportions. You try talking to him about decent children.'

'I shall have to, shan't I, when I go up to judge this festival?'

'If this festival exists anywhere outside his mind.'

The despair in that leaden sentence quietened Job. She looked up, brighter, more agile, feral.

'So you've no instant remedies, Mr Turner?'

'No. Nor did you expect any.' He clasped his hands. 'Mrs Moore, I honestly believe there's going to be an improvement in schools. The teachers will be in five days a week. They'll keep registers, take lessons, run clubs. This will be so, even in Bernard Brooks.'

'I doubt it. Just look what's happened this term. Schools like yours will feel the benefit. But his pupils see no reason either to attend or behave.'

'Even they realize the need to find jobs.'

'Do they? That may be so for your students. The majority at Brooks know quite well they'll soon be on the dole.'

'The youth opportunity . . .'

'Regarded by his riffraff as cheap labour for unscrupulous employers. No, Mr Turner, the heart's gone.'

'At least the teachers will be there to keep an eye on them.'

She shook her head.

'According to him his staff is a collection of the ineffectual and the inefficient.' He could hear Moore's rich voice behind the words. 'Anyhow, thank you very much for your time. I don't think it's changed anything. I didn't expect it would. At least you made me remember what Bertie was like when we first met.'

'Please let me know if there's anything I can do.' Turner spoke out of politeness, nothing more. He was defeated.

'Is it safe,' she began, and faltered, 'to take a little walk in these woods here round the Hall?'

'Now?'

'Yes.'

'It's still light. If not for long.'

'My shoes are not altogether suitable.' She held her feet out for inspection.

'I'll walk with you, if you like.'

'Would you?'

They donned scarves and overcoats; hers was new, sheep-skin-lined. Her car, he noticed, was splashed with streaked muddy triangles, as if she'd driven at speed through puddles.

Under the avenue of trees they walked silently and not fast. Mist hung half visible in the distance; bare boles and branches shone wet. A very few people called commands to dogs, their voices echoing.

'It's not really cold.' Sally Moore broke the silence.

'No. It's quite mild for late November.'

'We'll soon have Christmas on us.'

'Are you going away? It might be an idea. Suggest it. This is always a long, tiring term.'

'No. Bertie wouldn't countenance it. Are you?'

'I shall go to my daughter's on Christmas Day.'

'Are there children?'

'Yes. Two. Three and one.'

'Lucky man.'

Now they made their way uphill unspeaking between thickets which arched and dripped over the uneven lane. Their unhurried pace seemed companionable enough to preclude conversation. Between the trees the sky darkened. They came to a fork in the road.

'Do you want to go on?' Job asked.

She consulted her watch, with difficulty, screwing her eyes.

'Perhaps we'd better turn back.'

Downhill they picked up speed, glowed warm. Job Turner slapped the pockets of his coat. Sally's face became less grim. She flapped her hands with such vigour that he expected her to skip like an excited child. He increased his pace; she kept up with him without effort.

As they neared the Hall he noticed under the light a figure by the gate. Susan Smith. He called out loudly; Mrs Moore stumbled in surprise. Susan, turning, recognized him and walked towards the two and away from the wall. Job Turner

194

touched Sally Moore's elbow to guide her up the sideroad on which the girl approached.

'I thought it was you,' Job said. He made a brief introduction. The women smiled, nodded, saying nothing. 'How did you get on then? Last Tuesday?'

'Not so bad as I thought.' She gave a brief, sensible, chronological report of the examination.

'Who was the examiner?'

'I don't know. An elderly man. He looked bored stiff.'

'He made no remarks?'

'No. Just do this, do that. Very polite. Old-fashioned. Coughed a bit.'

'And were you pleased?'

'I can't tell. I don't much like the piano they have. But I didn't make any major mistakes. I was very nervous. My hands were sweating. How long is it before we get the result?'

'About Christmas, I hope. Mrs Waters will have it. Have you been in touch with her since Tuesday?'

'No.'

'Give her a ring, will you? She'd like to hear from you.'

'Right. I will. Oh, do you mind if I don't come to see you next week? We're terribly busy in the office. It will mean two late nights at least. And there's Christmas shopping now.'

'Is that a big time-consumer?'

'You'd be surprised.' They laughed, all three. 'I've made a start this afternoon.' She tapped her parcels, vigorously. 'See you, then.' She set off for the gate, not looking back.

Job explained his interest in Susan to Mrs Moore.

'Is she from Acton School?'

'No. The Holyoak, on the other side of the city.' He made further explanations, about Mr Smith's job, Susan's talent. By the time he had finished they had reached the East Lodge.

'Come in now, for a cup of tea.'

'You've wasted enough time on me, Mr Turner. Thank you all the same.'

'It's Saturday. My free day.'

'Then you'll need to go in and check your football coupon.'

They laughed. She unlocked the door of her car, thanked

him again, succinctly; her engine seemed loth to start. When it did, Sally Moore raised a gloved hand, pulled away, waving still. He watched her rear lights. A van rattled past in the direction of the Hall, diverting his thoughtful scrutiny.

# 19

One evening on his arrival home Job Turner found a letter from his youngest daughter, Hilary.

It had been a day like all the others at the Acton Comprehensive, full, busy, wearing, but ultimately, he considered, satisfactory. He recognized the handwriting on the envelope with pleasure and wondered what the girl wanted. She'd tell him something interesting for sure.

The letter was, in fact, comparatively short, and plain. Hilary had moved in, was living with a professor of mathematics. His name was Mohammed Ali Sadiq, and he came originally from Pakistan. He was forty-one years old, a professor at Imperial, had studied in Cambridge where he had been a research and full fellow, was a Fellow of the Royal Society. He was a widower, and the two daughters of his first marriage lived in Pakistan with grandparents who were well-to-do and not keen to send the girls to England to live with their father who had lost such orthodox religion as he once had. He was no longer a Muslim, but sometimes described himself as a doubtful deist. Extremely distinguished for his work on mathematical physics, he travelled a great deal to America; perhaps, she suggested, her father had heard the talks he gave last year on Radio Three. 'Ammy' wished to marry her, but she was slightly unsure about that at present, though they might possibly be wed, quietly and 'civilly', when she had made up her mind.

She wrote thus, Hilary claimed, because Alison had called in on them while she was visiting London for a conference, and had been 'shocked' to learn that Job knew nothing of the arrangement. 'So, Daddy, I'm putting it down in black-and-white, no verbal play intended, so that you know how everything stands.' Alison, doubtless, would fill in the details for him, on application.

Job Turner found himself sufficiently distressed by the news to put off the preparation of his tea. He was no racist, he thought; besides Professor Sadiq was obviously an outstanding figure. On the other hand, Hilary's tone was defensive; she had said nothing to her father in the first place, and presumably would have kept quiet had Alison not demurred. Did Hilary expect him to be angry, or shocked, or unreasonable? Was he, Job Turner the liberal élitist, a blinkered, ignorant ruffian his own daughter feared to confide in? He put the letter prominently on the mantelpiece for a reply.

While he was eating Alison rang to ask if she could call round that evening for half an hour to bring birthday presents from her family and from Hilary.

She arrived, as he knew she would, exactly on nine o' clock as arranged, put down her parcels and accepted a cup of tea.

'Don't open them until the day, Sarah says,' she warned.

'Are you very busy?' he called from the kitchen.

'No more than usual.'

'Susan Smith said they were up to the eyes in it, that she had to stay late nights.'

'I don't see why.'

Returning he put Hilary's letter into her hands. She read it, stood up to replace it.

'How long has she been living with this man?'

'The end of August, I think.'

'How long have you known?'

'A month, perhaps. When I wrote proposing to call on her.'

'Why didn't she say anything?'

'Perhaps she wanted firmer news, a wedding date for instance, before she told you.'

'Isn't cohabiting with someone news then?'

Alison frowned slightly.

'You're not cross, are you, Daddy?' she asked.

'I don't like being left out, that's certain. Did she think I'd disapprove?'

'Well, do you?'

He did not know.

'No man's good enough for one's daughters.' He gave

Smith's answer. Alison pressed him no more. 'Did you meet him?'

'Of course.'

'What's he like?'

'I thought he'd be rather small-boned, and delicate, but he isn't. He's big, six foot two, and a little bit fat. But he's got this marvellous bright face. Mischievous eyes. I think I shall really like him, when I get to know him. He talks quite quickly.'

'Chi-chi accent?' Alison's brows rose at his question.

'Yes, I suppose so, but he's lived in England for the past twenty-odd years.'

'How long has his wife been dead?'

'Five yeas, I think. She lived over here with him for some time, while the girls were small. She went back. Took the children.'

'Wasn't that unusual?'

'I don't know the details. She was ill, then, I believe.'

'With what?'

'For God's sake. Some kind of kidney trouble, I think. Or pancreas. I spent one night there with them. And an hour or two in the afternoon with Hilly.'

'You wouldn't be averse to some cross-examination.' They laughed together. 'Did Hilary seem happy?'

'Very.'

'Then why is she hesitating about marriage?'

'You know Hilly as well as I do. I guess she's thinking about her career. From casual remarks they dropped, I guess he's seriously considering emigrating to the United States. He's had offers. Apparently he's quite famous in his line, whatever that is. But if he goes she'd have to go with him, and if they started a family it might interfere with some of her projects. She'd find a job out there easily enough. But . . .'

'Are they in love?'

'That's difficult, isn't it? He's not a boy you know, and Hilly's not forthcoming on such matters, and never has been. They're fond of each other, admire each other. They seemed

199

to me, and I don't make myself out to be an expert, rather like an old married couple.'

Job Turner thought.

'Has she sold her flat?' he asked.

'No. She's let it temporarily to a colleague.'

'When do I get to meet the gentleman?'

'She sent a message that you can go down at any time. By arrangement. They'll be glad to see you; he has a nice little house in Chelsea. They can put you up.'

Alison talked on. Ammy was in some ways like Geoffrey, another big man. He'd acquired his nickname in Cambridge, a shortening of Abdul Abubul Amir, in the song. Both were good about the home and rather quiet. Both liked children. Sadiq was sad about his own family, felt responsible, inadequate, uncertain, but did not want to interfere at present. The girls were well looked after, well educated; the affluent grandparents would make all provision. He was frequently consulted. It had been tricky. He visited them, yes, but not often. He would have liked to educate them in England. Alison anticipated her father's questions. No, Ammy had not abdicated his responsibilities. There had been genuine difficulties. He wanted to act for the best. Alison was sharp. 'I know what you're thinking. That if he can leave the upbringing of his children in the hands of other people, however well intentioned, he's not much of a father.'

'There's something in that.'

'Oh, yes. But his wife had returned home. That's what she wanted when she became really ill. He couldn't deny her that. When she died, well . . . Her parents were not old; they'd plenty of money.'

'And the religious side?'

'He's not orthodox. But he respects Islam. He's like you. You're not much of a believer, but you can't throw off your Methodist childhood.'

Again they laughed; Alison said her time was up. 'I like a little of my husband's company every day,' she averred. Job did not try to detain her.

'Thanks for making her write,' he said.

'Encouraging her.'

200

They kissed; she punched his shoulder with small, hard knuckles encouraging him. She was Gillian's daughter.

At the door she said suddenly, 'You could do with a cleaning woman.'

'Is it as bad as all that?'

'Why don't you try Sandra Harper, Fred Greene's lady? You could do worse.'

Back in the house he walked his small rooms troubled and excited. If Hilary had children, they would have those beautiful dark Indian eyes, that black, straight, shining hair. Unless the father was a Pathan, which he might be: Job had seen frontier people with blue eyes. He wondered if Sadiq had retained traditional ideas about the place of women; Hilary would know that; she would not be put on. All at once his daughter seemed young and vulnerable, the girl who wrote poetic essays like those of her middle sister, but had been wedded to the certainties or precise probabilities of science and mathematics since the age of fourteen. Job did not understand her; he did not understand anybody. Gillian would have sorted him out, exposed his prejudices and fears in the plainest terms, and then comforted him. He took to his piano but lacked concentration. When he went to bed he could not sleep; he switched on the light, tried to read, but his brain skidded over meaning. He turned to the World Service on the BBC; they had nothing to offer him. He crept downstairs, made tea, carried it back. His mind spun; his feet were cold. The radio droned on.

His worry did not interfere with his work at the Acton School. He rushed about, made end-of-term arrangements, looked in at rehearsals, saw off November resits. He wrote to Hilary; it took three drafts on paper, but he expressed himself pleased, wondered if they would spend a day or two with him at Christmas, as he could just about put them up. Her reply, within three days, showed relief, was lively, charming, full of anecdote. Ammy had said that Job, in a photograph now in a position of some honour in their drawing room, looked a cross between a poet and a police superintendent. They could not come up at Christmas; she'd already refused an invitation from Alison, because he was off to Pakistan to see his

201

daughters, to deliver some lectures and to announce to his former in-laws his intention to marry Hilary. They had not yet decided on a date, but it might just possibly be Easter. He was to get his best bib and tucker ready. She was herself extremely busy and looked forward to the Christmas holiday to make big inroads into a research project she had engaged on. She hoped he was well; in fact she knew he was because Ally kept her up to date with the news. The letter sounded quite brilliantly cheerful and lifted his spirits.

On the same day he received a note from Bertrand Moore announcing that the festival Job had been asked to judge had been cancelled. Immediately Job thought of what Sally Moore had said: 'if the festival exists outside his mind'. He wrote back sympathetically saying that he himself had realigned his programmes, and offering his services whenever they decided to rejig the musical competitions. He made no mention of Mrs Moore; he had expected to hear from her, but had not done so. Their walk in the wood possessed some sort of worth, he considered, if only five minutes of spare time, a sheet of paper and an envelope, a second-class stamp, a millimetre of biro fluid.

Susan Smith appeared for her first lesson saying she had not done any serious practice, she had been too busy. They spent the hour on sight-reading and on the analysis of a Mozart sonata. She played well, vigorously, and answered with a cheerful intelligence. Refusing a cup of coffee, she confessed she had had no second thoughts about her performance in the examination, but in any case it was all over and done with, for good or ill. Susan seemed pleased with herself, but unwilling to share her delight with him. She retrieved her cycle from the back of his house, and pedalled off into the dark. When he mentioned work for the diploma, she had replied, 'Let's see how I've done this time first.'

He met Noelle Waters at a performance of part of *The Christmas Oratorio* at the university. She complained of the coldness of the weather, the thousand and one preparations necessary for a festivity as simple as theirs, the pains in a rheumatic knee. Oliver, her husband, beamed widely enough for both. 'I wanted to go to a hotel for the holiday period,'

202

he said, 'but Noelle wouldn't hear of it.' 'I should think not. I'd as soon throw money down a drain.' He invited them round for a drink. Oliver's diary, he noticed, seemed, unlike his, almost blank. Job sent them tickets for the final Music School Concert. His own time seemed completely occupied and he went to bed tired every night.

On the evening the Waters drove over to see him, Noelle questioned him about Frederick Greene and his bequest. She had sat for the first five minutes at his grand piano, playing a Brahms intermezzo. Job Turner now explained the old solicitor's position as best he could.

'Why did he choose Susan?' she persisted.

'Quite by chance. She was there. She had caught his interest. And he had this whim to do something personal, or out of the ordinary, with a small part of his money. The large bulk went to his son and grandchildren, but he wanted a thousand or two invested in an unusual way.'

'Why would that be?'

'It's difficult for me to say. He'd always, they tell me, a very keen eye for money or a bargain.'

'And you know,' Noelle answered, 'I agree with Oliver here that Susan is not everybody's cup of tea. She doesn't always put herself out to make herself pleasant.'

'He was a bit of an eccentric. I don't know whether or not he'd notice how Susan acted towards him. As long as she piped up, and played the piano well, that would do. He'd become interested in Elgar. In some measure I can take the praise or blame for that, and he often quoted the remark that Elgar made that no single person had ever helped him.'

'What about Alice Elgar, his wife?' Noelle demanded sharply.

'That was her privilege,' Oliver answered her, laughing. Noelle looked sour.

'I think Fred Greene perhaps equated himself with the composer. The end of Elgar's life was not happy. The young had turned against him. He said he had no pleasurable memories associated with music. His works were not much played, and to anybody with a skin as thin as Elgar's that would make him suspect he'd wasted his life. He couldn't, or didn't, compose seriously any longer, and he felt he'd been held back by lack of opportunity or help at the beginning of his career so that his period of musical fertility was not much over twenty years. It's a sad story.'

'All old people feel this,' said Noelle. 'We regret missed opportunities.'

'I don't think I do,' Oliver answered. 'I think I've just about managed all I was capable of.'

'Then you were lucky.'

'Or didn't expect too much. The war took five years and a half just when I was qualified. Made a change, I suppose.'

'And you came back.'

'Yes. I even enjoyed most of it. And it taught me to put up with discomfort.'

Oliver's cheerful stoicism affected his wife so that she sat in silent, patent gloom. Outside in the kitchen Waters spoke to his host. 'I've said the wrong thing again. Often seem to these days.' He did not appear much put out. 'She was engaged to a young chap in the RAF who was killed over Hamburg. She seemed to have recovered from it. But her mind plays on it now as it never did before. Retirement's done her no good at all.'

When they returned Noelle Waters immediately asked, as if she'd prepared the question,

'Did Mr Greene think he'd wasted his life?'

'I don't know. I doubt it. I think he regretted his lack of mobility, and perhaps his sense of lost position and power. But he had his moments. He was an actor, and he liked putting on a show for you.'

'So his interest in Elgar's decline was bogus?' Oliver.

'I don't think so. He understood it for the first time, and had the leisure to think about it. For instance, he regarded Elgar's attitude to women as futile. Elgar idealized women; not so Fred Greene.'

'Are you suggesting,' Noelle sitting straight, 'that he made some sort of sexual advances to Susan?'

'I doubt it. I very much doubt it. That's not the explanation.' Why the bravado?

'I never see Susan,' Oliver intervened, 'as a sexual, er,

204

woman. She's quite pretty, she's the right shape, but she's too unyielding, buttoned up.'

'She's engaged to be married.' Job.

'And you're an old man.' Oliver wheezed with laughter at his wife's clipped, realistic reproach.

'Susan must have impressed Greene in some way,' Noelle continued.

'Piano,' Job answered. 'He was surprised that an eighteen-year-old could play so much better than he could.'

'Yes. I see. You mustn't overrate her, though, Mr Turner. Really. As I've told you, I've had many pupils just as gifted as Susan.' There was no pleasing her.

The evening was not a success, left Job jumpy and depressed, uncertain whether Oliver's laughter or his wife's dejection disturbed him more keenly. He was surprised, therefore, a day or two later to hear Noelle say on the telephone that she had thoroughly enjoyed the visit, that it had done her good. 'It is not often, Mr Turner, that I have the opportunity these days to discuss serious subjects.' Job murmured gratification. 'You see Oliver and I are in no position to do so. Not now. We gave up important topics years ago. Now we can barely discuss the trivialities of everyday life without getting on each other's nerves. We've been married forty-odd years and it's too long. We're just skating in parallel expecting the next accident. And to come to you and talk openly about Elgar's disappointment, and how wrong he was about himself, and Mr Greene's eccentricity, it did me a world of good. We could never do it at home. We'd have been at one another's throats. But you provided the background, moved us sufficiently out of ourselves to raise these matters. We're both grateful. Oliver is often down, though he tries to present himself as otherwise. But we've talked about Elgar, and Turner, a great deal in these last few days.'

'You must come again.'

'That's most kind of you, but we mustn't expect miracles every time. Perhaps round about Christmas, if we may. You're something of a magician, Mr Turner. Oh, and by the way, I've started Susan Smith on Ravel's Ondine from "Gaspard de la Nuit". That'll give her something to cope with. You see I don't think it's much good arguing with her. I do better giving her another musical obstacle to tackle. Don't you agree?'

Mrs Waters rang off almost ebulliently.

He could not help being pleased, but hesitated about taking too much of the credit to himself. Noelle felt physical improvement and that lifted her mood. He wondered about the young man in the RAF, and how long after the death it had been before she married Oliver. Why had there been no children? A conscious decision? Regretted now? He visualized the thin, intense stick of a woman and her smiling husband, compared his notion of them with what they had said of themselves. She always, in the course of her conversation, flattered him: 'I wish I had known you before, Mr Turner.' That is what she had decided he wanted to hear. He compared the buoyant voice on the telephone with the shrivelled, miserable woman who had snapped at him by his fireside.

The term ended with the school play, *Twelfth Night*, with senior and junior carol concerts, the verse-speaking and lecture competitions. The assembly halls seemed more in use than the classrooms; his staff ran round with jaunty harassed faces; he signed end-of-term reports by the hundred; the morning post filled his wastepaper basket each day with advertisements, appeals and instructions; his deputies whirled in administrative circles, attendance ratios were high in spite of bad weather and colds. The Acton School seemed giddy with activity, and all of it beyond his control. Fatigued and delighted he staggered from one extravaganza to the next minor crisis. He came, by chance, across a young woman reading from Dickens's *Christmas Carol* to sixty juniors grouped round her feet in one of the gyms; why they weren't in their classrooms he'd no idea. He skulked behind a door enjoying every word, was furious to be dragged away to the telephone by the Head of PE. Later in the day he made a point of congratulating Mrs Darling, the teacher, on her performance.

'Brilliant,' he said.

'That's Dickens, not me.' She blushed, fetchingly.

'I was very taken. And so were the audience.'

'A-streams.' She had the two forms together, she divulged, to free a colleague who needed to repair damage to the scenery for the evening's play.

'You're quite an actress yourself.'

She looked at him closely, so that he feared he'd committed a gaffe, but she said nothing. He thanked her again; she did not appear gratified now, slightly embarrassed, moving from foot to foot. On inquiry in his office he learnt that Mrs Darling had spent the two years after her postgraduate diploma in a repertory company. 'Is she happy here?' he asked. 'Who is?' from the smiling secretary. One up, one down.

Job Turner had quickly come to terms with Hilary's news, and now he and his youngest daughter wrote or telephoned once a week. He enjoyed this; before they had corresponded on birthdays and at Christmas. Gillian had been much more assiduous in keeping in touch with her family, and had been free with advice. Hilary, like mother and sisters, had much to say for herself, and had a clarity and fluency he admired. After a strenuous ten minutes with her on the phone he blamed himself for missing this pleasure for so long. Hilary had delivered Professor Sadiq to the 'chopping block' she called it, ordering him to make a phone call to her father from Pakistan. The two men had exchanged polite remarks in praise of Hilary. Both had been relieved that this first family ordeal was now over; Hilary was much amused. In her next letter she had imagined Ammy as standing 'like an errant schoolboy outside the headmaster's room'. He had said, apparently, that he wasn't sure whether Turner was pleased with him or not. 'He only talked about you,' Ammy had said. 'He praised you in his strait-laced English way.' 'I'd have guessed that,' she had told him. 'I kept up with your father in my expressions of approbation,' Ammy had laughed back. 'I should think so, too,' Gill's daughter replied. Sadiq would now be back early in January.

Life seemed agreeable in these moments.

# 20

Noelle Waters rang Turner at his school with Susan's examination results.

He had just emerged from a flying visit to a speech competition where he had heard a fourth-form boy lecture on 'television comedians', a series of amateur 'impressions' much appreciated by the audience, though lost on him, followed by a dull account from a girl in 4B on the local canals illustrated by beautifully drawn maps to which she barely drew his attention.

Baffled, he was dictating the morning's toll of letters when Noelle Waters phoned.

'I've had Susan's examination marks,' she said. He could not deduce much from the voice and waited. She was in no hurry, baiting him.

'What were they like?' In the end he was forced to speak.

'So, so.'

She paused again.

'Perhaps you would like to find a paper and pencil to make a note of the details.'

He thanked her sarcastically. She continued her play.

'Are you ready now?' Noelle made him answer before she began to dictate, slowly, repeating each number thrice, thus: twenty-nine, twenty-nine, two, nine. She questioned him from time to time on his progress in taking down these figures. He curbed his impatience. When shc gave him the final figure, two marks above distinction level, she stopped again; he could hear her breathing.

'Good,' he said, 'good. She did us well. Thank you.'

'I thought you might be, oh, slightly disappointed?' The voice curled upward.

'In what way?'

'I thought,' she broke off again, 'you might have expected a higher total.'

'Doesn't that depend a bit on the examiner? And on a strange piano. What remarks does he make?'

She appeared now to have lost the form, muttering as one searching through a heavy file. This woman was putting him in his place, enjoying herself at his expense.

'Ah, here we are. Are you ready, then? "On the whole, an accurate and musicianly performance spoilt by a slight tendency to ostentation. A first-class technique." There. What do you think?'

'The last thing I'd have said about Susan.'

'What is?'

'Ostentation. Whatever else she is or does, she doesn't show off.'

Noelle did not contradict him. He gave her on request the number of Susan's office. They talked at random for two minues.

That evening, walking in the woods, he met Mr Smith.

'Congratulations, Father,' he began jovially.

'Oh, our Susan. That's good, isn't it? A distinction?'

'Is she pleased?'

'I suppose she is. She doesn't say much, or show much.'

'You'd have been whooping it up, then, would you?'

'I never passed anything with distinction. I didn't pass much anyhow.'

They talked about daughters, and understanding. At the end of five minutes when they parted, Job Turner felt rebuffed. Smith laid down the law too discourteously for comfort.

Job was glad to reach the last day of term. He shortened the lunch hour, and dismissed the school early to prevent drunken foolery. After the final bell, members of staff called in at his office to wish him the compliments of the season. He was surprised at those who appeared. No one stayed long; he kept his door to the corridor purposely open; not a few congratulated him on a good first term. Amongst the later callers was Mrs Darling. As she was about to leave, she turned back.

'I wonder if you would like to come with me to a party tomorrow evening.' Her fair skin blushed fiercely as soon as she had spoken. 'It'll be a very quiet affair. It's at the house of some people in Mapperley; they're called Simpson and are musical. It'll be a talk-fest.'

'No party games?'

'God, no. And nobody going bananas, either.'

'Do I bring a bottle?'

'That would be a good idea.'

'Thank you very much. Yes. I'd like to. That's most kind of you.' He did not know if he acted wisely. Mrs Darling looked disconcerted, as though she had not expected him to accept. Perhaps she had done it for a bet with some other young floozie. As they arranged the time and place of meeting, his secretary appeared at one door, and two senior heads of department, a man and wife at the other. He could not remember Mrs Darling's first name. She retired, in disorder. Job sat neatly at his desk.

Alison rang that evening, saying that Geoffrey would like to call round to see him, about the Greene bequest. He came out with Susan's result, and then his daughter inquired about his first term at the Acton Comprehensive. Job reported favourably.

'I'm glad,' she said. 'Your appointment there has been a godsend.' He expressed guarded surprise. 'Oh, you men.' She fixed a time for Geoffrey to call, and rang off, extraordinarily pleased. He was in her good books; he could tell, even over the telephone. It had been so with Gillian. When he had recovered slightly from Alison's approval, he remembered that he had not informed her that he was accompanying a young married female on his staff to a party. That might have wiped the smile off her face, but then one could never be sure with his daughters.

He idled about until eleven-thirty and was about to turn in when the telephone rang again.

'Oh, Mr Turner. It's Sally Moore.'

'Hello.'

'You've not gone to bed, have you?'

'No. Just thinking about it.'

'Bertie's gone up. He drank rather a lot. But I just wanted to tell you I'm still here. With him, I mean.'

'That's good.'

'I don't know about that. But we're still together. That chat we had was helpful. It really was. The best thing was it made me think what he was like when I first knew him. He helped me out no end, then. I thought he was marvellous. I suppose he was.'

'Would you like to come round again? In the holiday? Unless you're going away?'

'I'm not sure he'd like it.'

'Then I'll invite you both.'

'We'll see. We'll leave it for the moment, if you don't mind. At least we've got that long term over. But thanks once again.'

'Will you contact me?' he asked.

'I don't know. Let's see how things shape, shall we?'

Mrs Moore rang off, still murmuring thanks.

Next morning he rose at an ungodly hour, breakfasted and cleared up at his brisk, working-day pace, then pottered around with a vacuum cleaner. Mild weather with rain clouds darkened his windows. Thoughts of the evening party troubled him slightly, so that he grumbled out loud to himself. He would much prefer to stay in and read, or play the piano, or listen to music. At eleven Alison telephoned from her office to say that Hilary had decided to make a brief appearance in Beechnall on the Saturday and Sunday before Christmas, and that, therefore, he was to see to it that (i) he was clear to come over to lunch on the Sunday and that (ii) he had his Christmas presents for 'the London end' all packed and ready so that they could be loaded into the back of Hilly's car. He touched his forelock, and confessed about the party. Alison had laughed.

'Dirty old man, eh? Well, watch it. You're at a dangerous age. Who is the lady?'

'Linda Darling.' Alison gasped again. He had looked the girl up. BA Hons II, i, English and Drama, Bristol University.

'How old?'

'Twenty-seven.'

'H'm. Born between Phyl and Hilly. Well, come on, let's hear all about it.'

'There's nothing to hear. I've hardly spoken to her, just once to congratulate her on a class. I was utterly taken aback when she invited me out.'

'Ah, these scheming women.' Alison did not look on it seriously. She inquired about the venue, said she did not know the Simpsons, told him to enjoy himself.

'She's married, been married,' he ventured.

'And where's Mr Darling?'

'I've no idea.'

'The plot thickens. I don't handle divorce, but our Jon Tilney's very good. He'll sort you out.' She rattled on, pleased with the interlude. He asked her what he should wear. 'A suit, plain shirt and tie. None of your pullovers. You're fifty-seven years old, Joby, so nobody's going to approve of mutton dressed as lamb. And if a suit's unsuitable, then you're at the wrong sort of party. Run away at once, Darling or no Darling. I shall expect a full report when Geoffrey comes up to see you on Friday. My word, we are beginning to see life. That nice light grey thing with the red stripe is ideal.' She dropped the phone, still excitable, but assured.

After lunch he walked the woods for two hours keeping to the paths. He spoke to a man with a fox on a leash who drew back into the wet bracken to let him pass.

'Is it tame?' Job asked.

'Wi'th' family. Not wi' nob'dy else.'

He looked up on a street map Mrs Darling's flat and the Simpsons' avenue. When he arrived at the girl's home, she said she wasn't quite ready, and seated him in a small, warm room. Piles of books towered from the floor in an otherwise spick and span place.

'My first job,' she indicated the spaces either side of the chimney breast, 'this holiday, is to put up bookshelves.' She disappeared to the bathroom. 'Find yourself something to read. I shan't be long, but then again we don't want to be too early, do we?'

When she swept back into the room, her perfume pungent, she subsided opposite him.

212

'I hate to be the first there,' she said. 'We'll hang about, if you don't mind, for a few minutes.'

'Tell me about the people whose party it is.'

'The Simpsons. Yuppies, but nice. He's an architect; she runs a play-group. They're interested in drama, that's how I met them.'

After five minutes' practice she seemed less nervous, talked freely about her theatre club, the city, the school. She was dressed in a multicoloured dress, sewn in patterns of bright autumn leaves, which both suited her and yet was over-emphatic. Smaller than he remembered, she seemed bent on display, perhaps as a result of her histrionic training. A quarter of an hour later, he had refused a drink, she gave the word to leave.

'Are we going in your car or mine?' she asked.

'Mine's out there in the street.'

'I hardly touch alcohol, if you think that's an advantage.'

'I'll be sober myself, I promise.'

Without hurry she pulled on a dark blue coat which set off her fair hair, and flourished a bottle of wine still wrapped in tissue paper from the beer-off.

'We have to be careful round here,' she said, looking up. 'All sorts of strangers just walk up trying the doors.'

'Have you been burgled?'

'Not so far. It's a bit frightening, though, for single women.'

She made no attempt to impress him, spoke cautiously, even fumblingly again. Perhaps she regretted her invitation now. A striking young woman had invited her boss, a hundred-year-old autocrat, to escort her. He held the car door open.

They were by no means early on arrival. The host and hostess informed Linda that they thought she had forgotten. Mrs Darling introduced her guest as 'Job Turner, my head-master, so be careful.' They all laughed as their coats and bottles were collected. The hostess called him, he noticed, 'Mr Turner' as she provided him with a glass of warmish punch and an instruction to circulate.

The party seemed sedate, if noisily conversational, and middle aged. No music played, loud or subdued. The first group to whom Mrs Darling introduced him were being entertained by a small, moustachio'd man with an account of an audition he had recently suffered. Try as he might, Job could not determine either play or part. ' "I want you to read it as if it were written in some difficult, outlandish foreign language, Finnish or Estonian, which . . . " "So nobody will understand it, you mean?" I said. He had the grace to laugh, I'll give him that.' So had they all. The little man enjoyed his moment.

At one stage Job was backed into a corner by a balding conservationist who laid down the law about the iniquity of building across designated green belts. His thin face grew mottled with anger as if Job were responsible. On another occasion three furies canvassed his views on equal pay for women. They harangued and badgered him hard until Linda Darling appeared, introduced him as her headmaster, when they fell suddenly, unduly silent. 'They all teach at Bernard Brooks,' she explained later. 'Funny lot. They'll come back at you before the night's out. You see.' They did. Linda did not stay with him, but appeared at his shoulder from time to time like a good teacher making sure he knew what he was doing, did not venture too far out of his depth. Her acquaintance was wide; people listened to her with respect. She once quoted part of a poem he did not recognize:

> 'Did she in touching that lone wing
> Recall the years before her mind
> Became a bitter, an abstract thing,
> Her thought some popular enmity:
> Blind and leader of the blind
> Drinking the foul ditch where they lie?'

They were discussing some woman who, vociferous for good causes, showed affection only for her terrier. Talk had been malicious, but as soon as Linda began her quotation the whole emphasis of conversation, the room, his world changed for Job Turner. The others stood silent; one man closed his

214

eyes; it reminded Job of the prayer meetings of his youth. Linda laid a hand on his arm as she moved away.

'Yeats,' she said, answering his unasked question.

Her voice had returned to normality in the one word. While she recited she had called on other resources of timbre, he could not tell how. She had not spoken more loudly; other groups had continued with their chatter, but this five or six here only had been silenced, bound by the powerful lariat of words. It had been worth coming for that minute; Job, escort of the magician, stuck out his chest.

Just before ten they were wheeled into the bright kitchen where hot savoury rolls and samosas were on display with bowls of salad, roasted potatoes in the skins, pickles. Each guest was issued with a huge china plate and an instruction: We don't want any of this left. Linda Darling had led Job to the table.

'You haven't got much there,' she chided him. Her own plate was piled full. She ate with relish.

Job, truthfully saying how much he was enjoying himself, had barely taken his second forkful when a woman interrupted them by placing herself straight in front of them not a yard's distance away. She made a kind of bob or beck of apology towards Linda.

'Mr Turner.' Job looked her over. She was slim, thin-haired, pale, but the contents of her plate matched Linda's in plenitude.

'Mr Turner,' she continued. 'They tell me you're a pianist. Well, I've brought my harp to this party.'

'Angela Rees-Davies,' Linda elucidated. Job recognized her now; she led the Harmonic Orchestra, the Midlands Sinfonietta, the Bach Society, the Linden Players.

'Jenny Simpson said you'd accompany me. It's a violin, actually. My harp. Would you?' Linda was blushing again, the source of information.

'Depends what you're doing.'

'Nothing out of the way. That Kreisler–Pugnani Praeludium and Allegro. And a Handel sonata. A major. You'll have all of two minutes to look them over.' On Job's agreement Angela lifted her plate. 'First things first,' she said. 'I'll fiddle my way though this, and come and collect you. By the way the Rioja's going down it won't much matter what notes we play.'

She had gone.

'Did you not know her?' Linda asked.

'I've seen her often enough. At concerts. I've never actually met her.'

Angela Rees-Davies returned after the serving of fresh fruit salad, Black Forest gâteau and coffee when she, Mrs Simpson and Linda led Turner to a small room upstairs. Angela tuned; the other two women talked about an outing to Stratford. On the first chord of the Praeludium Turner knew real refreshment, as the sound of the violin ricocheted from the walls in the confined room. He concentrated, forgot all to match the soloist's breadth of tone.

'Perfect,' Angela said. 'You'll enjoy the drawing-room piano much more than this. Bigger altogether. Let's nip through Handel.' They performed as soon as they appeared downstairs, were applauded, almost coarsely called back to an encore. People pushed to congratulate Job. The party grew noisier; wine glasses were held high. Turner found himself describing a silver effect in the sky often observed, he pontificated, among rain clouds on windy days in November. The music had made a large man of him. He restricted himself to one glass of wine, but heard himself claiming, Linda at his elbow, that 'silver' was unarguably the most beautiful word in the English language. Other choices were excitably canvassed; one pedant opined that it needed the wealthier 'gold' to bring out silver's full 'richesse'.

'And see the gold air and the silver fade
And the last bird fly into the last night.'

Linda silenced them all again with her lines. The Delphic oracle had no more reverent auditors. Job Turner rustled up his common sense. 'There is a perjorative connotation. Thirty pieces of silver.' He felt inordinately pleased with himself. He'd be a credit to Alison and her mother.

He listened with pleasurable absorption to arguments about

216

feminist novels, the date of an election, the reasons for frequent misprints in newspapers. The merits of the local schools were discussed, aged parents, investments, SDI, AIDS, Opera North, 'The Blind Watchmaker', expensive cars. One of the Bernard Brooks trio spoke knowledgeably and hoarsely about schizophrenia; not long after midnight the party began to break up. Turner, by no means fatigued, inquired from Linda Darling whether she was ready for home. She consulted her small gold watch.

'I suppose we'd better. I've got my Christmas shopping to start tomorrow morning.'

They collected coats, thanked host and hostess, shook hands with the few still voluble guests.

Outside they felt the cold immediately, like a toothache. Cars still skimmed the back streets.

'I've not enjoyed myself so much for years,' Job told her once they were on the way.

'I'm glad I asked you, then.'

'We used to give parties when my wife was alive.'

'Not now?'

'I live in a shoebox.' He explained about his house, and the grand piano, and Oak Villa. She sat quietly huddled in her coat so that he thought she might be asleep. When she decided that he had had his turn, she offered in exchange that she was going to stay with a sister over Christmas, and this meant clearing up the shopping in the next two days.

'Give me a ring when you're back,' he said, on the pavement outside her flat.

'Is it too late for you to come up for a cup of coffee?' she asked.

'It is, I think.' He had given the right answer. She bobbed forward and kissed him, on the lips, but sisterly, then dodged indoors, unringed left hand twinkling. Job Turner sat for a minute in his car until the light came on in her flat. He had spoken the truth when he had said he had enjoyed himself, but was surprised that he had not known any of the twenty or so people at the party. They were his sort of folk, careful readers of the newspapers, prepared to hear Handel violin sonatas as a means of pleasure, and yet with the exception of

217

Angela Rees-Davies he had not seen one of them before, at concerts, the theatre, the university, charitable functions, or on the streets.

That, he supposed, meant little. He lived a restricted social life. But his own powers of observation were to blame, had atrophied. Until he had come by chance across the Scale I teacher's reading of *A Christmas Carol* he had known nothing of Linda Darling, a member of his staff, a superior woman who could quote poetry without embarrassment and walk into a room like a tragedy queen. Job shook his head. Now Mrs Darling had invited him out, and he . . . It was too late to make firm commitments, but he felt pleased with himself, as if he'd won a small prize in a local raffle.

By the time Geoffrey Greene came round at the weekend Job had dispatched his Christmas cards, bought and wrapped up the remainder of his presents.

'Don't boast,' Geoffrey advised. 'You're certain to have more from people you've not sent to.'

The son-in-law sat massively in his armchair, smiling, huge, benevolent, at ease, as unlike his father as could be.

'Has your Susan Smith made her mind up about these lessons yet?' he inquired.

'I've hardly seen her this last week or two. We've been neglecting each other since her exam. But now she's had the result, we'll have to make her mind up for her. I shall see her on Tuesday.'

'Did she do well?'

'Distinction.'

'That's good. It will encourage her. From what Alison said, the girl seemed to be blowing hot and cold about going on. Is that so? There's no time limit to the bequest, but the money might run out if she leaves it too long. I'll invest it as profitably as I can, but . . .' He spread his hands. 'If you think it will do any good, I'll see her down at George Square.'

'She won't be frightened by the inside of a solicitor's office, that's for sure.'

'I've no intention of frightening anybody. Just explaining. Making it absolutely clear. But it's only a suggestion. You talk to her on Tuesday, and I'll do my bit if it's necessary.'

Job liked Geoffrey, his large frame, his modest assurance, intelligence, sobriety, dress sense. The son-in-law inquired about progress at the Acton Comprehensive. Turner gave an unflattering assessment.

'We're pleased about that,' Geoffrey answered, considering, wiping his chin. 'Alison especially. We saw Ferguson, the education officer, the other night, he and his wife are clients of mine, and he was full of praise. "Job Turner doesn't court trouble. He'll face it if it comes, but he doesn't go out looking for it." Alison was delighted.'

'Good.'

'She was worried about you, you know.' Geoffrey spoke with extreme diffidence. 'After Gillian was killed. "Daddy doesn't say anything. He just puts up with it all, and it can't be good for him." That's why she pressed you to change houses. She thought this place wasn't altogether suitable, but it was there, it presented itself, and it winkled you out of Oak Villa. She thought the removal would give you something to occupy yourself with.' He laughed quietly. 'She also thought you'd be out again before very long. She was so worried.'

Job nodded.

'She was afraid you might not manage without Gillian. We discussed it, time without number. "Don't be misled by his appearance," she'd tell me. "Because he looks calm and collected, that doesn't mean he is. He adored that woman, depended on her." '

'That's true.' Geoffrey had never spoken as openly as this to him. Job did not resent it.

' "He didn't realize, either, how much she admired him. I've seen her listening to him playing the piano and her eyes shone." That's the way Ally talks of you. Makes me feel a bit inadequate sometimes, when she's summing me up.'

'She's very like her mother.'

'I'm sure. She knows it. "We all had music lessons," she says, "but we all turned in the end to the dry dust of the law, and the probabilities of maths and sciences. Mother's girls".'

'There was nothing dry about Gillian.'

'You don't need to tell me. She smartened me up with a few questions when Ally first brought me to Oak Villa. We were much of an age. Well, she'd be about seven years my senior. But she wasn't letting me get away with her ewe-lamb without a struggle. I used to pull her leg, you know. "Alison's marrying me, not the other way about," I'd say. "I'd be ashamed to admit it," she'd answer. I loved talking to Gill and I love talking about her.'

Job Turner sat, moved, near tears, uplifted. Opposite, Geoffrey Greene, huge and still as a temple Buddha, spoke in seriousness as if proximity, this small room, the dim lights, the warmth gave him leave to be quietly frank.

'Ally thought it would be the end of you. "He'll wither".'

'She didn't tell me.'

'Of course she didn't. And like all balanced people she's just that little bit afraid of her father. So she advised you about conveyancing and storing furniture and letting Oak Villa and invited you to Sunday lunch. As solicitors we often have to give advice people don't want to hear. They want to follow certain courses because these touch an emotional strain or chord in them. They'd sooner lose sometimes, than not try. And we have to talk them out of it.'

'Do you succeed?'

'Not always. No. They sometimes go off and consult somebody else. But the reason I'm telling you this roundabout rigmarole is that we try to argue them out of it by reference to the strength of their case in law. That's why they pay us. But it's oblique in my eyes, because they are acting in the way they are on account of some emotional urge, based not on justice, not even on money, and God knows that's got plenty of clout with most of my clients, but in some trauma that has nothing to do with the business in hand. I'm no psychologist, but when I've pointed out with all the force I can that they have no chance to recover, that they'll just be wasting their money and my time, they don't seem able to accept it. "Go home and talk it over with your wife, your husband, for a day or two," we say, or "I'm not really prepared to do this for you, because I'm so convinced we'll get nowhere," you can see them rage or stagger or add another wound to their vulnerability because we, the friends, the trusted advisers, have betrayed them. They are incapable of accepting plain common sense. In the same way Ally talks to you about selling houses, because she can't bring herself to voice her fears, or make or watch you face your problem head on.'

'I think I take the point.'

'The parallels aren't exact. It's the emotional element. In plain words your daughter loves you even when she's pushing you into something you don't want or criticizing you for your shortcomings.'

'Yes.' Job felt reassured.

'Not that she thought Gillian was perfect,' Geoffrey continued, voice deep, bland. Job had never known him so open. The shyness had gone. 'Or you, for that matter. "He let Gill get away with too much," she says, "because he felt guilty, because he thought he and marriage and family life had prevented her from achieving her full potential. He should have laid down the law more often. Or lost his temper".'

'Is that right?' Job, genial.

'Moderately so. My father barely concealed his contempt for my mother. Nor did she appear to notice. And yet he depended on her a great deal.'

'Did he know that?' Job asked.

'To some extent. Though he never allowed it to influence him very much. He chased after his investments and women. And did so to the day of his death.'

'Didn't your mother mind?'

'I expect so. She resented it and got used to it. Presumably she decided that her status as wife and mother was better than the alternative. She had me.'

'She didn't try to set you against your father?'

'She didn't need to. I was there already. In fact she calmed me down from moment to moment.'

'You weren't afraid of your father, then?'

'Terrified, at one time. He had a very short fuse. But then I came to realize that I was more useful to him than he to me. He could have cut me out of his will, and that would have been a nasty reprisal, I admit, but even so, I could earn my own living.'

'Did he threaten to disinherit you?'

'To give him credit, he didn't. Even after the upset of my mother's testamentary high jinks. But he wasn't a generous man. That's why this bequest to Susan Smith surprises me. It's a bit out of character.'

'Was it sexual attraction?'

'One thing you soon learn in my trade is how many forms sexual attraction assumes. So I don't know. Did she make any advances, would you say? Is she that sort of girl?'

'I shouldn't think so.' Job could not be honest about Susan yet.

'Alison was a bit troubled about you and the girl, you know. When you first started giving her lessons. You talked about her a good deal. Too much so, according to Ally. She thought you were so lonely, so wrapped up in your loss, that your judgement had gone, and you were investing your all in a dubious enterprise. "Nobody can be as good as he thinks she is," she'd say. "Not even a female Mozart." I don't think she saw the danger as sexual; it was rather that you'd either demand too much of the girl and drive her round the twist, or become steadily disappointed in the way she developed. "He's obsessed," she said. "He's bound to come a cropper." So she was delighted when Bruce Ferguson pushed you into the new job. "It's just what he needs. He's competitive for all he says. And it will occupy him properly. Take his mind off one fallible pair of hands." '

'She never said anything of this to me.'

'No. We'd often discuss it, though, at home. "Go and tell him," I'd say, but no, she couldn't, wouldn't. "He's a grown man," she'd begin, and then shake her head. In our trade the number of grown, settled, mature, integrated men who make utter bloody fools of themselves in all sorts of ways is legion. As she well knows.'

'Are you included?' Job asked.

'I lack your drive. I bumble about. And I have a young wife and children. And the awful example of my late, lamented father. I'm too easily satisfied.'

'Will Alison mind your telling all this to me?'

'No. I think not. She loses her wool with me sometimes, but she does think that arguing a case out is the best way of proceeding. I don't think it's altogether her legal training, either. It's this basic assumption that the more you know about a matter, the better able you are to make up your mind.'

'Do I detect some reservation on your part?' Job, enjoying himself.

'Yes. Sometimes you can't get to the bottom, to the necessary information. Human beings are not simple; complexity tangles with complexity. I could never make out, for example, what drove my father. He was a good lawyer, and he amassed a great deal of money outside his legal practice. His father wasn't poor either. They loved lucre. Even at the end of his life, when he'd nothing to do but play the piano, he'd study the financial pages and the property market. He'd less energy by that time, of course. He was a bit of a dervish as a younger man, I guess. In the last year of his life he was conducting an affair with Mrs Harper, his home help. You knew that?'

'Yes. He told me.'

'He would. He left her five hundred pounds for faithful service. And to put her in her place.'

'Alison, you know, suggested that I took Mrs Harper as a cleaning woman.'

Geoffrey pulled a comically lugubrious face.

'Did she now? And that reminds me. Alison said I was to inquire how you got on with the young lady from your staff who took you to a party.'

Job gave a brief, guarded account, and then answered a few questions.

'Did Alison approve?' Turner asked when his son-in-law had finished.

'She doesn't want you to do anything silly, she says.'

'Does she think that likely?'

'Not exactly, but she was, is greatly worried. Gillian's death. You all on your own. This stiff upper lip of yours. She thinks something will give or blow up somewhere.'

'Do you?'

Geoffrey Greene stroked his chin, this time with stiffened fingers.

'Since you put me on the spot, yes. It's a possibility. I've

223

seen it happen. On the surface you're a sensible, intelligent, self-contained man, but . . . But. That's why Ally hopes this new job at Acton Comprehensive will keep you so occupied that you won't have time, energy or inclination to do anything daft.'

They stared at each other. Though Geoffrey repeated what he had already said, the reiteration set a constraint between them. The son-in-law saw this at once, smiled, rubbed his hands together and said,

'Tell me something. This Linda Darling of yours. What's the most attractive thing about her?'

'Oh, well.' Job acted genial doubt. 'One thing comes to mind. She quotes poetry in public without any embarrass-ment.' He frowned. 'I've missed out on poetry. We learnt some at school, read some for exams. "Sohrab and Rustum", "Adonais", "The Deserted Village" and so on in an anthology for School Cert. And always we were asked to set four lines or so for musical examinations. For voice and string quartet; for four-part choir, SATB; for baritone with piano accompani-ment. I was interested, tried to make out what was being said, meant, or felt, but they were crumbs, bits and pieces.'

'You could have gone and looked them up,' Geoffrey chided.

'I could, but I didn't.'

'And now you've found a lady concordance who'll serve you with quotations. You do like her?'

'I hardly know her.' Job glibly purveyed an account of the Dickens reading.

'And you enjoyed the party, her company?'

'Thoroughly.'

They watched each other, as in a court room.

'Oh, come on, man. Are you going to see her again?' The *bonhomie* did not sit easily on Geoffrey. 'I have to ask you,' he said, more normally. 'Alison's bound to quiz me.'

'She's away over Christmas. I invited her to telephone me when she returns. That's where it stands.'

'Alison says you're to bring her up to see us, if you want to.'

'I'll think about it.' Job sat as uncomfortably as an

224

adolescent. 'She seems an interesting girl, has been married before, but I don't know anything about it. I don't know why she invited me to the Simpsons' party. It may well have been a joke or a dare amongst these young women on my staff. She expected me to refuse, and then was lumbered with me. But you're the expert on the wiles of the younger female.'

'In my case Ally made it quite clear what she wanted, and what I should do. I don't quite know how, looking back, but I was in no doubt at the time. But I'll say this for myself, because nobody will say it for me, I wasn't afraid of intelligence or a forceful temperament.'

'Or beauty.'

'Well said, Father.'

They laughed, self-consciously, but talked on, knowing enough had been broached for one evening. In the end Geoffrey shouldered his overcoat, and the men stood in cold darkness outside, listening to the wind flicking twigs high in the wood.

Job Turner, back indoors, washed the coffee cups.

He stood at the sink, sad and confident. He deliberately recalled the cruel news of the death of Gillian, the scarifying loneliness, day-long delirium, the shuddering, shouting unbelief that it could have happened to him, the first frequent breakdowns into tears, hammering of fists on his bed as he knelt not in prayer but in a mad wrestling match to master himself and his grief, but now it was as if it had happened to someone else. Still he missed Gillian; still even in his lodge which she, to the best of his knowledge, had never seen, he half expected her to open the front door, to breeze in with baskets and carriers of shopping or some titbit of scandal or point to be put and argued. He grudged her death, the waste, but had after two, three years made a truce with the knowledge. He feared that illness, defeat, depression, age might disinter his sorrow, with intensity again, and he be left defenceless, but he managed each day at a time without his jewel.

Geoffrey's sentences had steadied him. He felt Alison behind the lawyer's shy, deep words, but she had sent her husband with the message, not delivered it herself. That

225

cheered Job. Some place was left for him, some purpose. His daughters loved him; he had loved Gillian, and loved her to this minute.

He dried his hands on the tea towel, stepped outside his front door once again to listen to the thrash of twigs in the darkness above his head. Tears prickled, wetted his cheeks, dripped. He wept in silence, not far from happiness.

# 21

Next day Job Turner stocked his freezer, bought a small Christmas tree, practised on Frederick Greene's grand and waited for Susan Smith.

The girl arrived on time complaining about the cold. While she warmed her hands, he asked what she thought about her examination result, and she replied dully, evasively, with a crooked smile. She had looked up, she said, 'ostentation' in the dictionary, but she and her father had concluded that all recitals were a form of showing off.

'You didn't think it fair, then?' Job asked.

'I didn't throw my head and hands about like some of them.'

'The word surprised me, but at least he gave you a distinction.'

'Just about. I didn't much like the piano. But I didn't play too many wrong notes. My dad calls me "swankpot" now.'

'But he's pleased?'

'Very likely.'

Job looked at her kneeling on the hearth rug in front of the coke fire. He had just finished speaking to his daughter, Hilary, on the telephone; they wrote or rang once a week now. She said she missed Ammy, but worked such long hours that she just about managed to tumble into bed at night and slept immediately. She used Saturday afternoon to shop and Sunday morning to clean; he was lucky to catch her in this evening, but she'd come to a decent halting-place in her work, and was writing a long letter in reply to the one of Ammy's that had arrived this morning.

'Does he write a good letter?'

'Marvellous. He's very, oh, alive. And knows all the questions I want answering. I might be there with him. He writes to me half an hour every day and sends it off every fourth.

That's just like him. Very methodical, knows exactly what he's about. Sits down to his desk exactly on time. But his letters are so colourful and vivid, with so many twists and turns and imaginative curlicues, it's quite fantastic. You don't know what to expect next. They say his mathematical work's like that, from what I can make out, full of leaps and bold advances. Not that I understand it very well.'

'And is he similar in real life?'

'I suppose he is, when you get to know him. Witty and tumbling over himself. You'll find him rather quiet, a bit like Geoff for a start. Old-fashioned. A gentleman.'

'And underneath there's all this mathematical activity boiling up.'

'And verbal.'

'You're lucky.'

He inquired what he should buy Ammy for a Christmas present. She suggested ties and handkerchiefs and said she'd choose them for him, then there'd be no mistakes.

'You're just like your mother.'

'And isn't that a compliment?'

The ten minutes of conversation had left him so cheerful that he was prepared to argue optimistically with Susan whatever her obstinacy. The girl now stood, sufficiently warmed, ready to move towards the piano.

'Before we start, Susan,' he said. His jaw had tightened; he did not usually call her by name. She looked up rather sheepishly, mulishly, but without apprehension or misgiving. 'My son-in-law spoke to me yesterday about Mr Greene's bequest to you.'

Briefly he set out the position. She listened, upright, left thumb tucked into the top of her jeans. 'He thinks you should begin now in case the money runs out.' Job added explanatory sentences to put off her reply rather than to enlighten her. Her face, pale enough, pasty, had something of her father's about it, slightly jowled, obstinate, on the lookout for trouble. She was licking her lips. Neither was in a hurry. Susan waved an arm, an unintelligible signal.

'I've some news for you,' she said.

'Good or bad?'

'Good. Douglas and I have decided to get married in January.' She stood proud.

'Congratulations. Well done. Why the change of plan?' He must acquiesce in cheerfulness.

'He's got the house now. We can move in next month. It seemed silly just to hang about with no good reason. And, besides, we can put Mr Greene's piano in.'

'It's good news, it really is. I'm delighted for you.' He bent forward to kiss her; she put her arms round him. 'This calls for a glass of sherry.' He kissed her again, and she released him. 'Sit down while I search for the glasses.'

They faced each other schooners in hand, his dry, hers sweet, ready to lift them.

'Congratulations. Here's to a long and happy marriage.' They drank.

'Douglas says I must start straight away on my diploma.'

'Is that so? What he says goes, does it?'

'He realizes how much of my time it will take up, every day when we get back from work, and at the weekend. Or at least he says he does.'

'And he's prepared to put up with it?'

'He'll bring work home, he says. And do shopping and the dusting.'

They sipped again, formally, half raising glasses in a second toast.

'When do I get to see this young man?'

'Tonight.' She smiled, as one in control. 'He's coming to pick me up at nine o'clock. He's staying the night up at the Hall with us.'

'Are your parents pleased?'

'Um. So they say. My dad doesn't make much of a song and dance about such women's things.'

They moved to the piano. She explained that Noelle Waters had presented her with an old German book of Mendelssohn pieces and told her to prepare the Andante and Rondo Capriccioso, Op. 14, on her own, without instruction. 'You've got to learn to play things for yourself.'

'How long have you had on it?'

'A week.'

'And you're still doing the Ravel?'

Susan sighed, laughed, said it was so, ruefully, pulled a sour face.

'Mendelssohn, then.'

'What's that German mean?' she asked, delaying.

'Appeared in print at the latest in 1833,' he translated. 'How old was he?'

'I've no idea.' She shook her head.

'Born 1809.' Susan did the arithmetic. 'Away you go, then.'

She played with great dignity, and aplomb, the andante cantabile, while the presto danced sharp, swinging with rhythmical bite. She corrected her mistakes immediately, ended with brilliance.

'That was a good week's work,' he admitted.

'I like it,' she said. 'But I might, just, might,' she spoke each word slowly, mischievously, before rattling on to the end of the sentence, 'get fed up with it, so I thought I'd master it first.'

They both laughed. He took her through some bars again, to the profit of both.

'You need another week or two,' Job said. 'I think it'll be worth it. But you were very good.'

He lifted the book from the stand, found the Fugue from the Characterstücke, Op. 7.

'Let's have a bit of counterpoint,' he ordered.

'You need a German dictionary with every piece in this book,' she said.

'Ernst, und mit steigender Lebhaftigkeit. Serious and with mounting liveliness. Just like you and your life.'

She slapped his knee as he sat by her, and began the Fugue.

Susan did not find too many difficulties, but they were discussing the structure of a passage when the doorbell rang.

'Life interrupting art,' he said, rising. She sat at the keyboard and started to play again demonstrating independence. She could hear Job Turner talking to Douglas outside, but continued at the keyboard until they entered the room. Then she stopped in mid-bar. 'We've introduced ourselves,' Job said.

Douglas Middleton sat, on invitation, in one of the big

chairs. Susan perched by him on the arm proprietorially. When Job offered the couple sherry, they refused, opting for coffee. Douglas had looked to Susan for the lead.

Job lifted his cup, wishing them a long and happy life together. While he had been in the kitchen he had heard them whispering seriously, but could not make a word out. On his return the conspirators fell quiet.

Douglas looked clean, and thin, and nervous, scattered a biscuit crumb or two. He spoke rather slowly, with a northern burr, but very precisely. As he sat, his kneecaps poked sharply into his tightly pulled up grey trousers, and his hands and wrists protruded to abnormal length from the sleeve of his unbuttoned anorak. His mousy hair was short, parted, school-boyish and he wore gold-rimmed glasses.

They thanked him and Susan cheekily asked if he were going to offer them any advice. 'Everybody else does.'

'I don't know whether I'm qualified.'

'How long were you married?' Douglas asked, surprisingly.

'Almost thirty years when my wife was killed.' He'd come out with it, that last word, unthinking.

'Did you ever quarrel?'

'Yes. Sometimes. Though the quarrels were indicative of something else. If I was troubled about my work I'd be more likely to take umbrage at home. But you learnt to be on the lookout for that.'

'Do your parents have rows?' she asked Douglas, suddenly swooping on him.

'They must do. But they keep it away from me. In any case, my father's pretty easy-going.'

'Your mother's got a paddy,' Susan said.

'She soon tells us if anything's wrong, that's true.'

'I did as I was told.' Job, smiling.

'I don't believe that, Mr Turner.' Susan now. 'If any man knows his mind it's you.'

'I know my mind in one or two small fields. Otherwise I'm a reed shaken by the wind. And in the home, it's proper that the wife is the initiator.'

'We shall both be at work.' Susan.

'I'm not saying that the husband should do nothing about

231

the house. But even when my wife was out working she'd establish herself in a commanding position. Of course, I was only too willing to play second fiddle at cooking, present-buying, letter-writing. My wife was very energetic.'

'Where did she work, Mr Turner?' Douglas keeping his social end up.

'At the university. She was a lecturer in the education department. She'd been a biology teacher.'

'And your daughters followed her? In their careers?'

'Well, Phyllis is a doctor, and Hilary a biochemist, so, yes. Alison, the eldest, is a solicitor, like you. I think you've met her.'

'No, but I've seen her husband at Law Society meetings and so on.'

'One fixes a pattern, before long, in a marriage. I spent a lot of time away with choirs, perhaps unfairly, but it made my name known. These mutual arrangements don't always work out. How can they? Snags crop up, interests clash.' Job Turner felt he had said enough; these words were useless except insofar as they stressed the formal enjoyment of this celebration. 'When Gillian died,' he concluded. 'I was a lost man.'

The faces of the young people fell. Both stared at the carpet.

'She had made herself indispensable to me. Not in cutting sandwiches or polishing sideboards or organizing holidays. I needed her there, with her body, her ideas, her criticisms, her comfort. We needn't be saying anything. We might be working away in different rooms, but I knew she was about, that before too long we'd be having coffee together, and she'd come out with something interesting, or put her arms round me, or smarten me up. She was a remarkable woman. I was lucky.'

'Was she a musician, Mr Turner?' Douglas.

'No, not really. Interested. This view that married couples must always have identical interests is nothing like right, in my view.'

'That's good,' Susan's bright voice. 'Douglas is tone-deaf.'

'I don't believe it.'

232

They laughed, the three of them, as if some anxiety had been lifted.

'You think we're wise, then, to marry straight away?'

'Yes. As far as I can judge. You're both going to be working hard; you'll be establishing your place in the firm, and Susan'll be practising. You'll support each other. You won't be starting a family.'

'Is that a drawback?' Susan now.

'I speak as one who thinks, mark that word, that he enjoyed every moment with his children. But they're a tie, especially to a teenager.'

Susan blushed, mouth thin, as if he'd spoken out of turn.

'The younger you have your children, the sooner they're off your hands, and you're free.'

'I think freedom when you're young is preferable. You haven't the money or the opportunities that financial security brings, but you've energy, and, uh, enthusiasm, flexibility.'

'Besides you might have a dozen.' Douglas beaming at his pleasantry.

'You can put that idea right out of your head.' With her father's glum voice.

They talked, affably, for half an hour. Douglas made a favourable impression. He was shy, but he knew his mind, for instance, about house purchase, and could put his views with a forcible politeness. Turner was not surprised that Gerald Frogmore, the principal of his firm, thought highly of him. Douglas guessed he might take over the firm's court work in due time. He saw the disadvantages, but said he'd like a shot at it. Life seemed good.

When Susan thought it was time to be going, Job suggested that she should play the Mendelssohn to her fiancé. 'On Mr Greene's piano.' They moved into the next small room, and the two men, pressed into the wall, battered by the sound, watching her flying hands.

'I like that.' Douglas.

'Some silly mistakes.' Susan ignored her young man, spoke to Turner. 'It's like a battle with this piano.'

'You won, though.'

Job congratulated them again; Douglas thanked him for all

he was doing for Susan; Susan smiled. She seemed gracious, adult, modest, at ease, mistress of ceremonies. Turner had never known her in that mood before. Almost regal, stately, slightly distant, she was no longer an eighteen-year-old. Perhaps thoughts of marriage or the Mendelssohn had changed her.

Job Turner accompanied them to the door.

There a further transformation took place. The young couple linked arms on the path, and laughed out loud. He accompanied them to the garden gate, and listened to them as they turned right along the lane. They had not travelled thirty yards when they began to run. Like children escaping from school they chased hard for no good reason. They had forgotten him.

Job looked at bare trees, ear cocked still to the runners.

Ten o'clock, within a minute. He went inside, locking up, to the television news, the great outside world.

When two days later he described the young people's running to Alison, who had taken a day off from work to complete her Christmas shopping and visit her father, she seemed delighted.

'Goodness, I wish I'd that sort of energy.'

'You have.'

'I have not. The au pair rolled in last night at three from a party, and she's up this morning none the worse for it, still mangling the English language, arguing with nanny, and cooking herself a full English breakfast.'

'Is that good?'

'The girl's a fool, but I envy her.'

Job Turner had received that morning an invitation from Angela Rees-Davies to play the Beethoven 'Spring' Sonata with her in Retford in January, and a card with berries and robins and an accompanying note from Linda Darling. She had one more day of shopping, hair-restoring and house cleaning before she set off for her sister's and chaos. On her return she'd ring him; she'd need to after all the din and disobedience. She scribbled her hurried love. Under the four lines of Christmas jingle on the card, already apologized for, she had written, 'I don't think you should set this to music

234

or you'll end up another John Bacchus Dykes, "catspawed by an indolent poem" (Geoffrey Hill's "Fantasia on Horbury"). All my love, Linda.' She impressed him, this woman. She commanded, like Gillian, regions of knowledge barred to him. It attracted. He could not deny it.

Alison was now describing her Christmas arrangements. All was cut and dried, even attendance at midnight mass, Anglican for them, Catholic for the au pair. His daughter delighted in arranging the world to her will.

'I'm glad Hilary decided to come up. She works too hard, that girl,' he said.

Alison began to reminisce steadily about her sister, and how she had lived at one time with a research student who had taken to drugs. Hilly had done her best to drag him back; he was clever, on a postdoctoral studentship at her college, and she had been desolated when she saw finally she could help him no longer, would have to drop him if her own career was not to suffer.

'It half killed her. She'd all this work for her Ph.D. on hand, and then home to Jonathan Sears and his lunacy. She had Phyl in to see him, and they, she and Martin, recommended some consultant. Jon's parents didn't want to know anything about it. And poor old Hilly thrashed on, nursed him, got her doctorate, kept appearances up at this end. God knows how she did it.'

'I'd heard the name Jonathan Sears, but I didn't know any of this.'

'Don't let on to her that I've told you, then.'

'Did your mother know?'

'No. Hilly wanted you both kept out of it. She was near frantic, but she kept her head. It went on for over a year. There's a lot to be said for your daughter, my man.'

'For all of them. What happened to Sears?'

'He died. In the end.'

He was shaken by the information. He and Gillian had realized that something was amiss with Hilary, had discussed it, but put it down to overwork and worry about her research.

'Why didn't she tell us? Or at least, tell Gill?'

'She didn't think you'd understand. You'd have given her

sensible advice she didn't want to hear. She was specially frightened of what Mum would say. "You never know with Dad," she said to me, I'd gone up to see her pregnant with Sarah; "he might just have an inkling".'

A tear started down Job Turner's face, shocking him. He dabbed it away.

'We live and learn,' he said, covering up. 'Will she be all right with her Ammy?'

'I expect so. You'll like him.'

'Will they have a family?'

'I imagine so. In time.'

Alison's short sentences seemed to mock, as though she feared she disclosed too much, as well as to reassure. Her expression was benevolent.

'Thanks for telling me all this. I just didn't . . . I'm surprised Gill knew nothing.'

They talked about Alison's children, and he praised Geoffrey.

'Oh, he's a good man. He's marvellous with the kids. It surprised me. He's nothing like his father, thank God.'

'Does he take after his mother?'

'No. I don't think so. I never met her. But I guess, from what he tells me, he isn't. He's a freak, genetically speaking.'

'By the way, I've had a good clean round here. Did you notice?'

'I did. Frightened of my willing the egregious Mrs Harper on to you, were you?'

'You know . . . ?'

'About her and old Greene? Oh, yes. He boasted to Geoffrey.'

'Not to you?'

'He'd more sense. And while we're on the subject, how's your love-life? You and Miss Darling?'

'Mrs.'

Job produced the note and card. Alison's alert glance took all in in a few seconds.

'She's setting her cap at you.'

'Is that good?'

'You're a sly old devil. Come on, now. Is she nice?'

236

'Oh, yes. But I've explained all this to Geoffrey. I hardly know her.' Again the recital, with *élan*, on his part, of the Dickens' episode; Alison listened, slim fingers clasped, her face long-suffering, humorous, saintly, sceptical.

'I take it,' she inquired, 'that's it's not usual for the young ladies on your staff to quote lines of poetry to their headmaster?'

'Well, no.' He courteously matched her in irony.

'Beware.' They burst out laughing. He remembered many passages like this with Gillian, when she'd attacked his theses by polite ridicule. Alison looked at the card again. 'What's "Horbury" here?'

'It puzzled me, until I looked it up. Place in Yorkshire. It's the name Dykes gave to his tune to "Nearer, my God, to Thee."'

'Nearer, my God, to Thee. Is that how she thinks of you?' Not a glimmer on Alison's face betrayed her mockery. 'You'll have to watch it.' She relaxed, comically. 'How did you meet Gillian?'

'She was in a choir I ran.'

'Love at first sight?'

'Fairly. You know what I'm like. Cautious. Not breaking my neck.'

'Is this Linda like Mum?'

'I don't think so. No. She's young, of course, Younger than you. I don't think so, at all. But there's nothing to it, really. As yet.'

'That's what they all say.'

They talked on about Gillian; tonight his daughter was in no hurry to leave. She was easy, comforting, confident from the report her husband had brought back. They were interrupted by the telephone. When he returned she was out in the kitchen washing their cups.

'Mrs Darling?' she shouted. 'Wishing you goodbye?'

'No. Another of my lady friends.'

Sally Moore had invited him round for coffee. On the first day of the holiday Bertrand had consulted her and rung up an expensive hotel in Torquay where they were to spend Christmas. The hotel, the first he had tried, had just received a cancellation. They were lucky. Bertie had done all this; it was unheard of. Usually she was left, with garbled remit, to make arrangements. He was pleased with himself, went humming about the house, had dug a small square in the garden, and so she had decided to issue this invitation.

'He may have another engagement.'

'Then it will be you and I together, love.'

She had sounded extraordinarily pleased with herself, and as he explained all this to Alison his own spirits danced.

'Your own, your very own Samaritans,' she said. 'My, we are making progress.'

'I'm not optimistic about them,' he admitted in face of his cheerfulness.

'Latet scintillula forsan.'

'Scintillula,' They laughed together again. She translated, to make sure. When that was over, Alison looked at her watch, said it was time for home, issued instructions to congratulate the young couple on their engagement, to bring Linda round to see them, if he thought fit. At the door, she asked,

'Are you thinking of leaving here?'

'The Lodge?'

'The Lodge.' She might have been addressing her three-year-old.

'Why do you ask that?'

'Fred Greene's piano for a start. It does crowd you out. I just wondered.'

'I could sell it, could I? The house, I mean. It's not forbidden?'

'You could. There's nothing against it in Ian Turner's will, once you've actually lived here.'

'You think it's served its purpose, do you?' he asked.

'I don't think any such thing. But it's a touch cramped now. Of course if you decided to marry your Linda,' Alison held up a hand to stem his protest, 'or anyone else now you've got the idea, you could always move back to Oak Villa. Which you have kept. Against my advice.'

'I wouldn't want that. It's Gillian's house.'

'She wouldn't want you bothering yourself with such

238

considerations. I can just hear her. "It's almost super-stitious." ' Alison imitated well; a very little modification of her own voice sufficed. 'Still, that's in the future. Geoff was pleased as punch when he came back from talking to you the other night. He shies away from overt stirring of emotions, but somehow the pair of you had . . . well . . . had managed something. You're in his good books, and in mine.'

'He's a good man. He does me well.'

'Not the only one.' She squeezed his arm, kissed him. 'It's far too cold to be standing out here baring our souls. You scuttle in.'

'I like to hear the wind in the top of the trees, and not feel a breath down here.'

Alison took up an actor's stance, exaggerating, face comical.

' "With the help of a surgeon he might yet recover and yet prove an ass." There you are. A quotation from the classics from your own dear daughter. How's that then? Not quite up to Mrs Darling? Never mind.'

She kissed him again, dashed away to her car, sped off.

Job Turner stood by his gate. The wind, high up, obliged. From the far side of the road Susan Smith's father, dog at heels, called a rough goodnight.

Turner felt the cold, suddenly, and slipped inside, locking up against the world.